fluorescent MUD

eli howey

FLUORESCENT MUD by Eli Howey | elihowey.ca | Publishers: Maggie Umber, Raighne | Publicity: Melissa Carraher | Production Design: glint | Published by 2dcloud | 3364 S. Lituanica Ave #1R Chicago IL 60608 | 2dcloud.com | Distributed to the Trade | In the U.S. by Consortium Books Sales & Distribution | www.cbsd.com | In Canada by Publishers Group Canada | www.pgdbooks.ca | Orders: (800) 283-3572 | First edition, March 2018 © 2018 Eli Howey | All rights reserved. No part of this book (except small portions for review purposes) may be reproduced in any form without expressed written consent from Eli Howey and 2dcloud. | Library of Congress Control Number: 2018939429 | ISBN: 9781937541446 | Printed in Korea

We would like to acknowledge support from the Toronto Arts Council and the Ontario Arts Council for the writing and artistic creation of Fluorescent Mud.

TORONTO ARTS COUNCIL | **FUNDED BY THE CITY OF TORONTO**

ONTARIO ARTS COUNCIL
CONSEIL DES ARTS DE L'ONTARIO
an Ontario government agency
un organisme du gouvernement de l'Ontario

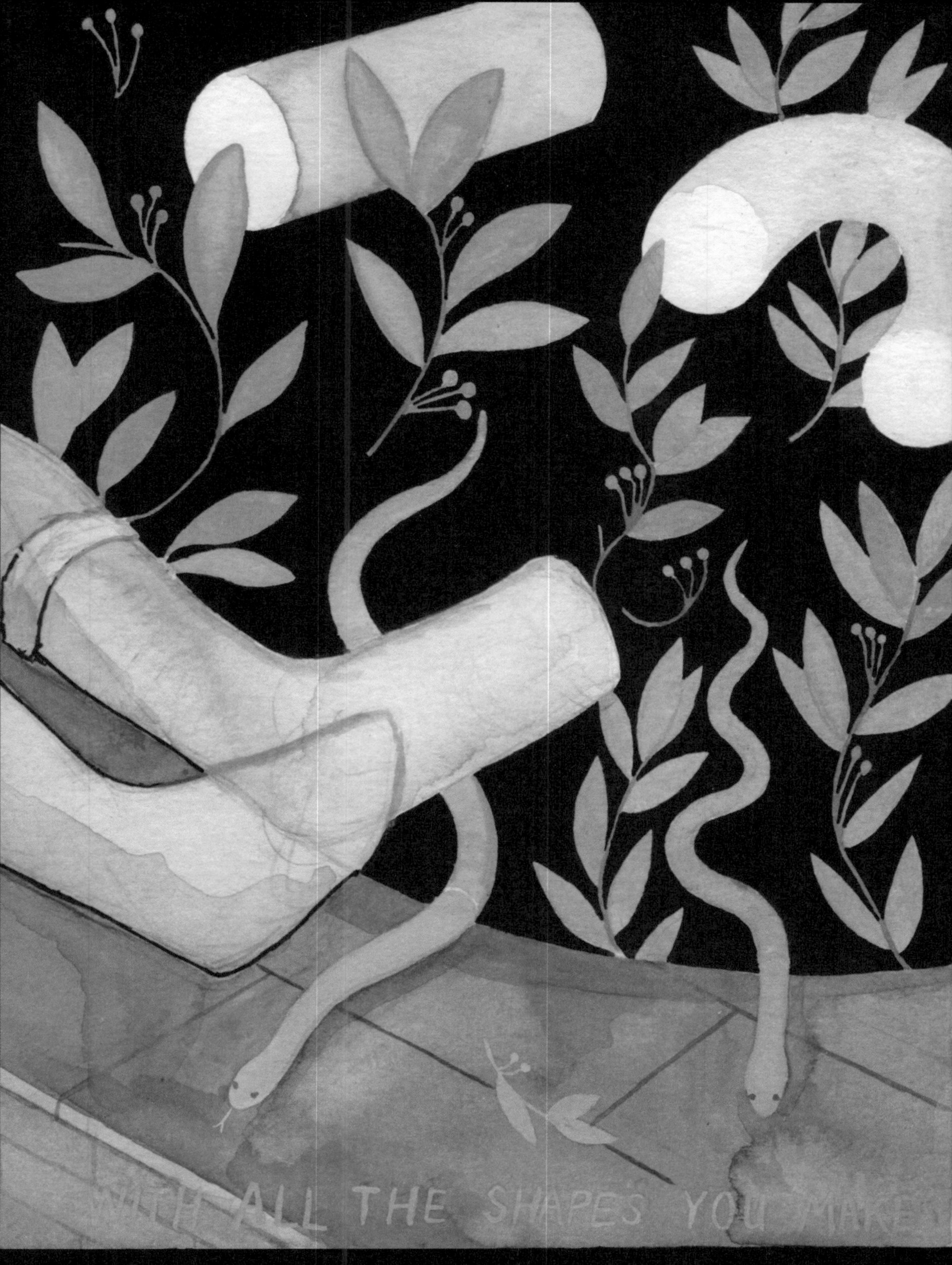
WITH ALL THE SHAPES YOU MAKE

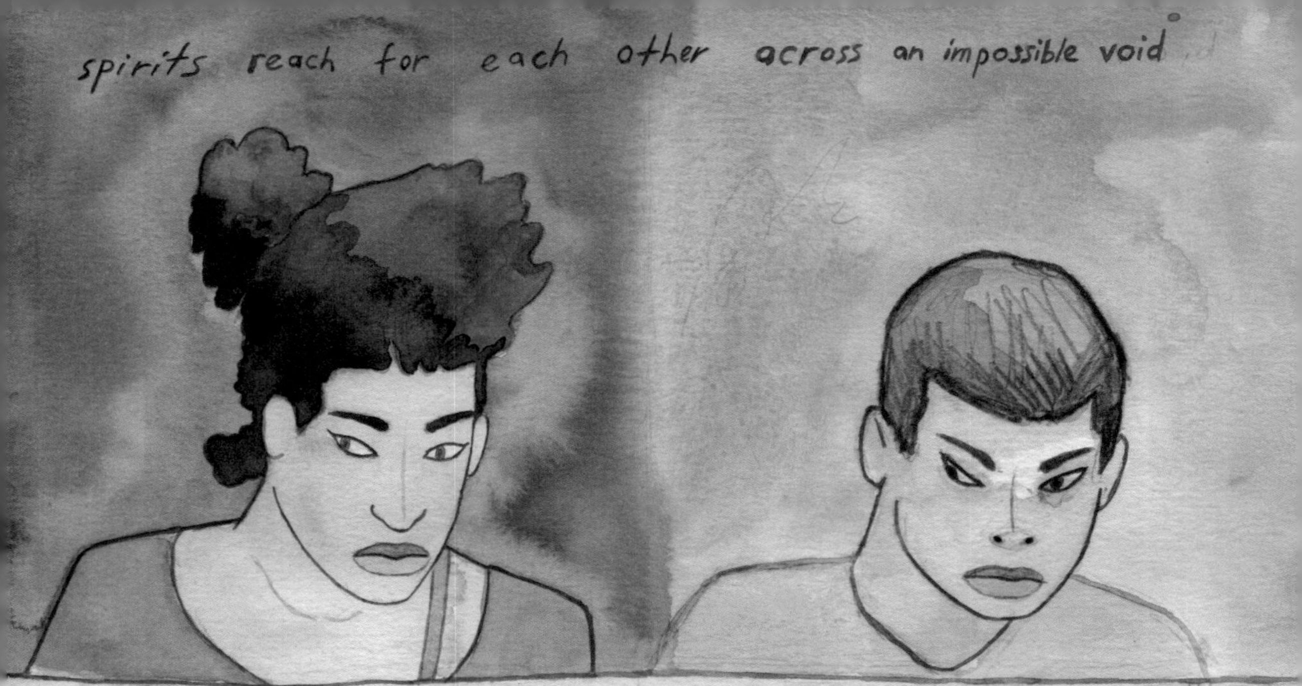
spirits reach for each other across an impossible void

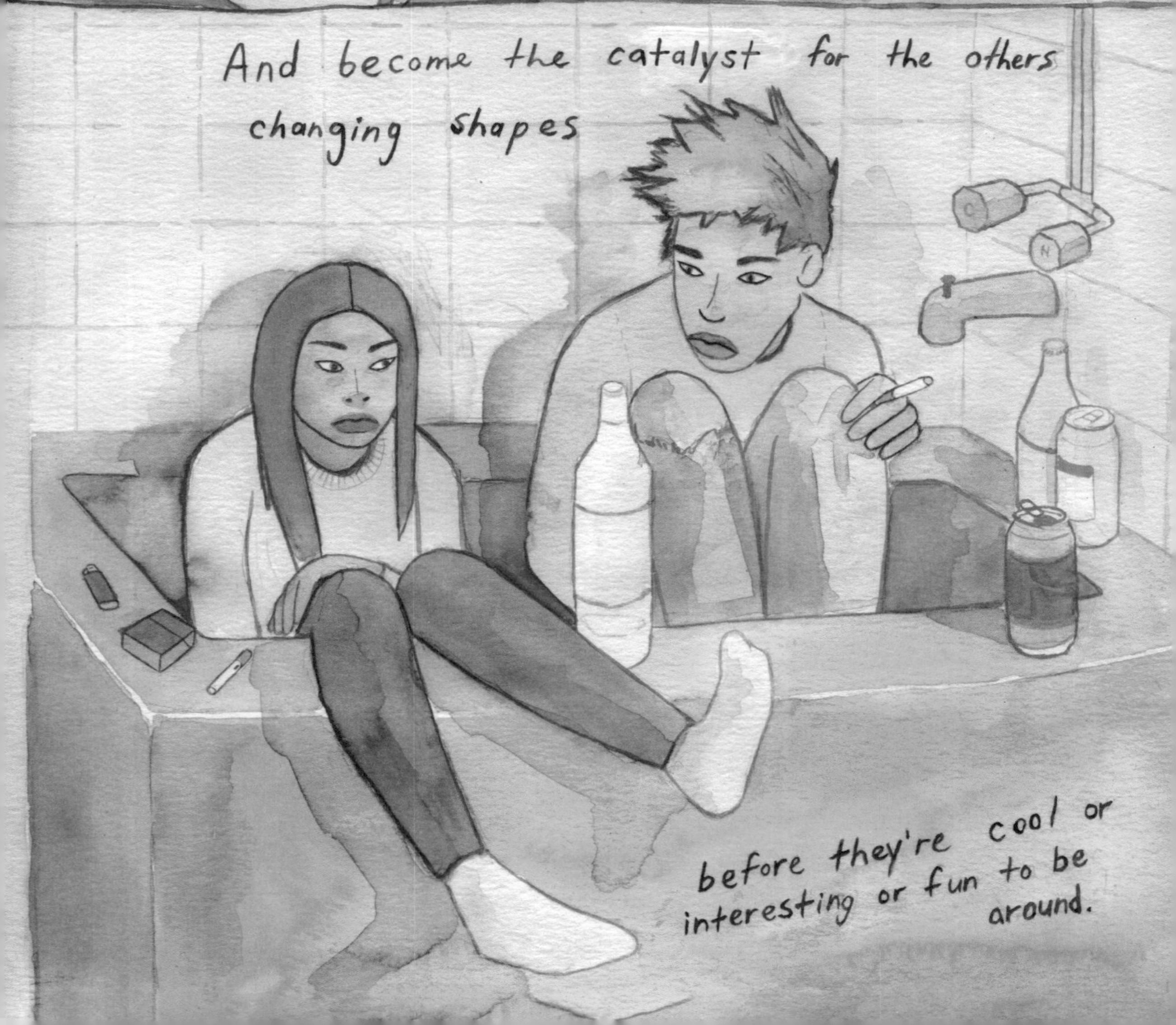
And become the catalyst for the others changing shapes
before they're cool or interesting or fun to be around.

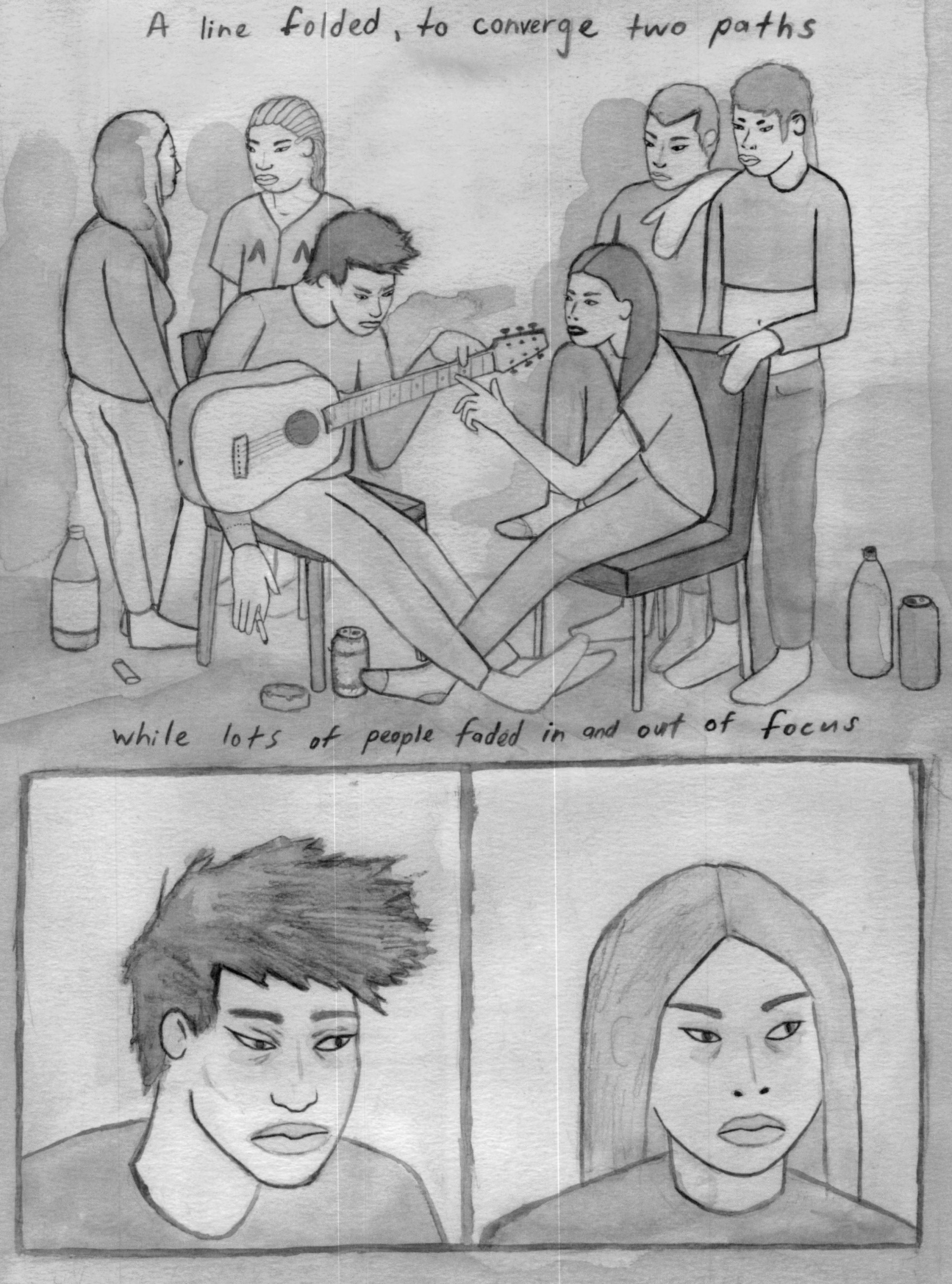
A line folded, to converge two paths
while lots of people faded in and out of focus

I started to notice the further away I got from my town, the easier it was to show the unfamiliar pieces of myself. Walls started peeling back around formless baggage and I started forgetting to hide.

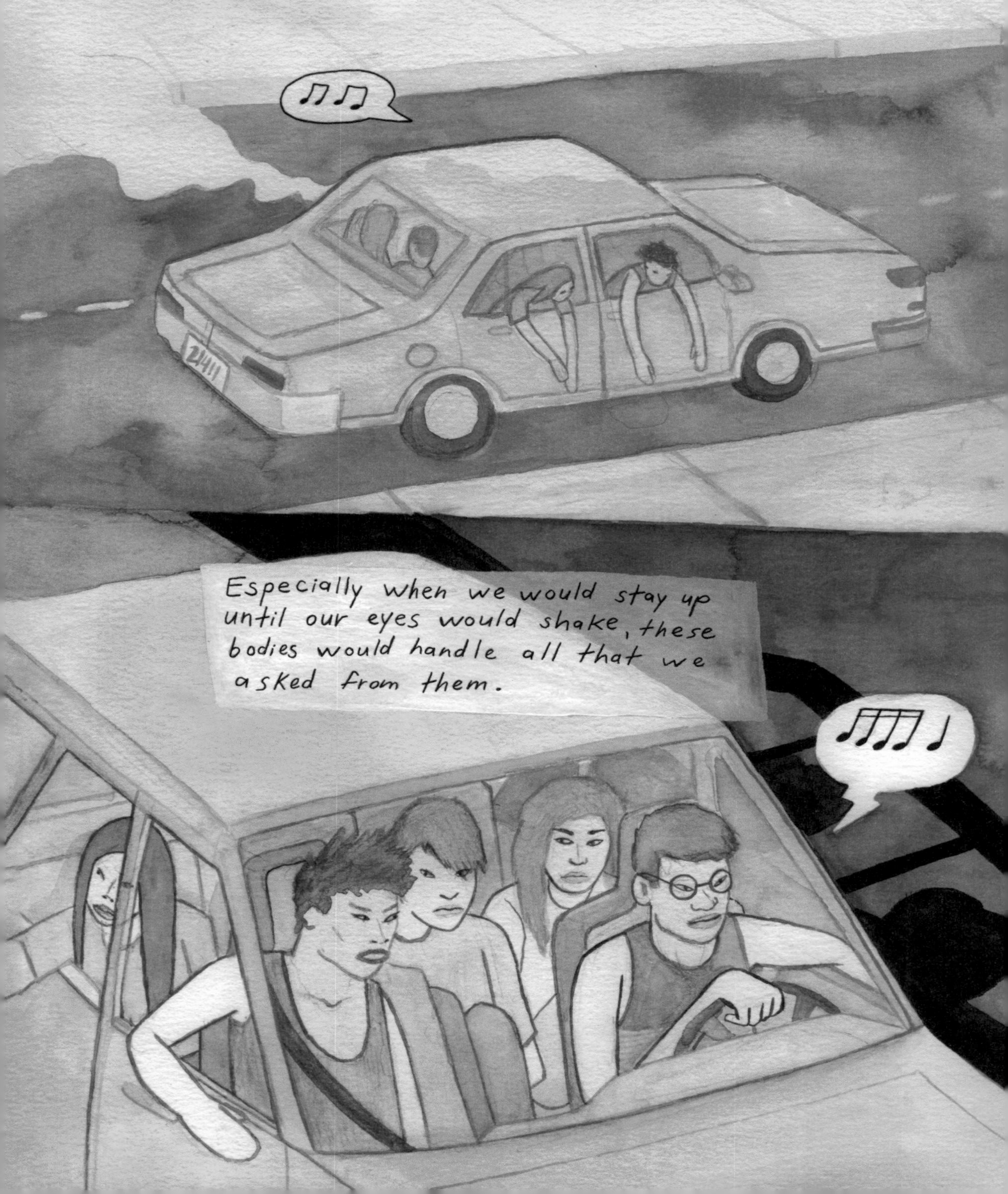
2411
Especially when we would stay up until our eyes would shake, these bodies would handle all that we asked from them.

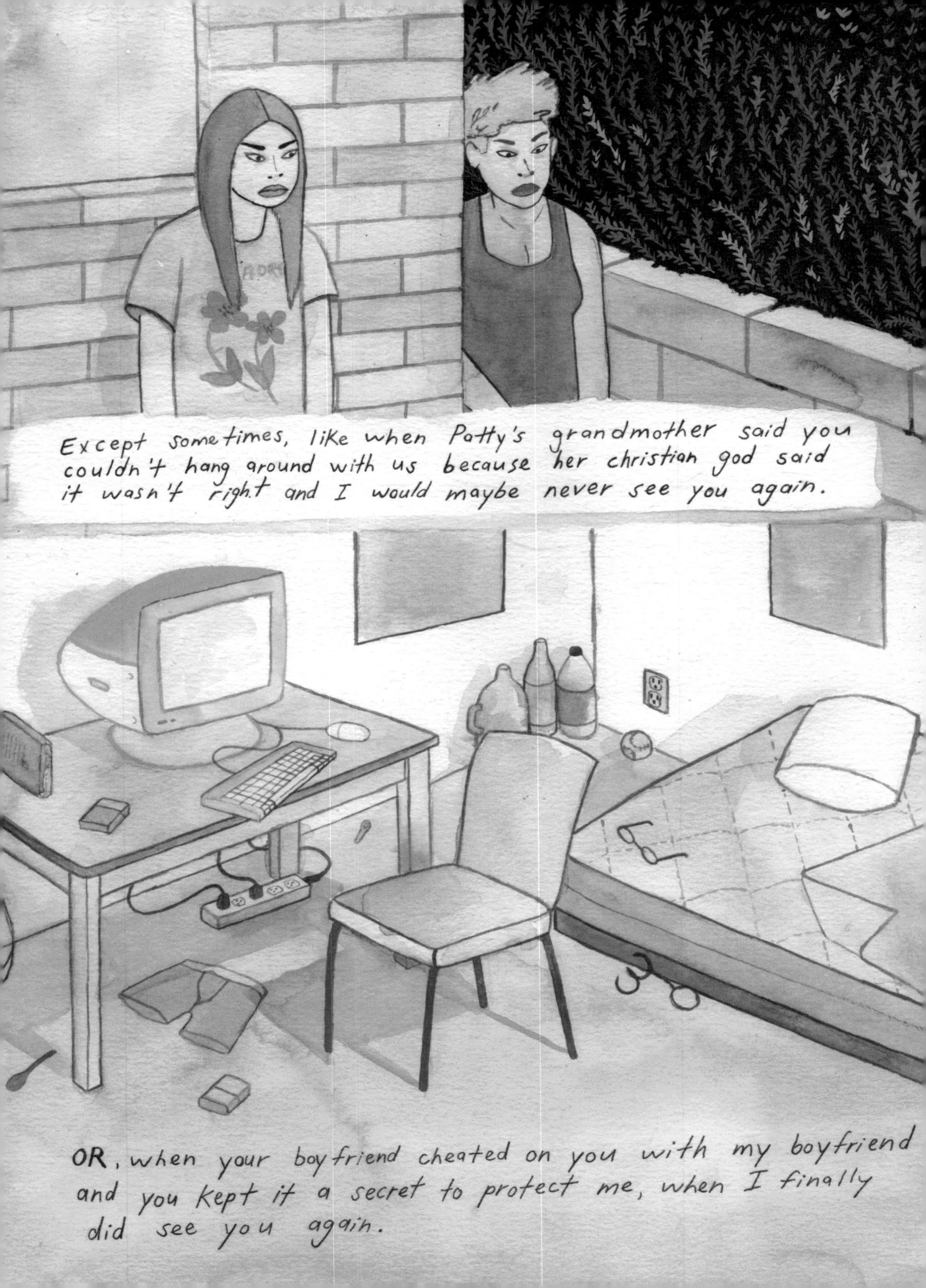
Except sometimes, like when Patty's grandmother said you couldn't hang around with us because her christian god said it wasn't right and I would maybe never see you again.
OR, when your boyfriend cheated on you with my boyfriend and you kept it a secret to protect me, when I finally did see you again.

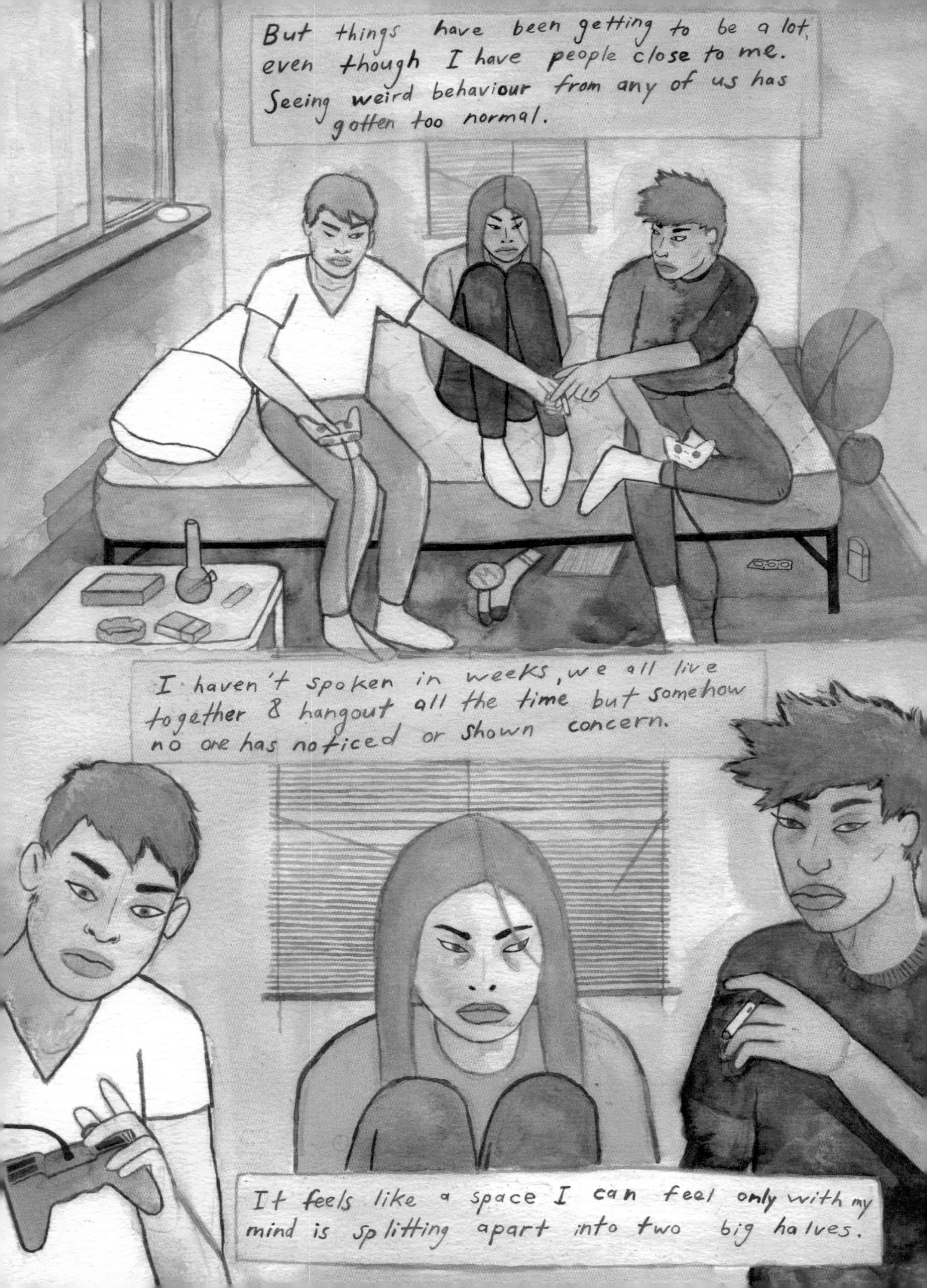
But things have been getting to be a lot, even though I have people close to me. Seeing weird behaviour from any of us has gotten too normal.
I haven't spoken in weeks, we all live together & hangout all the time but somehow no one has noticed or shown concern.
It feels like a space I can feel only with my mind is splitting apart into two big halves.

I try to move but it comes out as a twitch.

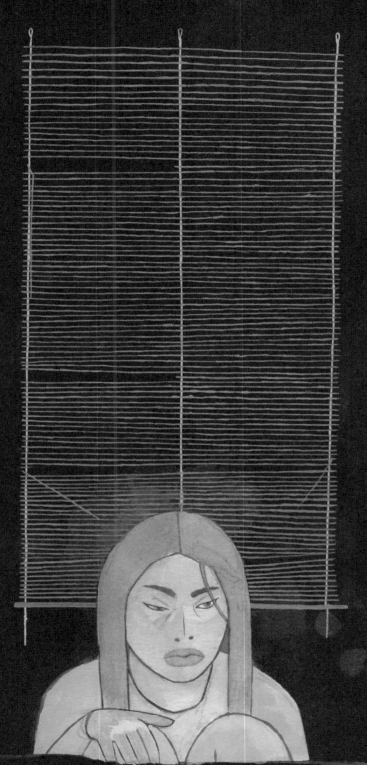

I try to say words but the thought and action don't connect.

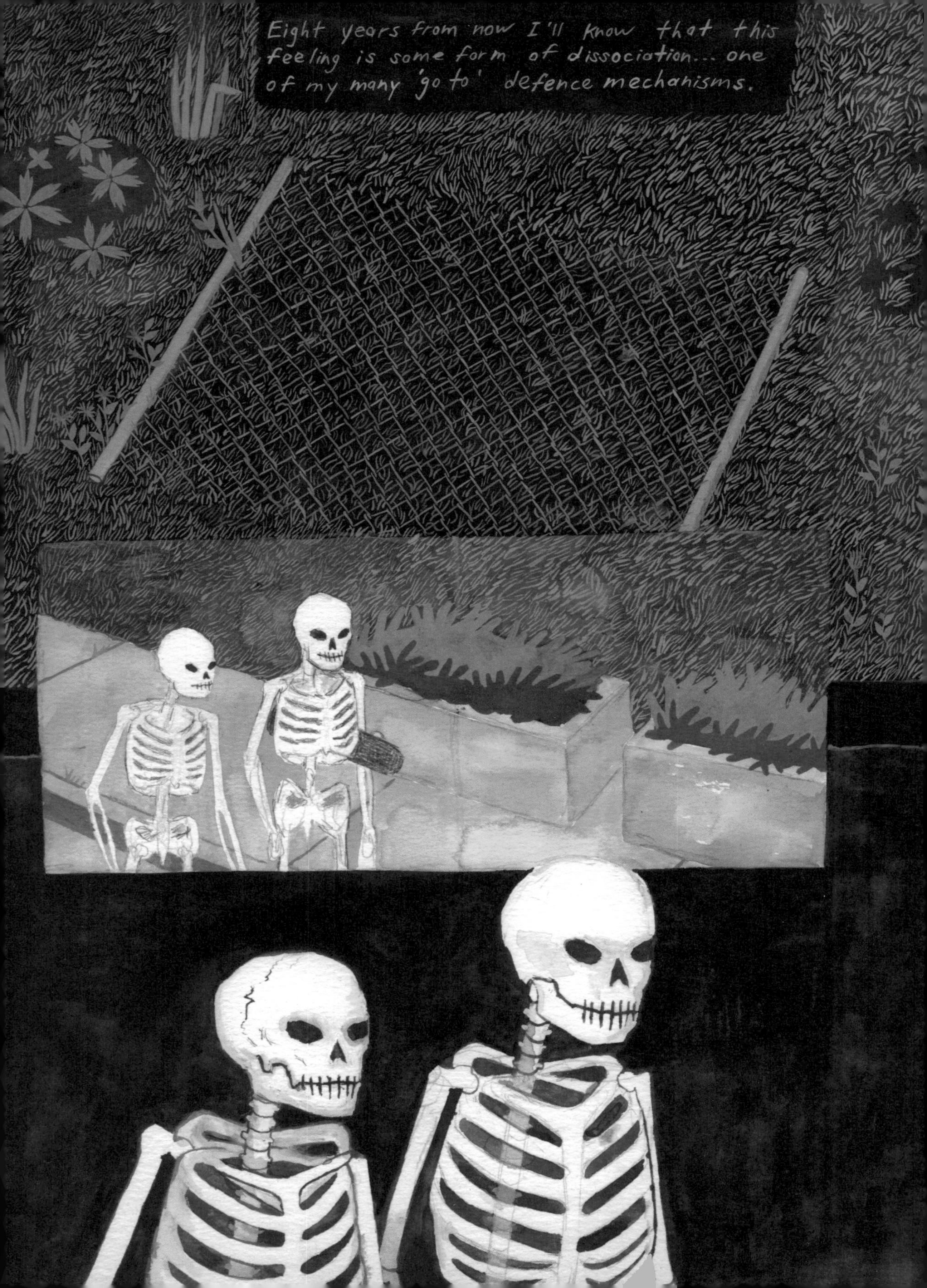
Eight years from now I'll know that this feeling is some form of dissociation... one of my many 'go to' defence mechanisms.

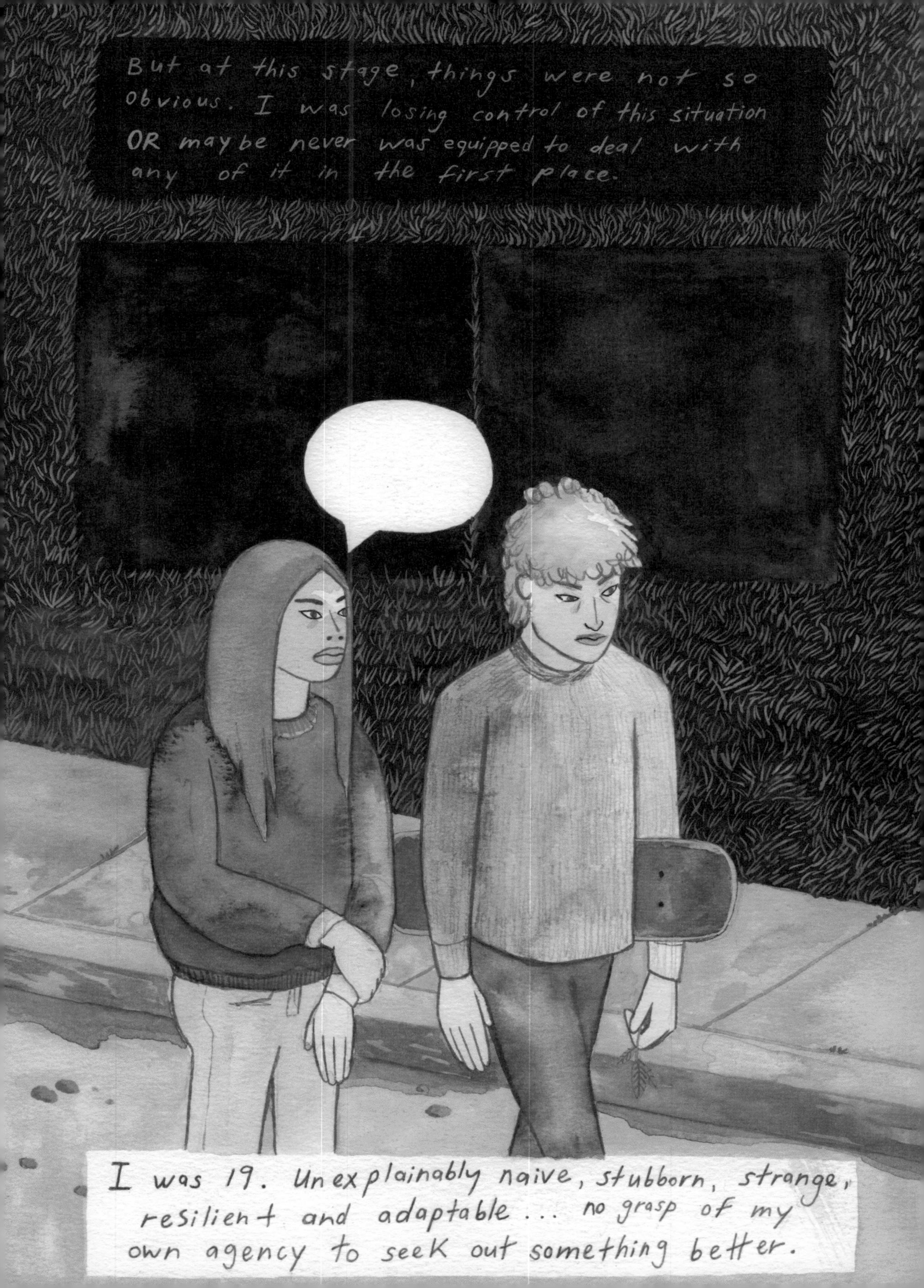
But at this stage, things were not so obvious. I was losing control of this situation OR maybe never was equipped to deal with any of it in the first place.
I was 19. Unexplainably naive, stubborn, strange, resilient and adaptable... no grasp of my own agency to seek out something better.

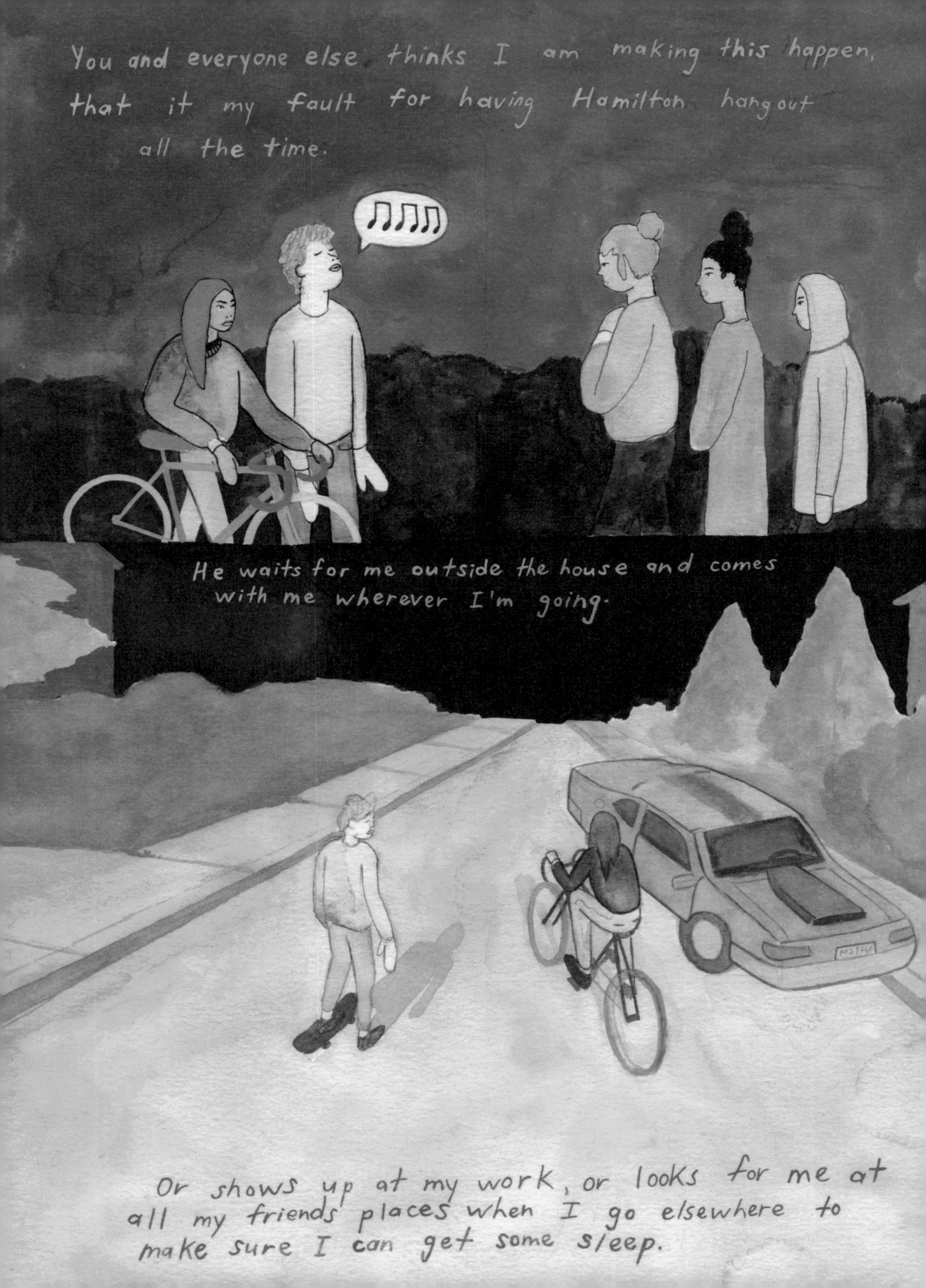
You and everyone else thinks I am making this happen, that it my fault for having Hamilton hangout all the time.
♫♫♫
He waits for me outside the house and comes with me wherever I'm going.
Or shows up at my work, or looks for me at all my friends places when I go elsewhere to make sure I can get some sleep.

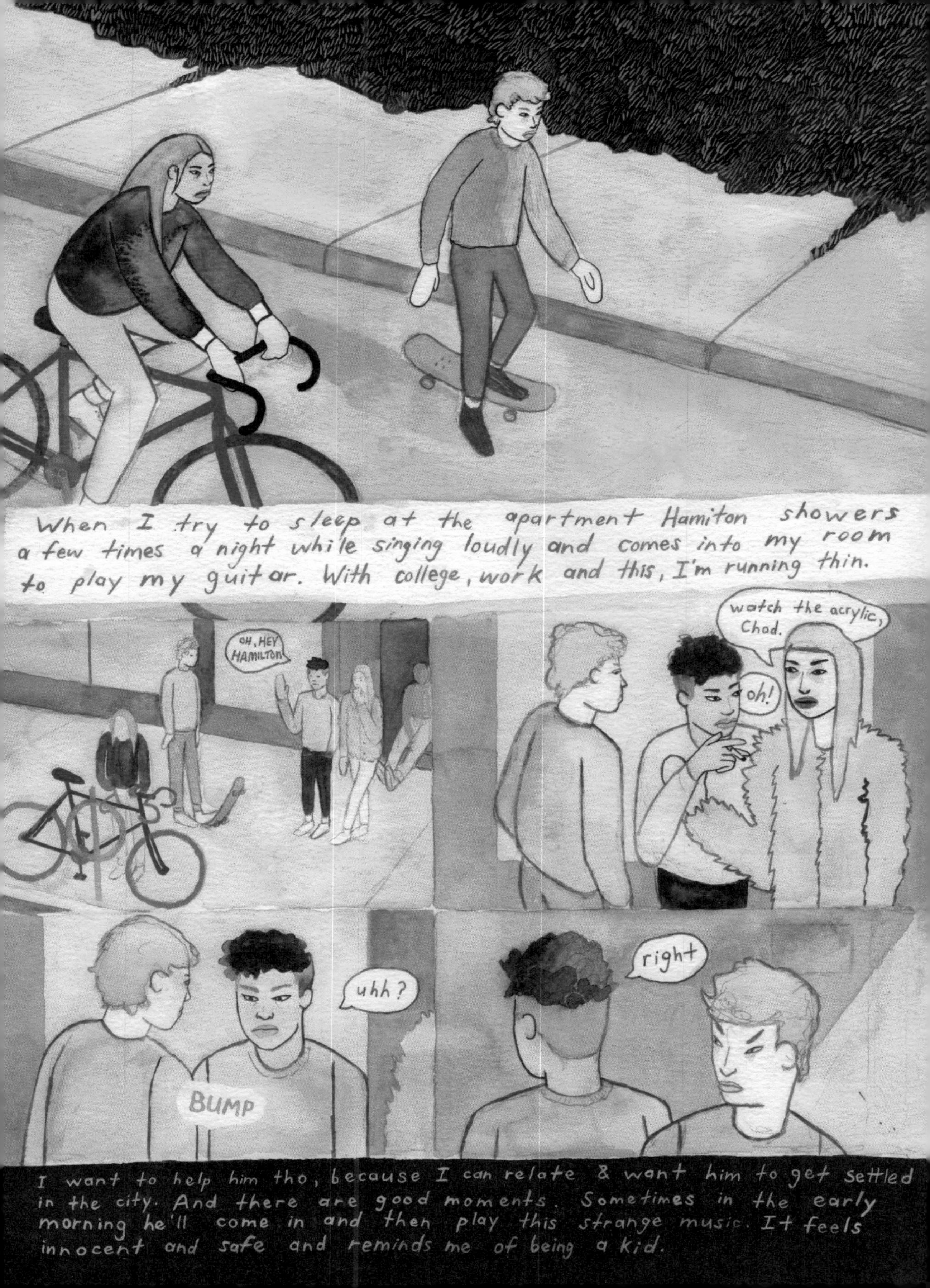
When I try to sleep at the apartment Hamiton showers a few times a night while singing loudly and comes into my room to play my guitar. With college, work and this, I'm running thin.
OH, HEY HAMILTON
watch the acrylic, Chad.
oh!
BUMP
uhh?
right
I want to help him tho, because I can relate & want him to get settled in the city. And there are good moments. Sometimes in the early morning he'll come in and then play this strange music. It feels innocent and safe and reminds me of being a kid.

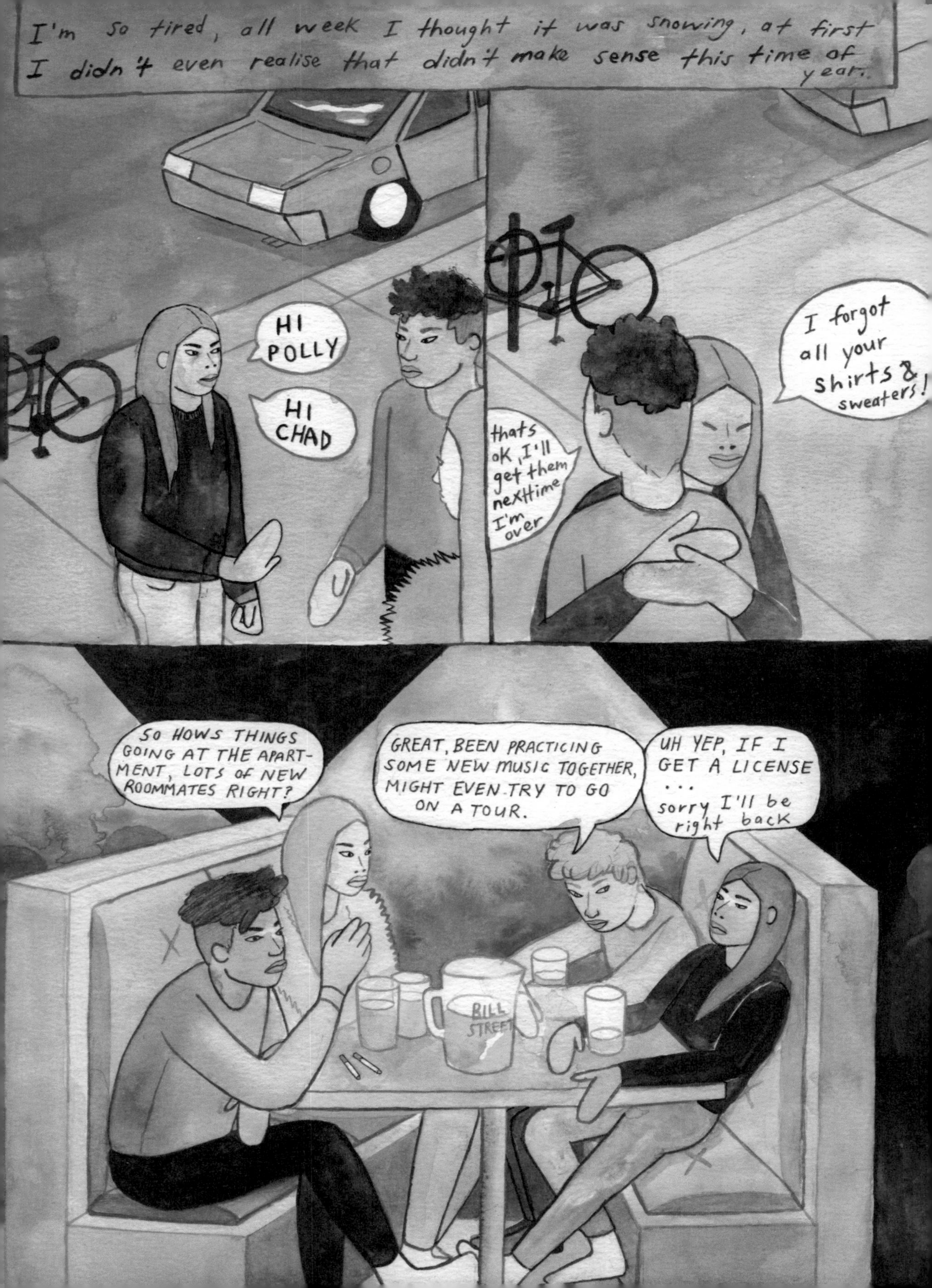
I'm so tired, all week I thought it was snowing, at first I didn't even realise that didn't make sense this time of year.
HI POLLY
HI CHAD
I forgot all your shirts & sweaters!
thats ok, I'll get them nexttime I'm over
SO HOWS THINGS GOING AT THE APARTMENT, LOTS OF NEW ROOMMATES RIGHT?
GREAT, BEEN PRACTICING SOME NEW MUSIC TOGETHER, MIGHT EVEN TRY TO GO ON A TOUR.
UH YEP, IF I GET A LICENSE . . . sorry I'll be right back
BILL STREET

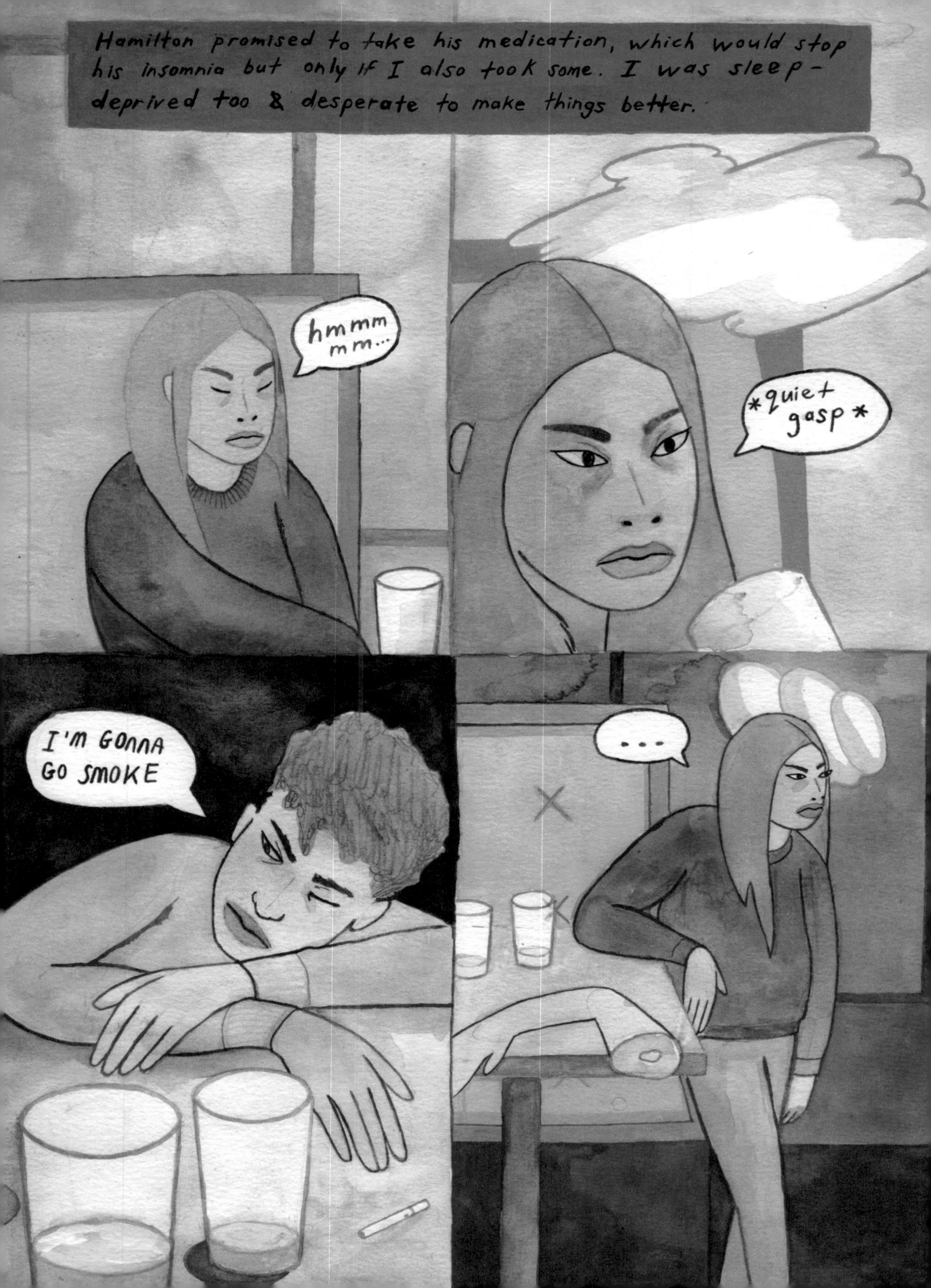
Hamilton promised to take his medication, which would stop his insomnia but only if I also took some. I was sleep-deprived too & desperate to make things better.
hmmm mm...
quiet gasp
I'M GONNA GO SMOKE
...

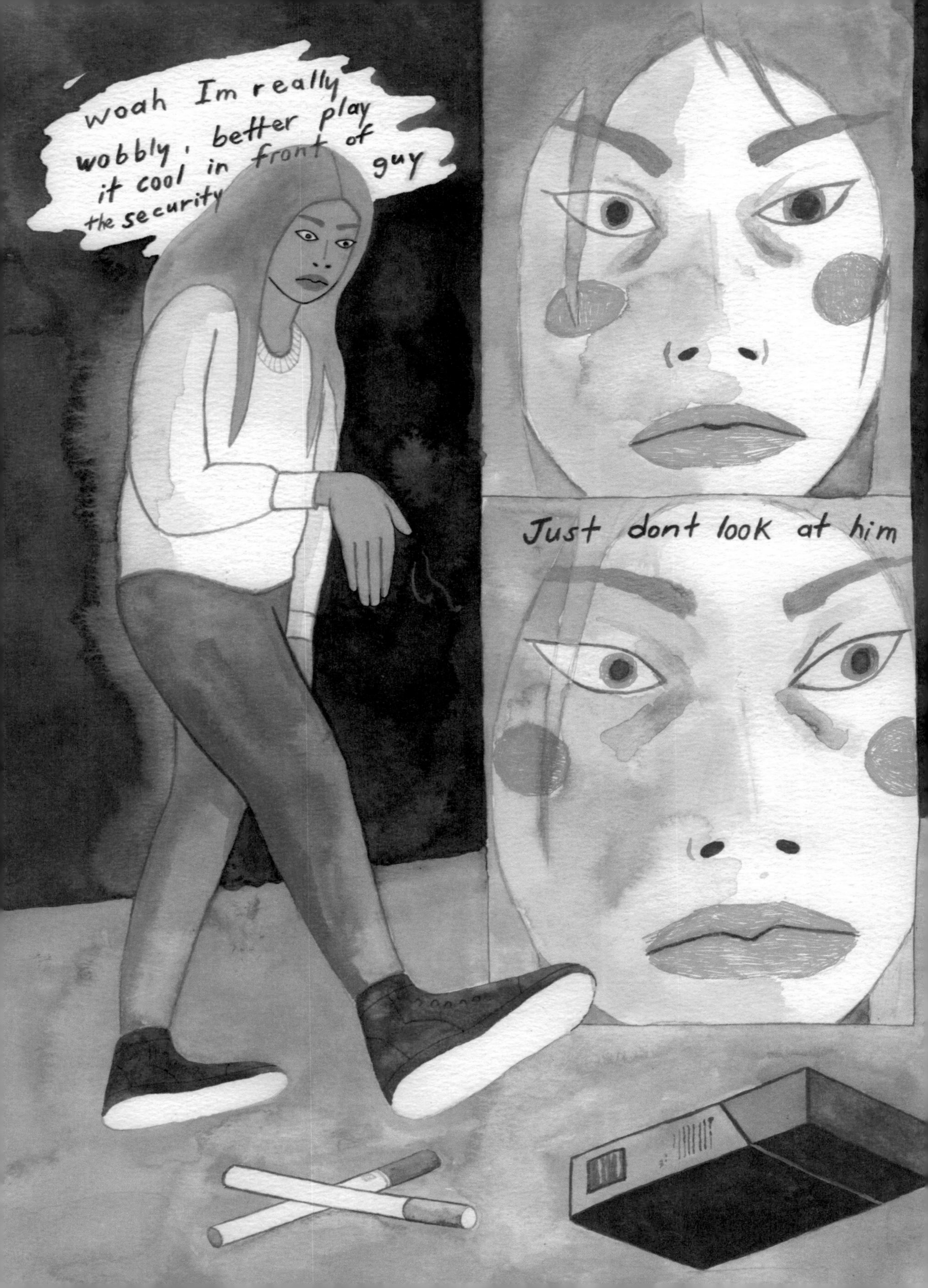
woah Im really wobbly, better play it cool in front of the security guy
Just dont look at him

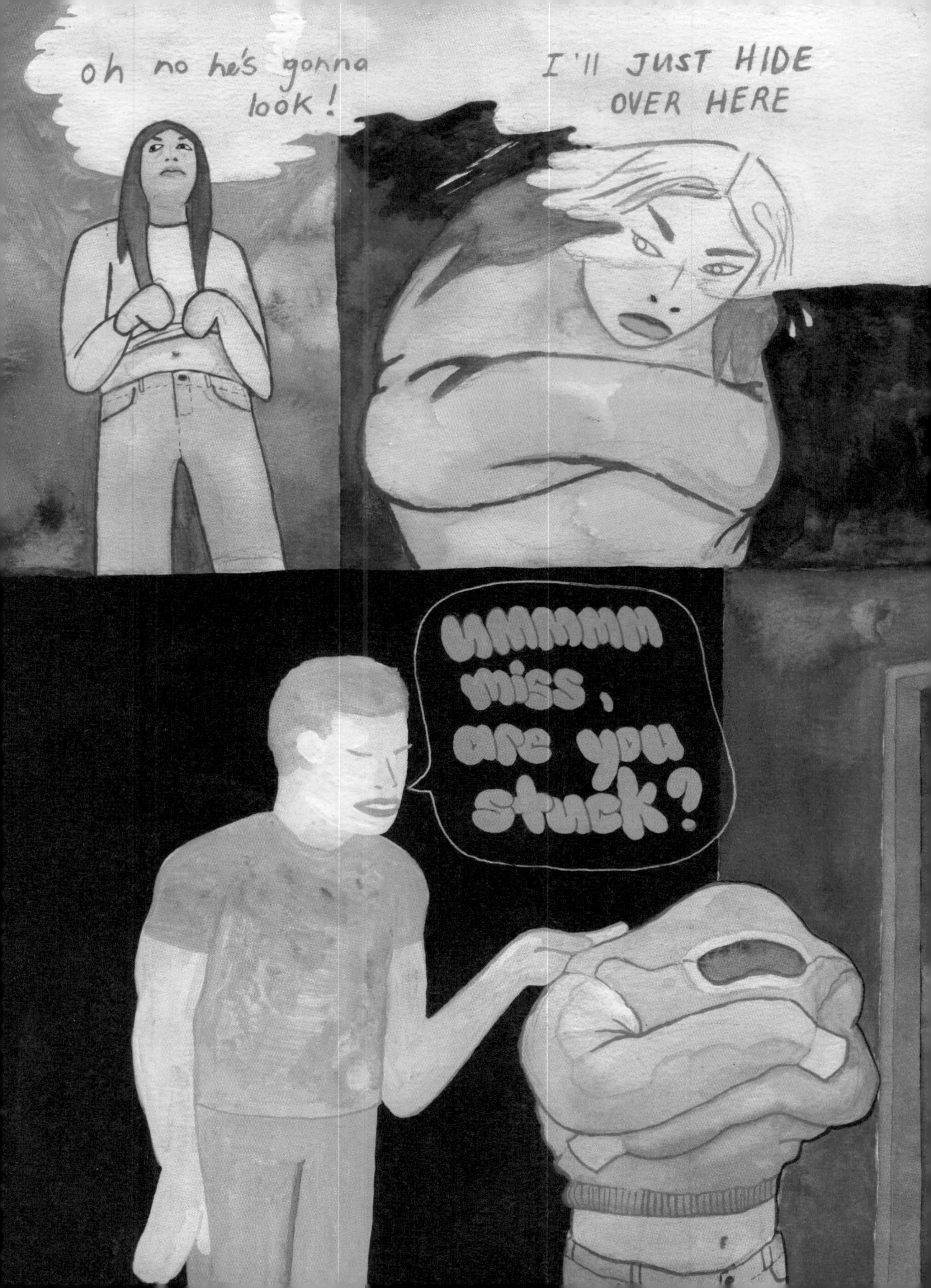
oh no he's gonna look!
I'll JUST HIDE OVER HERE
UMMMMM miss, are you stuck?

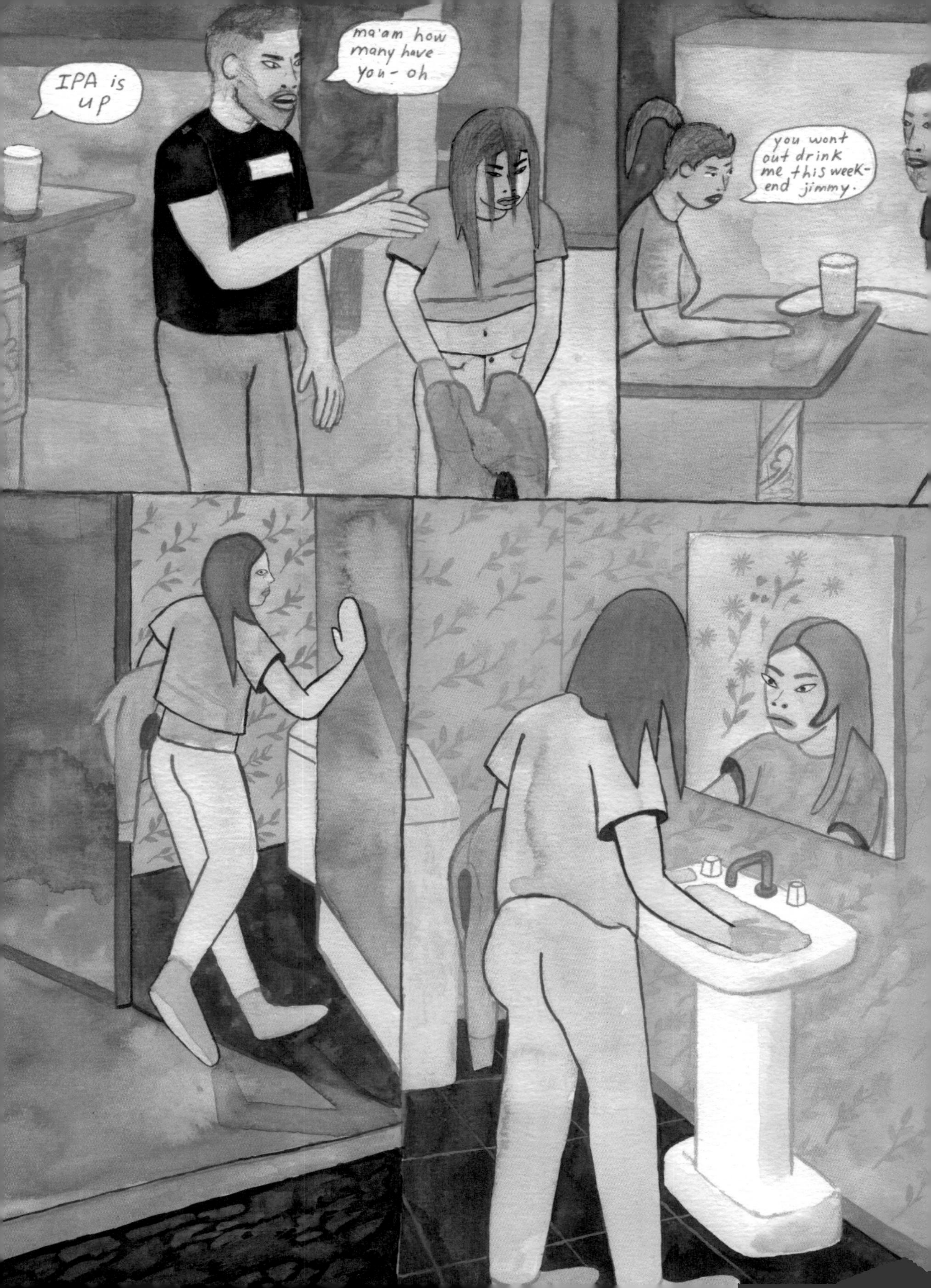
IPA is up
ma'am how many have you- oh
you wont out drink me this week-end jimmy.

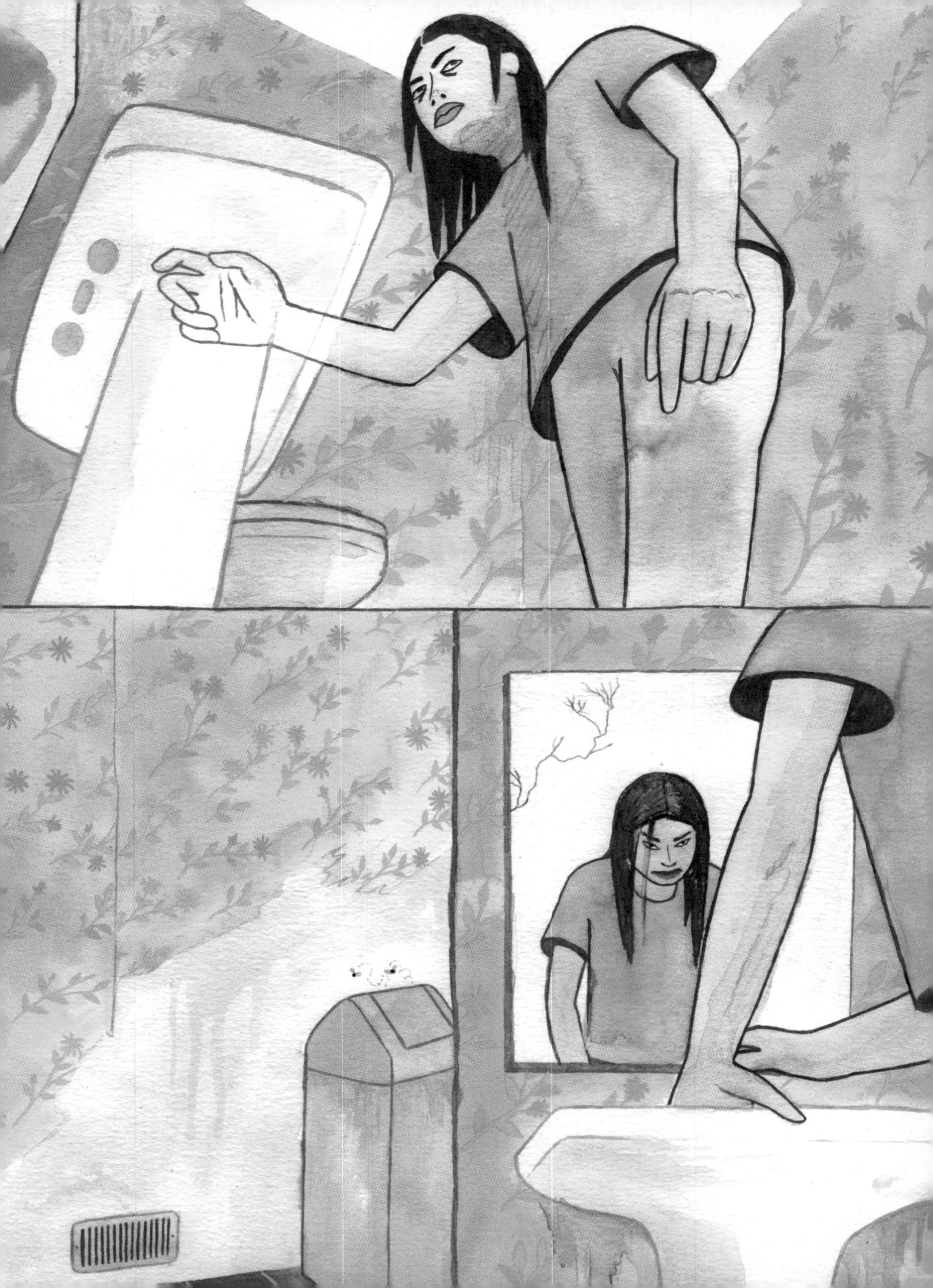

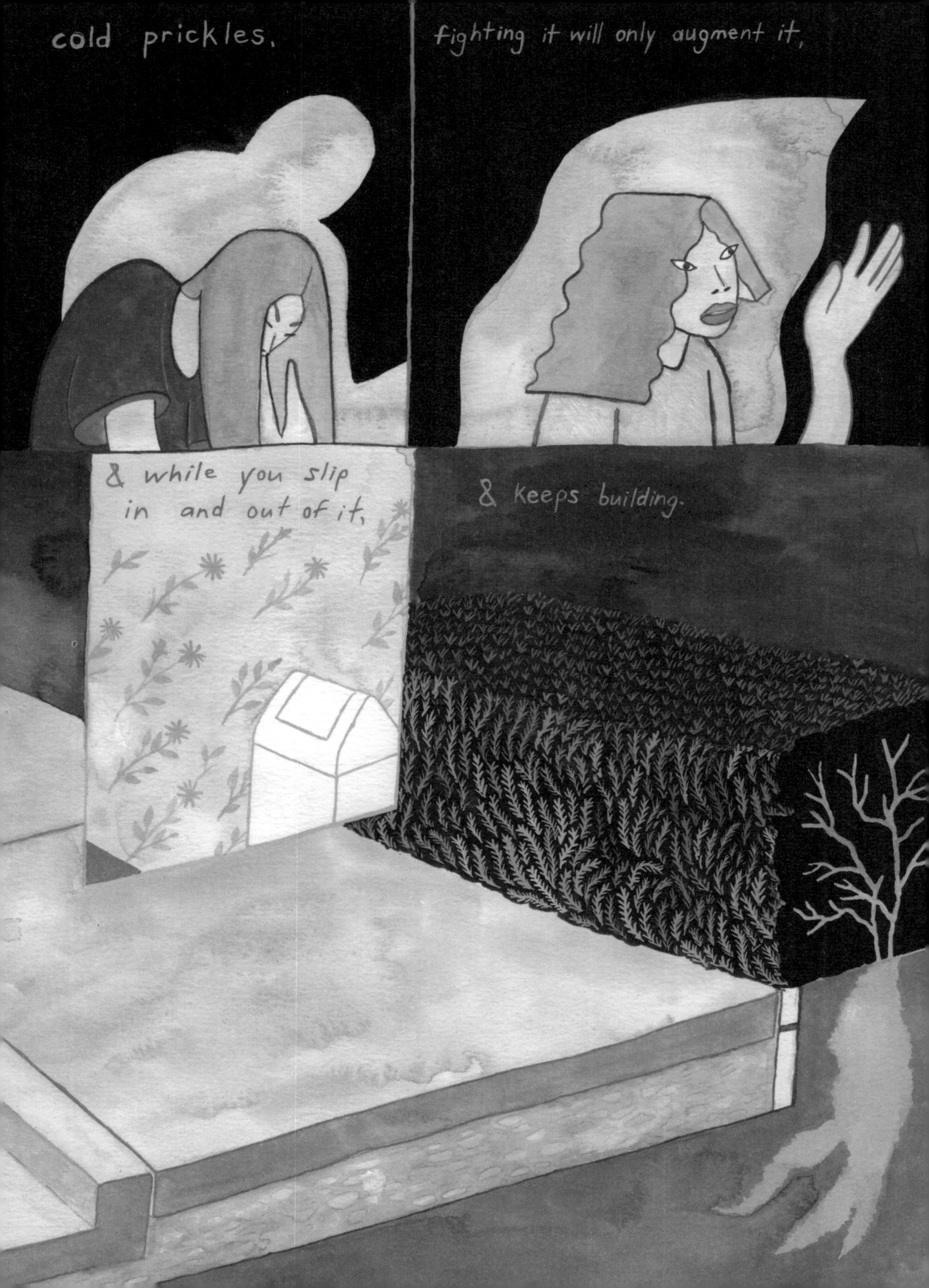
cold prickles,
fighting it will only augment it,
& while you slip in and out of it,
& keeps building.

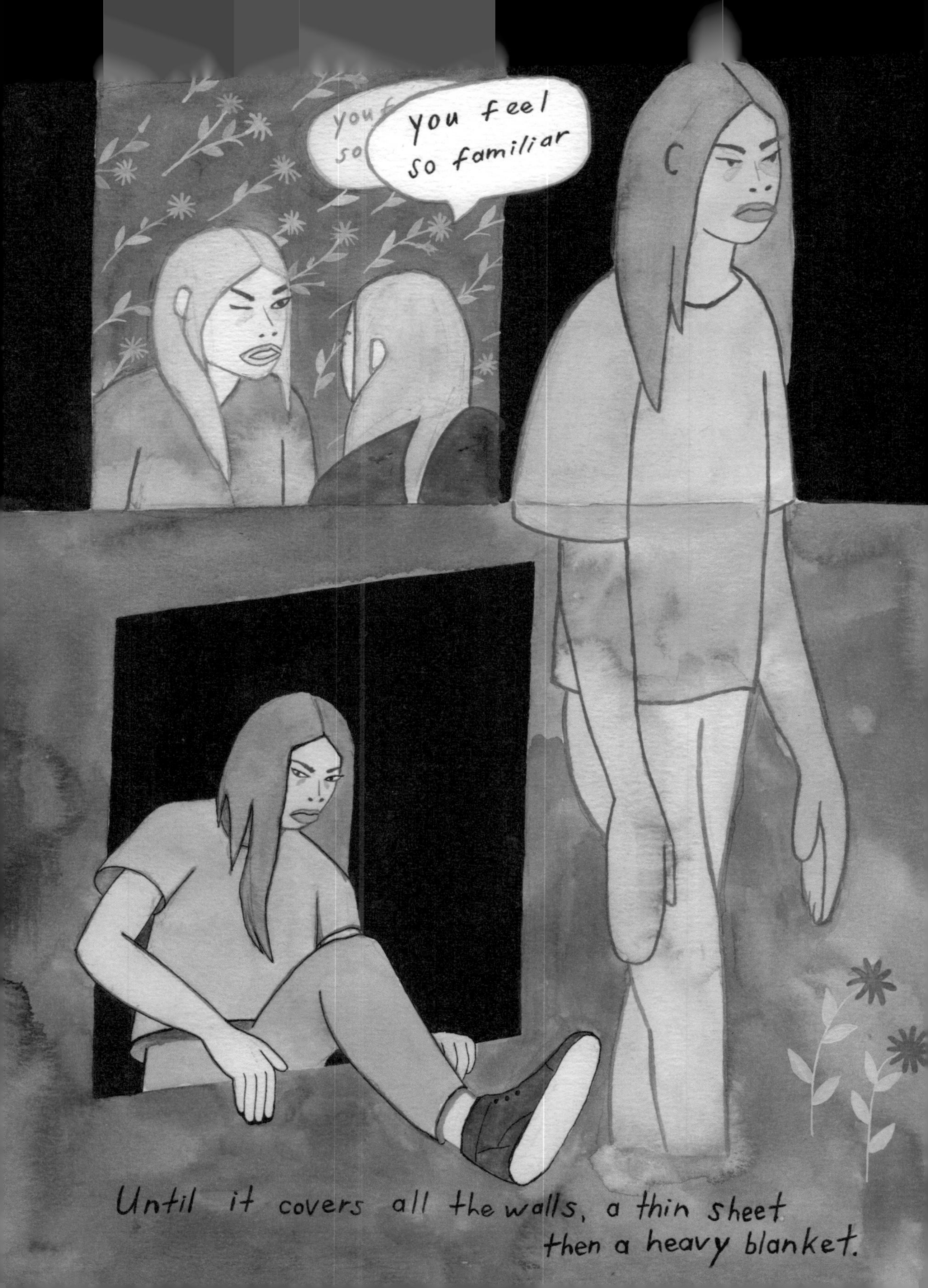
you feel so familiar
Until it covers all the walls, a thin sheet then a heavy blanket.

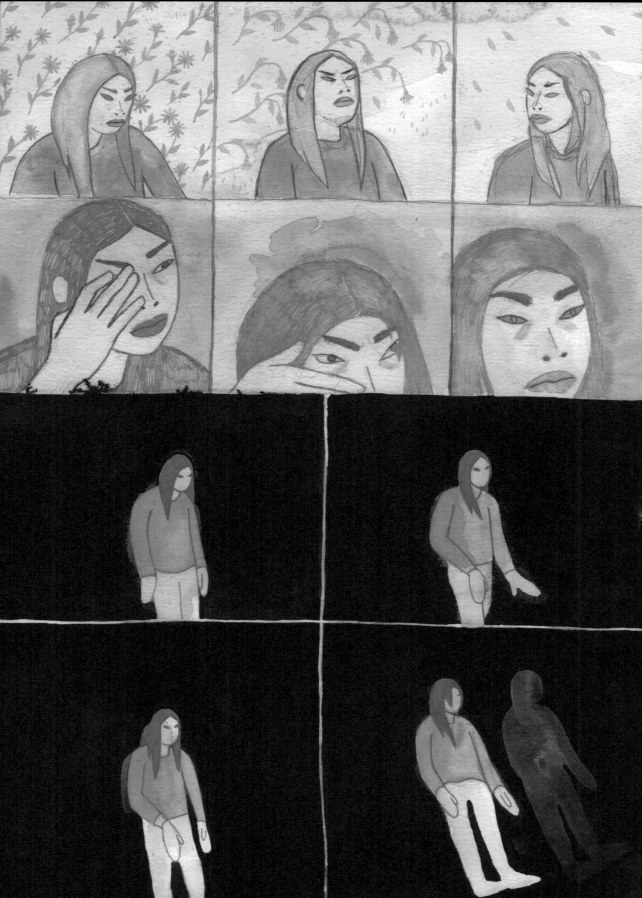

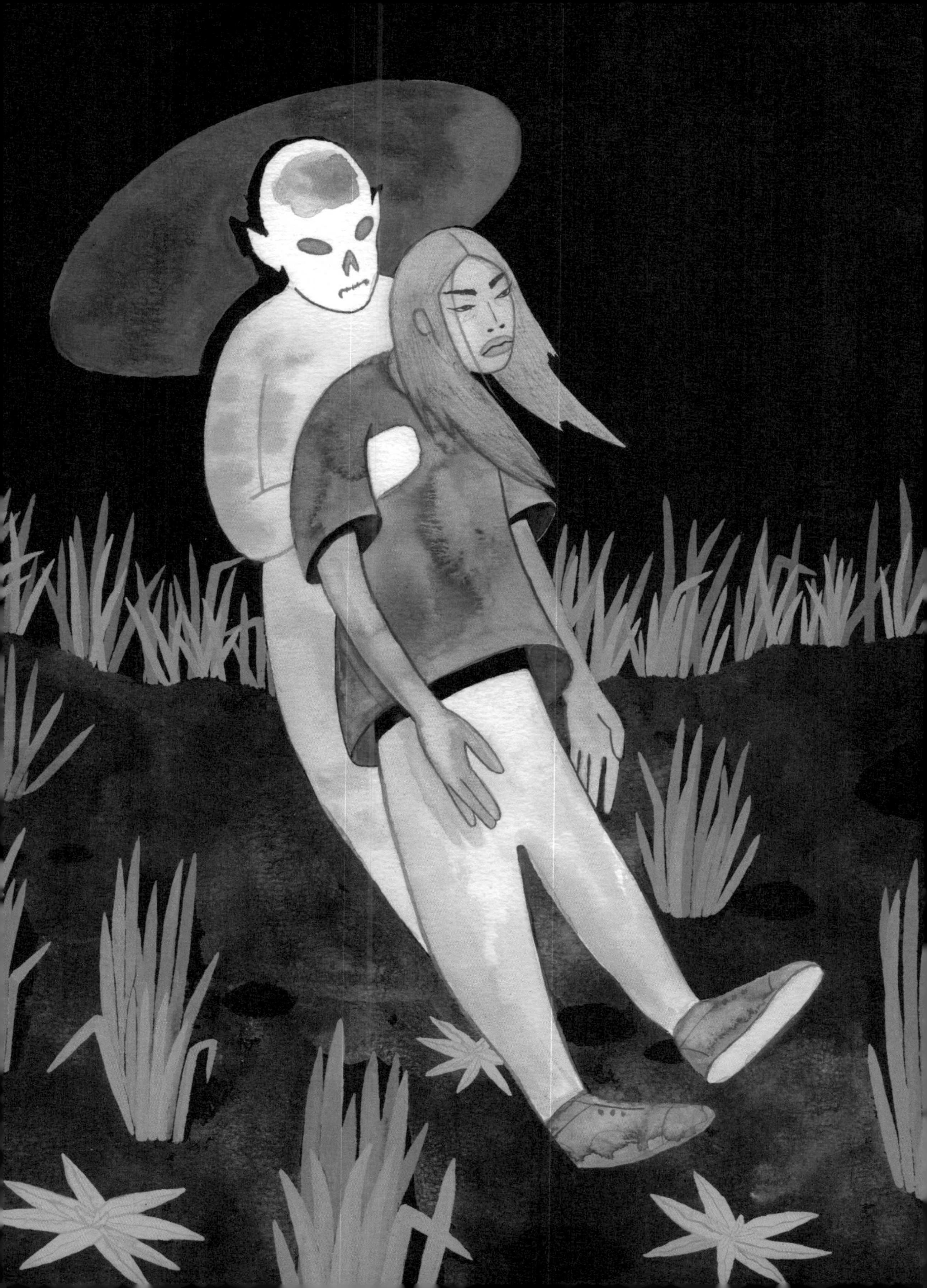

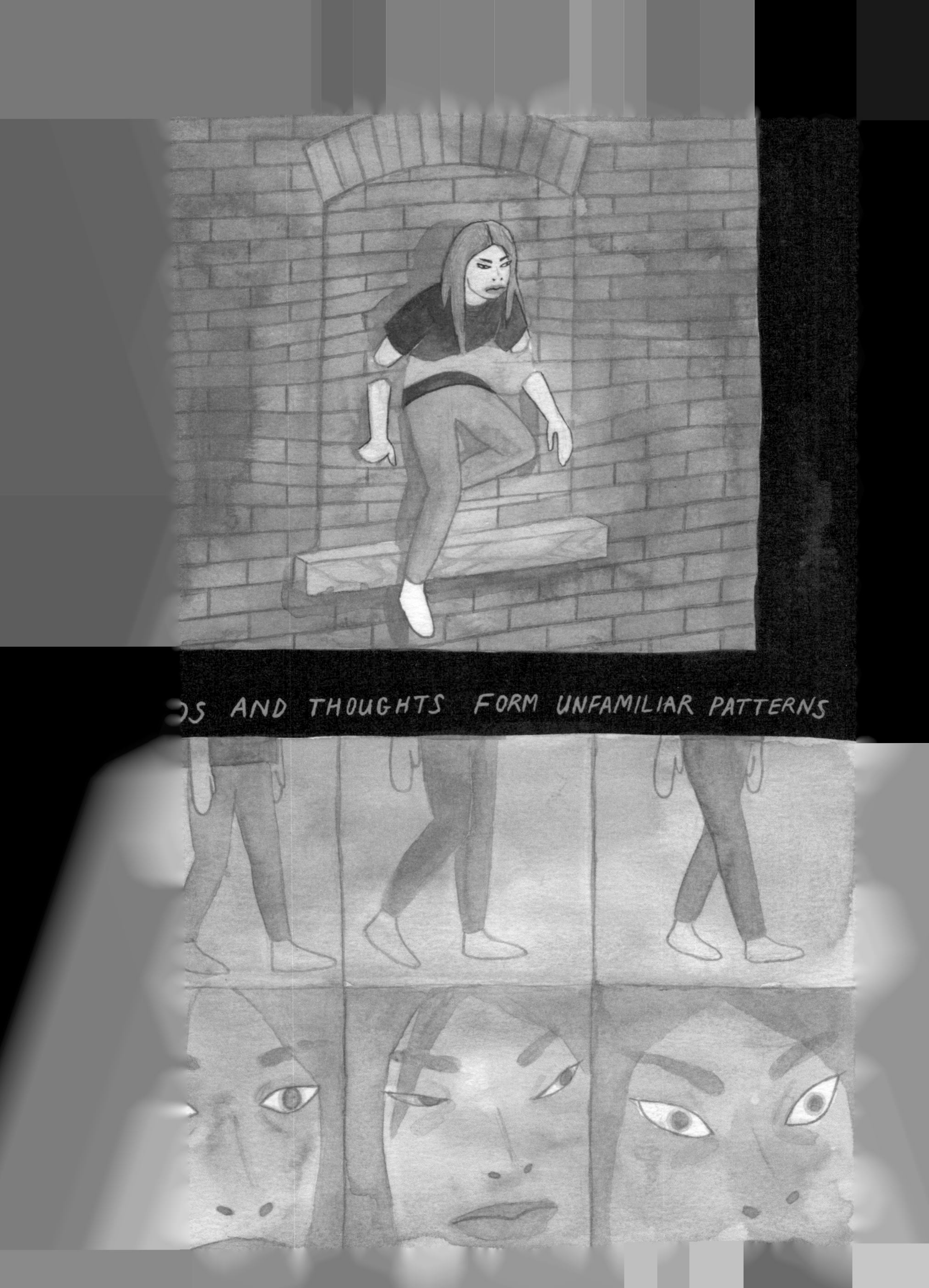
DS AND THOUGHTS FORM UNFAMILIAR PATTERNS

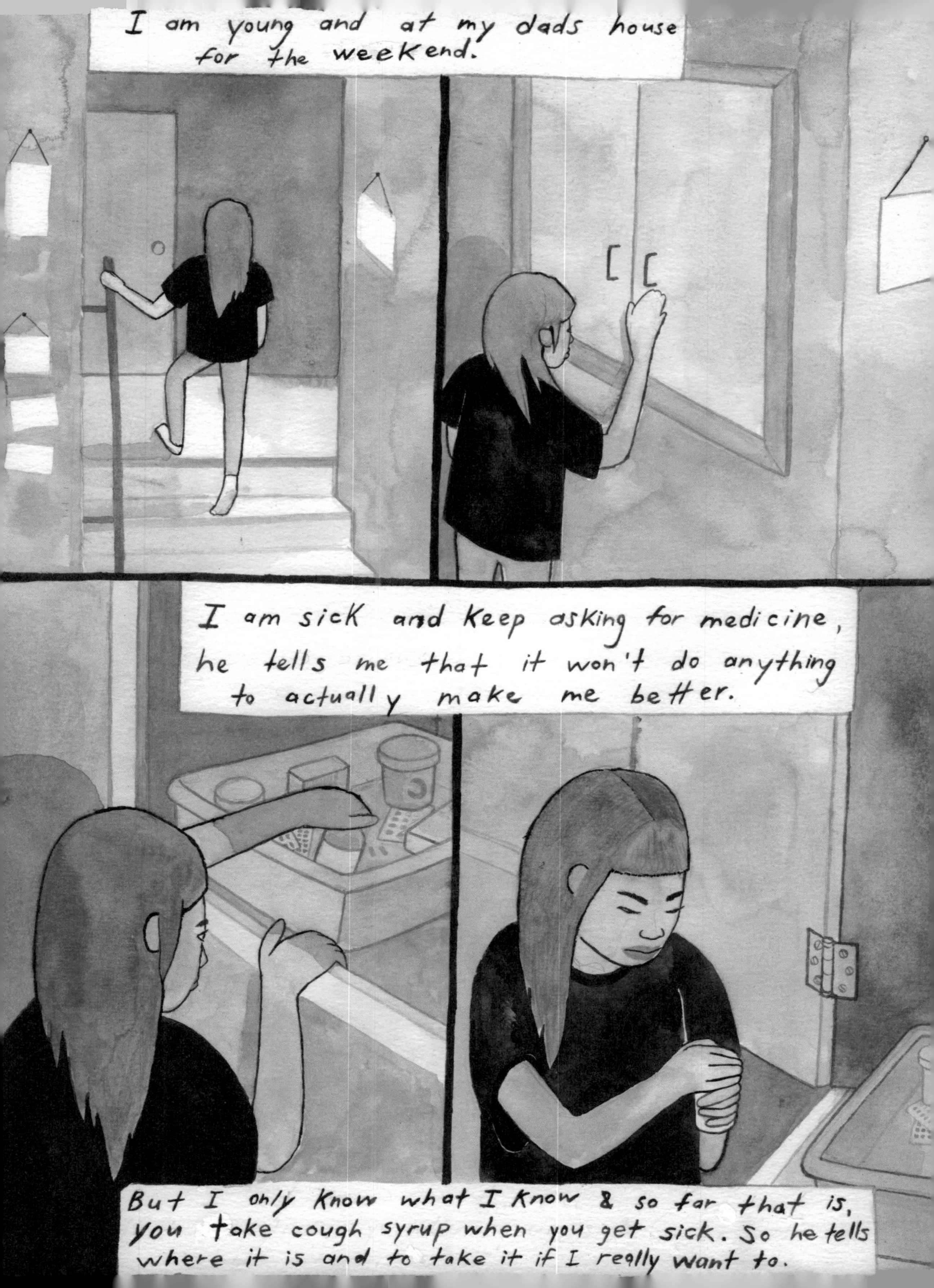
I am young and at my dads house for the weekend.
I am sick and keep asking for medicine, he tells me that it won't do anything to actually make me better.
But I only know what I know & so far that is, you take cough syrup when you get sick. So he tells where it is and to take it if I really want to.

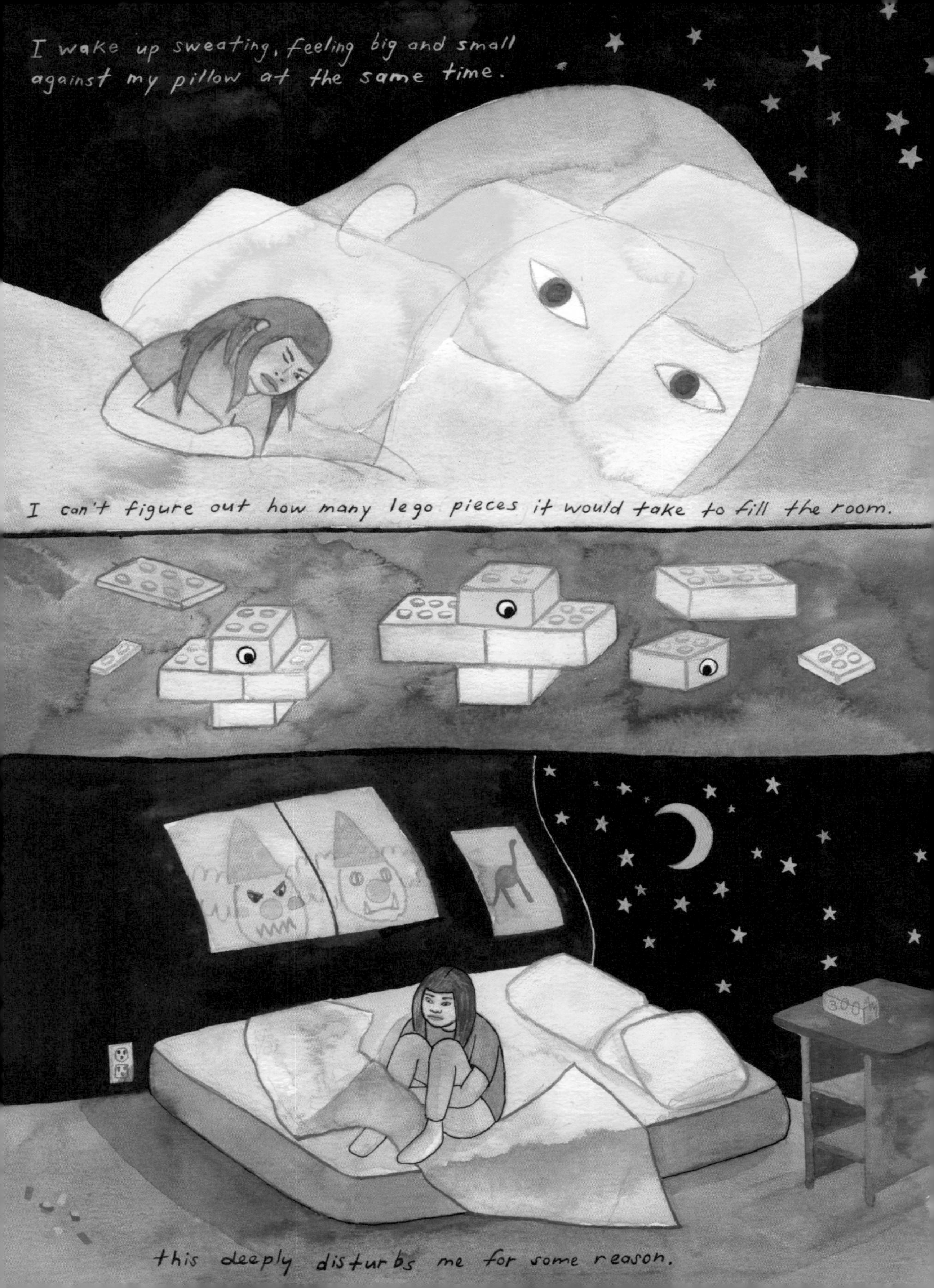
I wake up sweating, feeling big and small against my pillow at the same time.
I can't figure out how many lego pieces it would take to fill the room.
this deeply disturbs me for some reason.

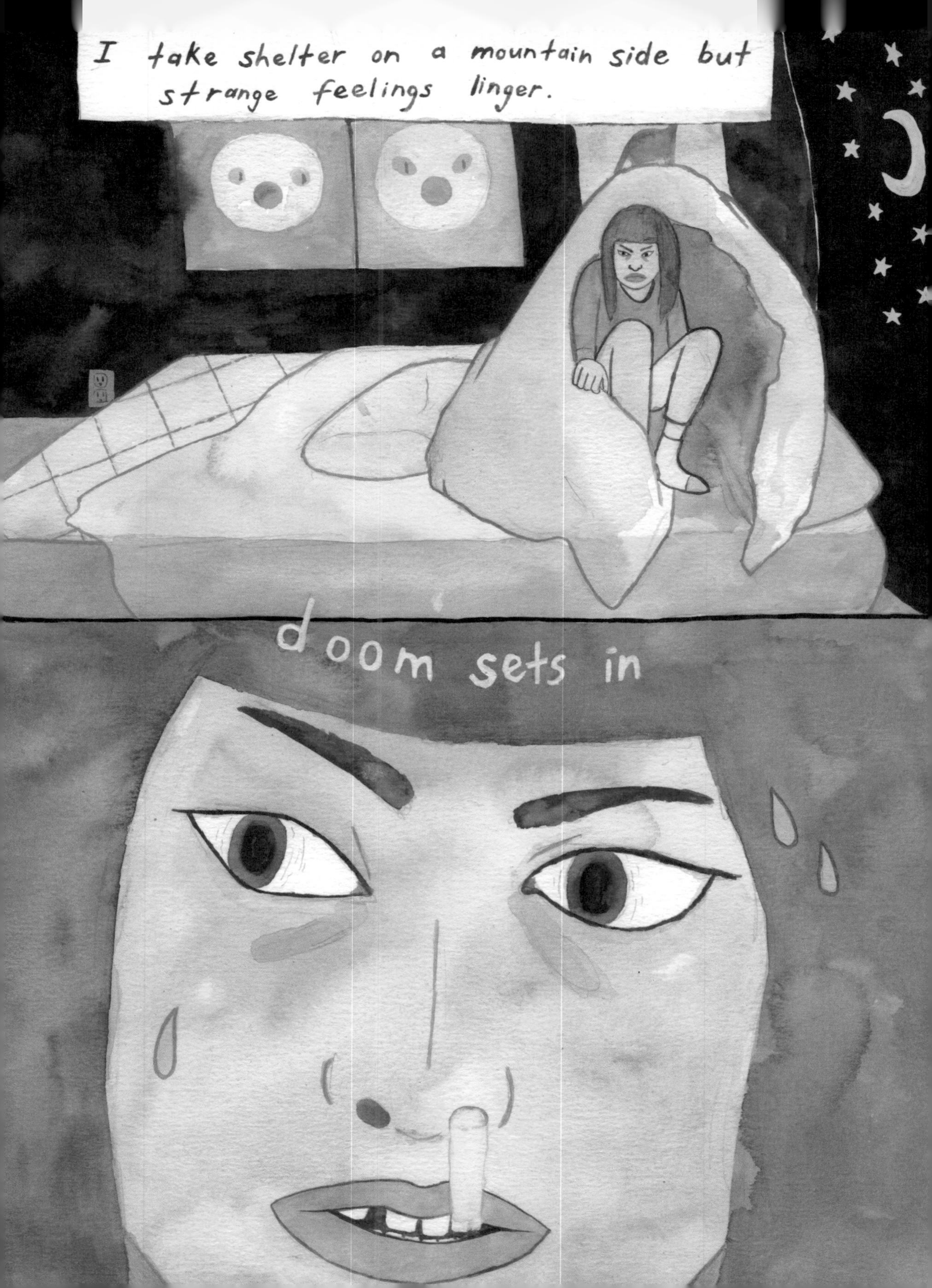
I take shelter on a mountain side but strange feelings linger.
doom sets in

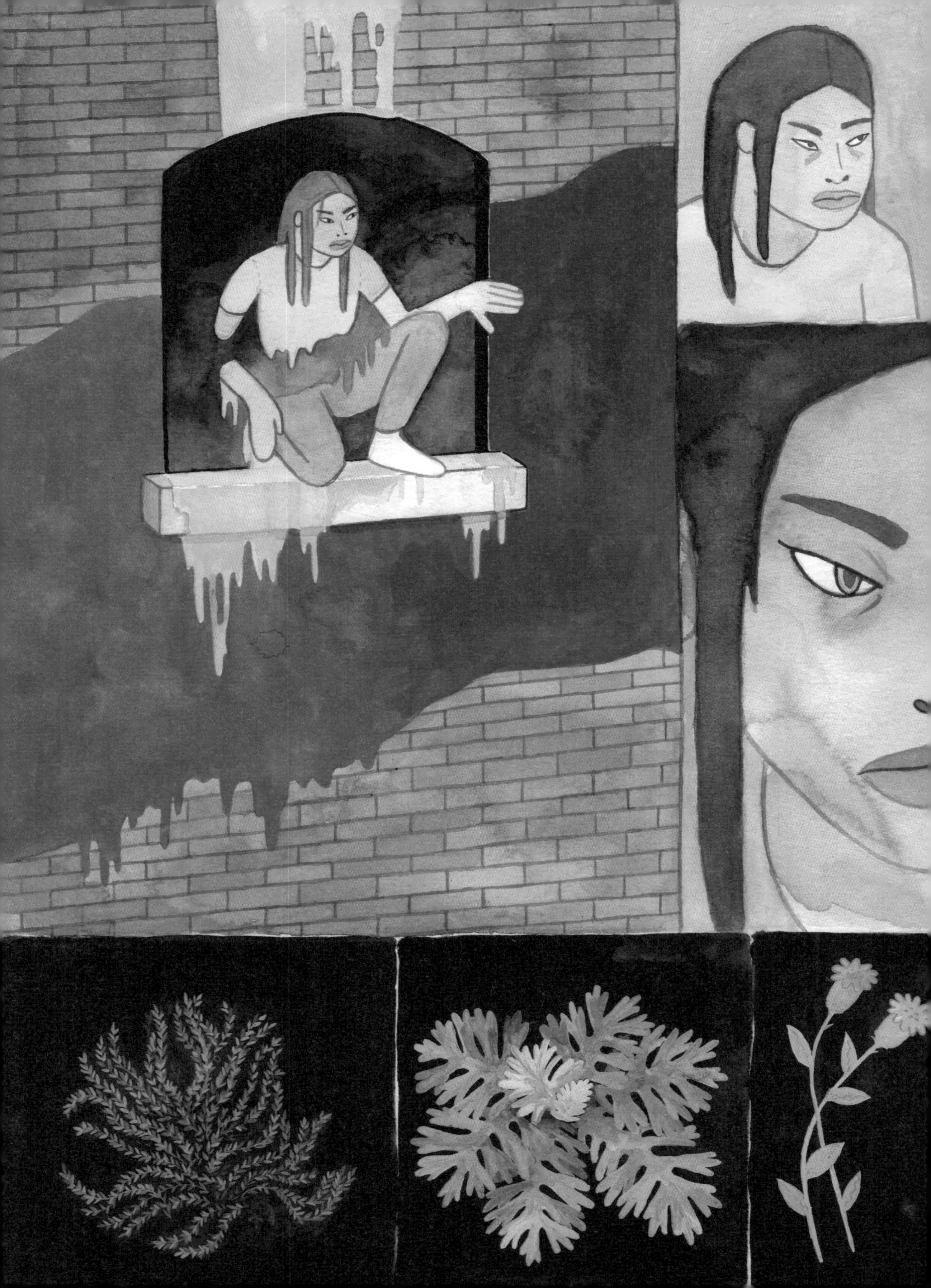

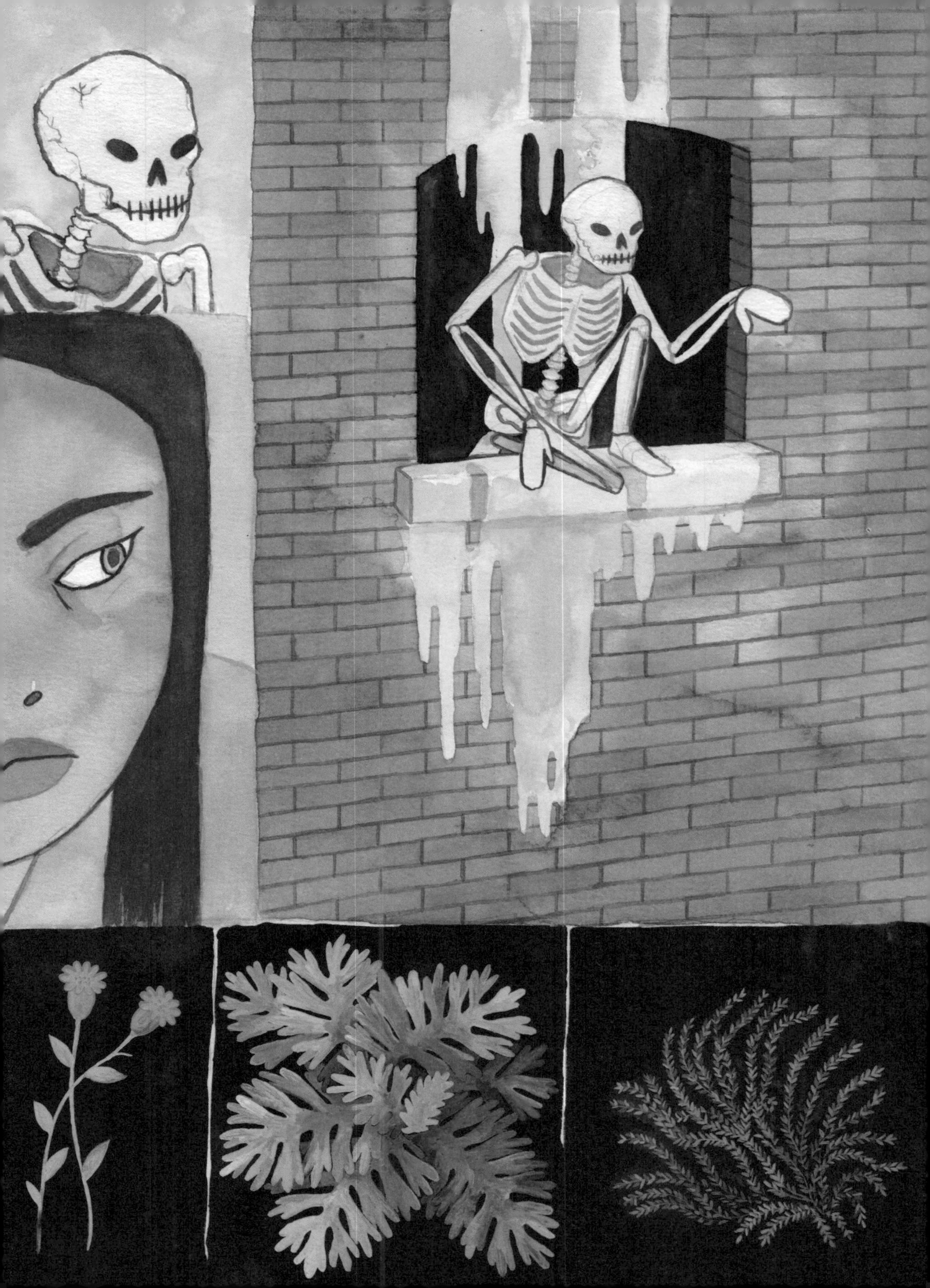

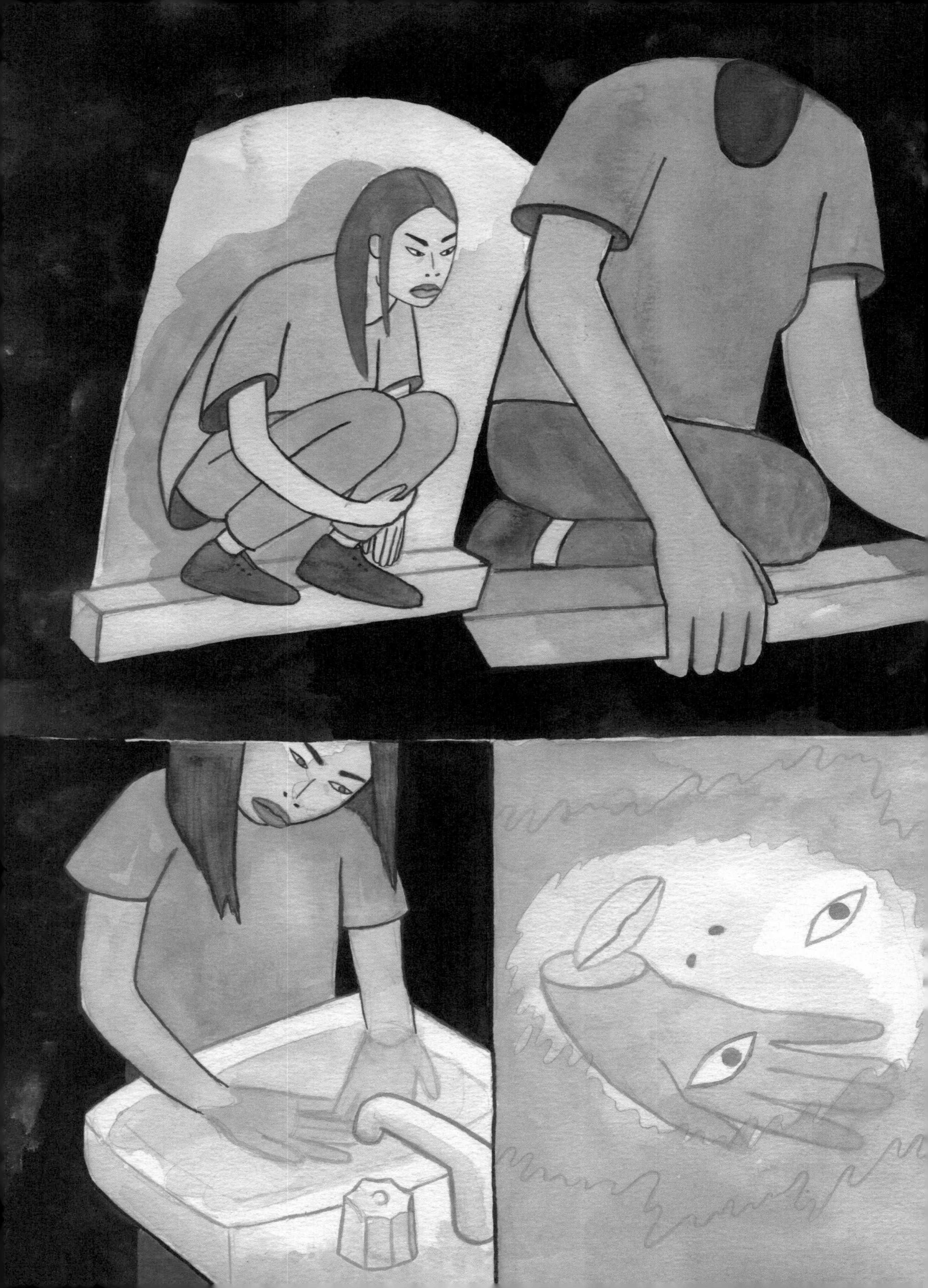

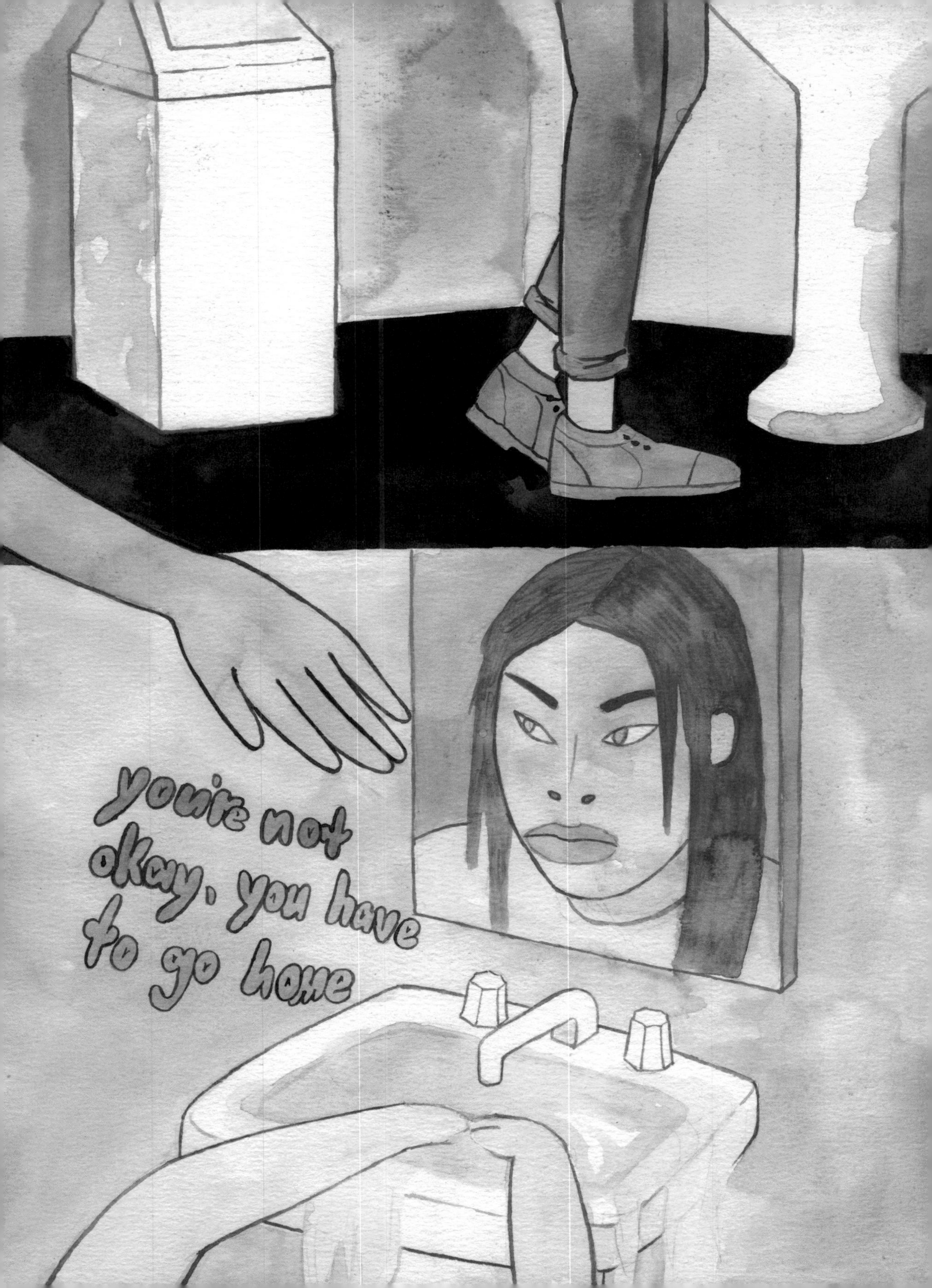
you're not okay, you have to go home

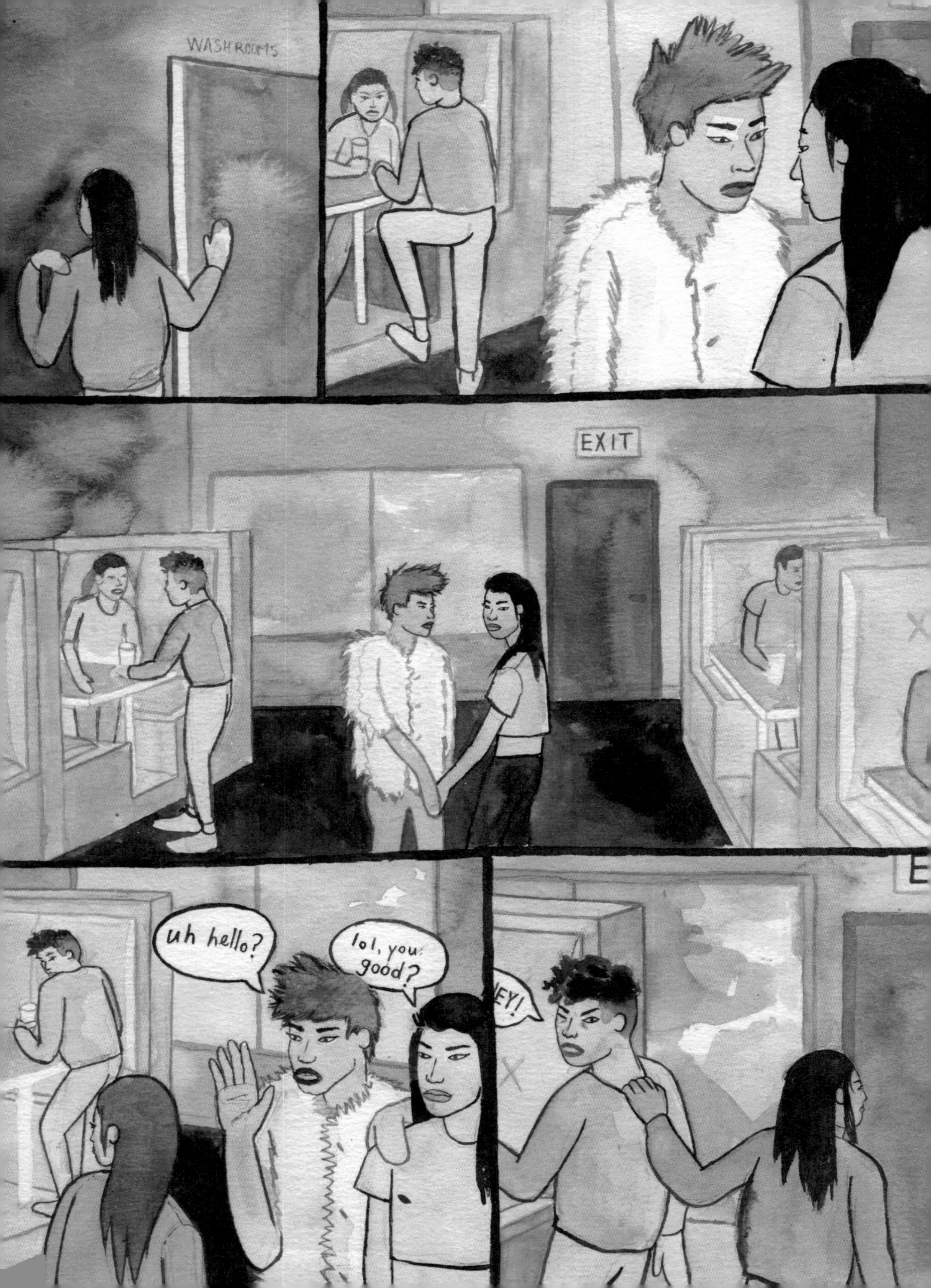
WASHROOMS
EXIT
uh hello?
lol, you good?
EY!

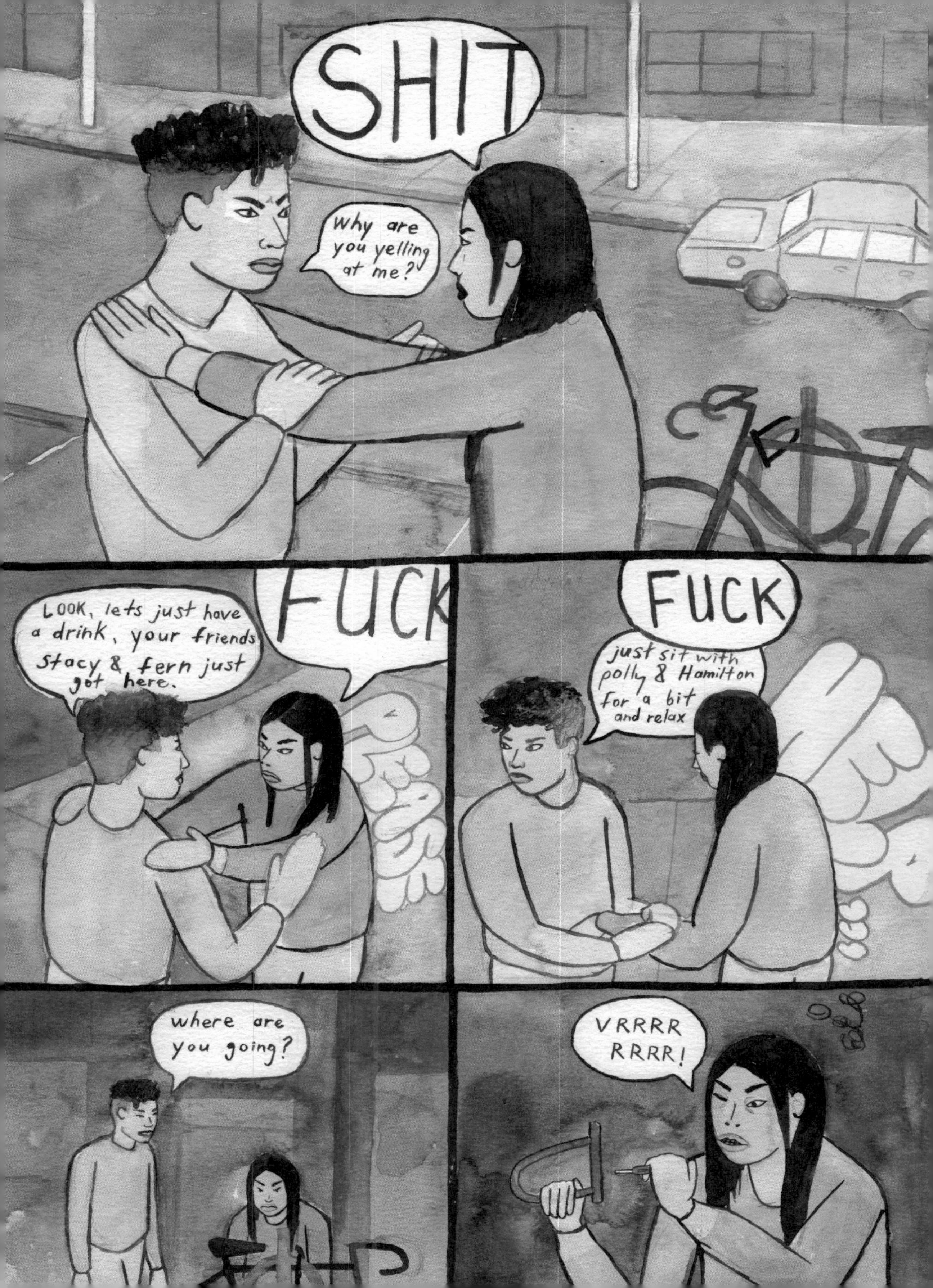
SHIT
why are you yelling at me?
LOOK, lets just have a drink, your friends Stacy & fern just got here.
FUCK
FUCK
just sit with polly & Hamilton for a bit and relax
where are you going?
VRRRR RRRR!

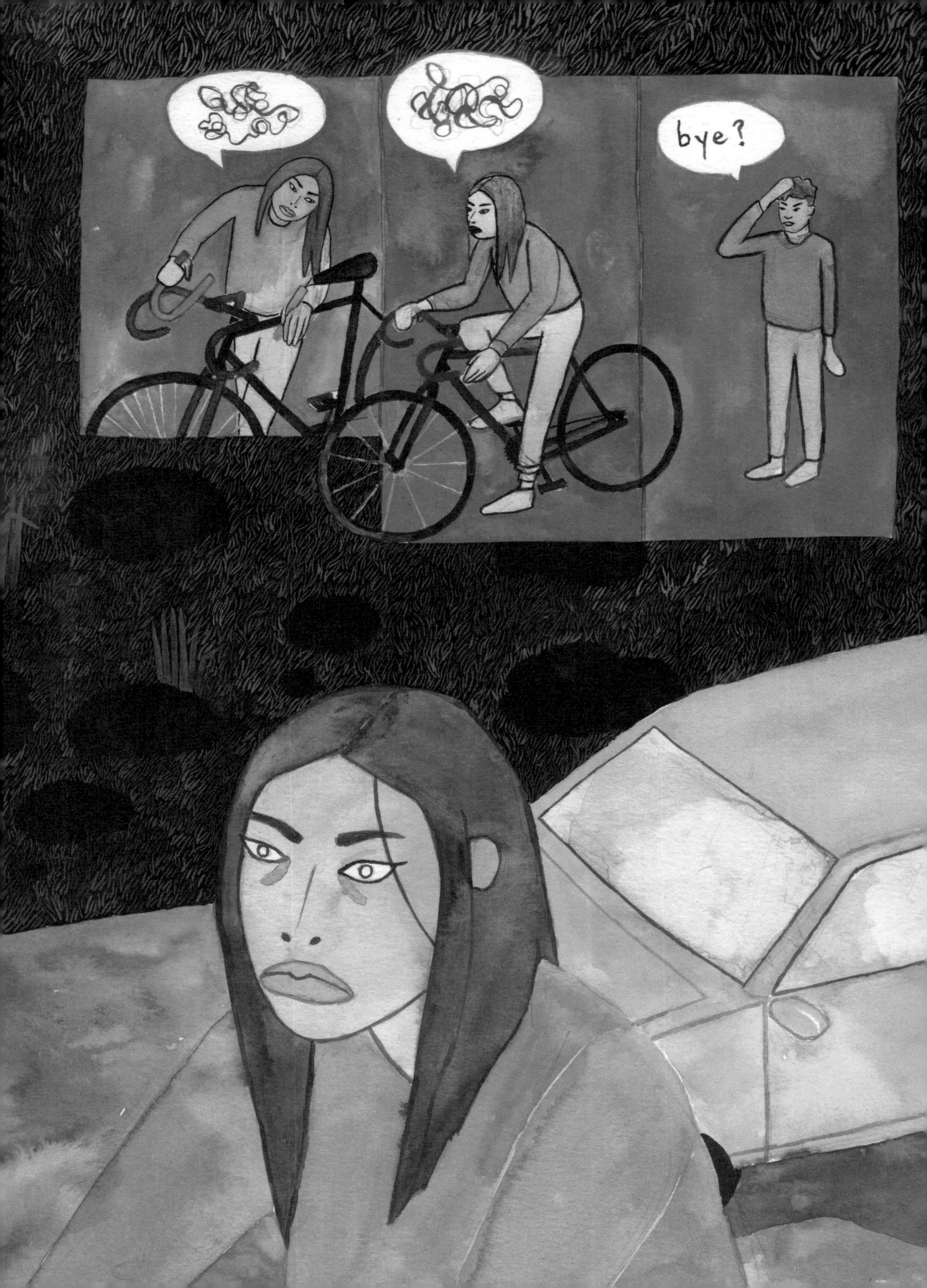
bye?

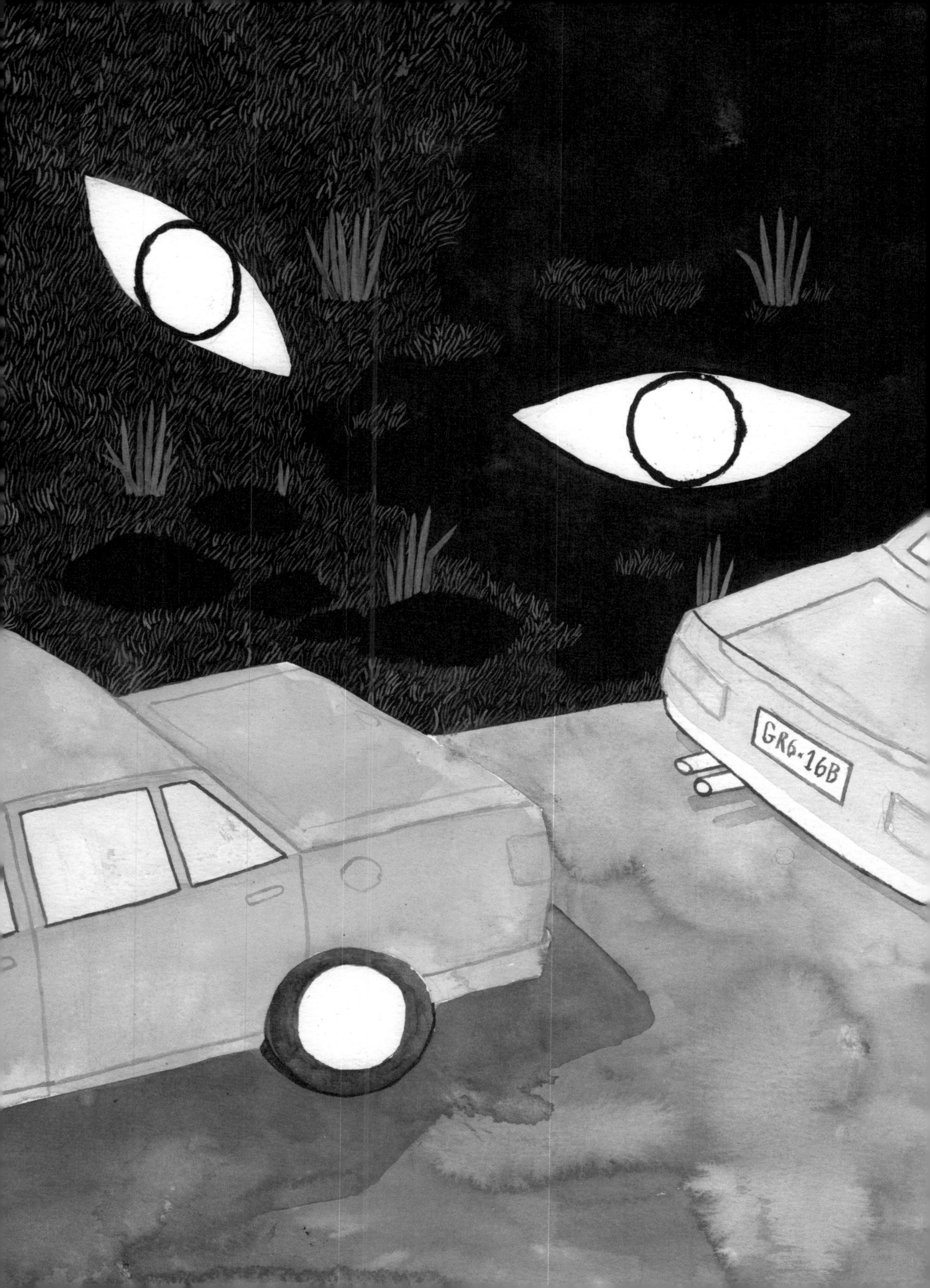
GR6-16B

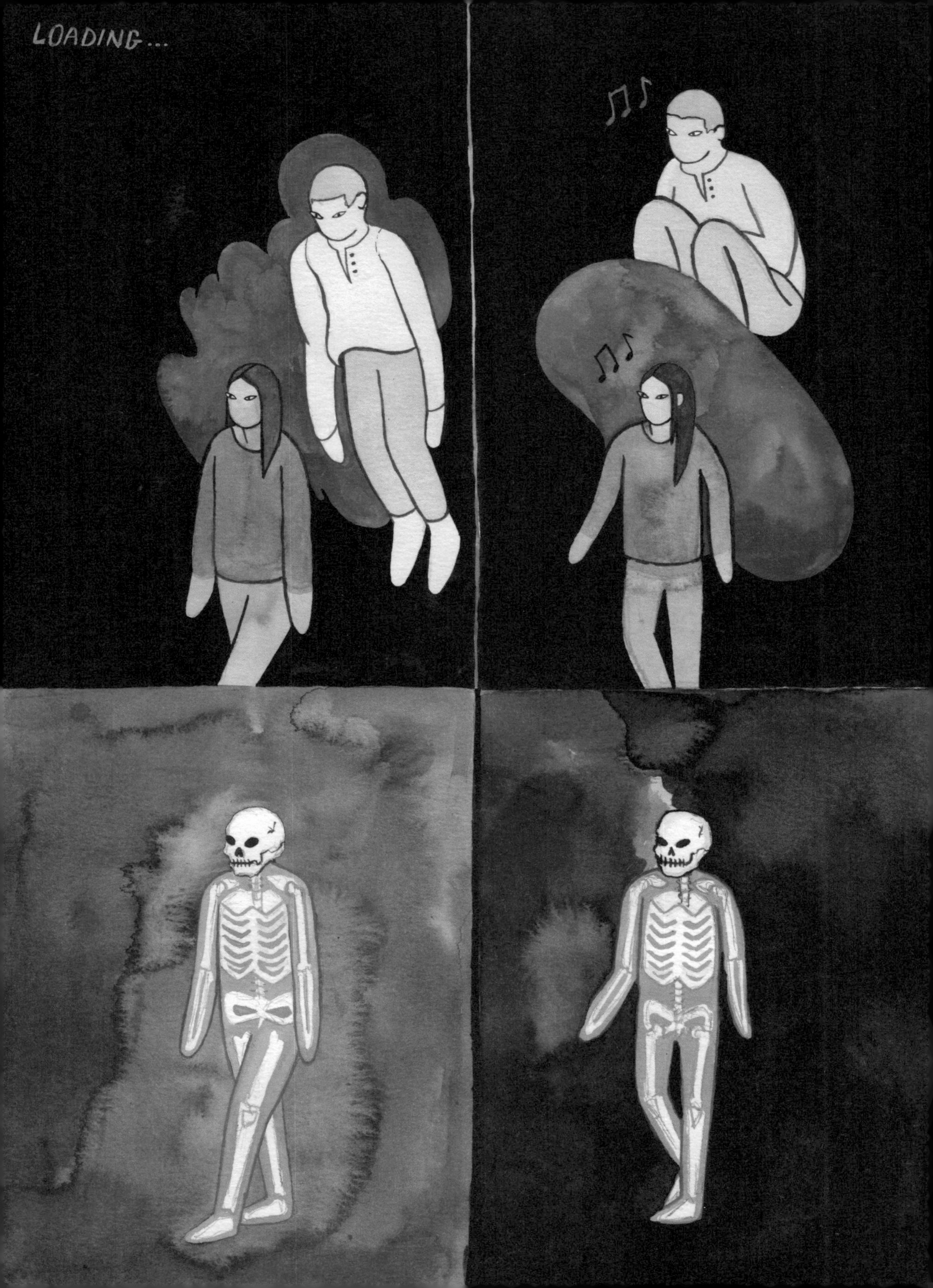
LOADING...

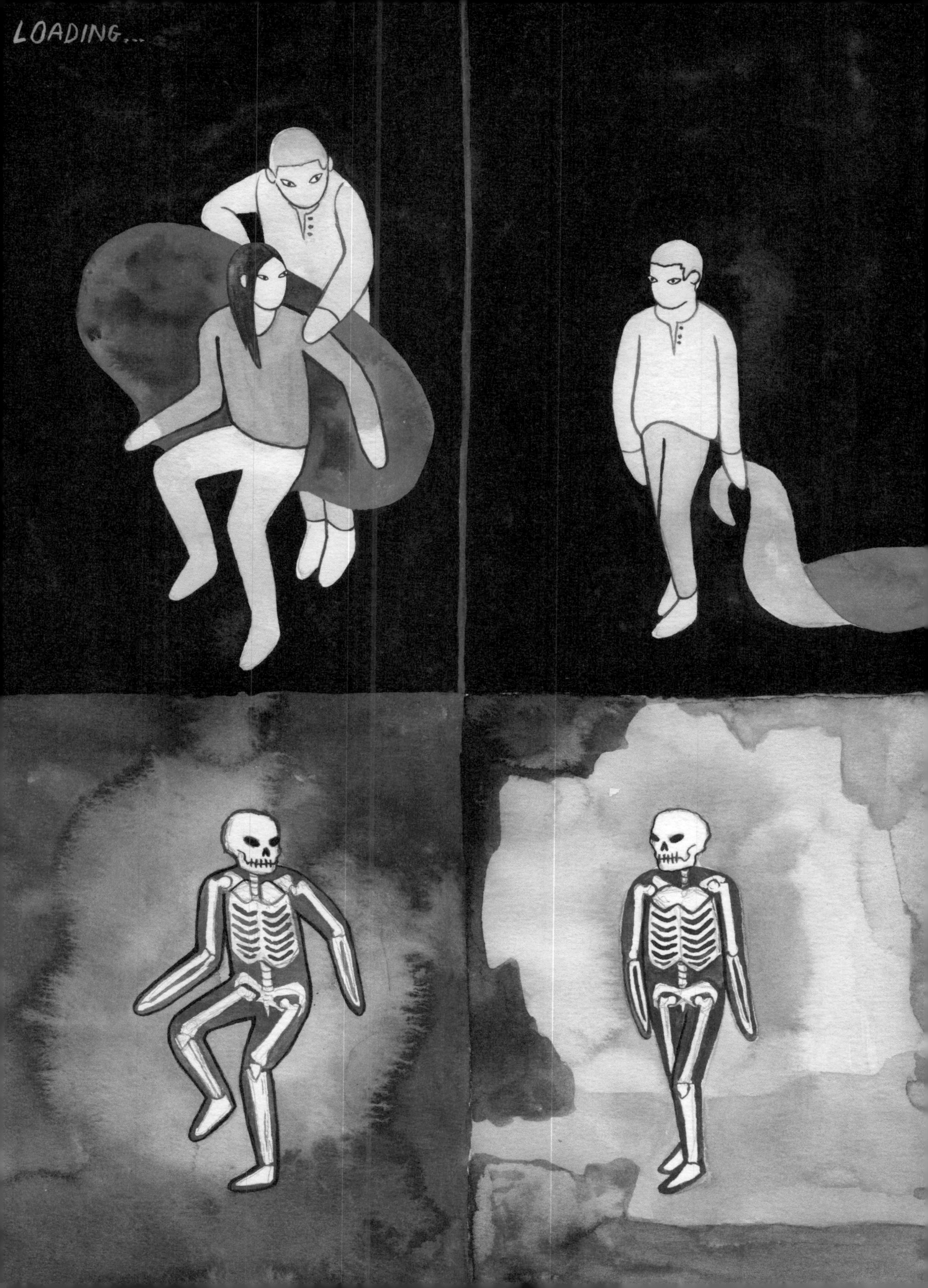
LOADING...

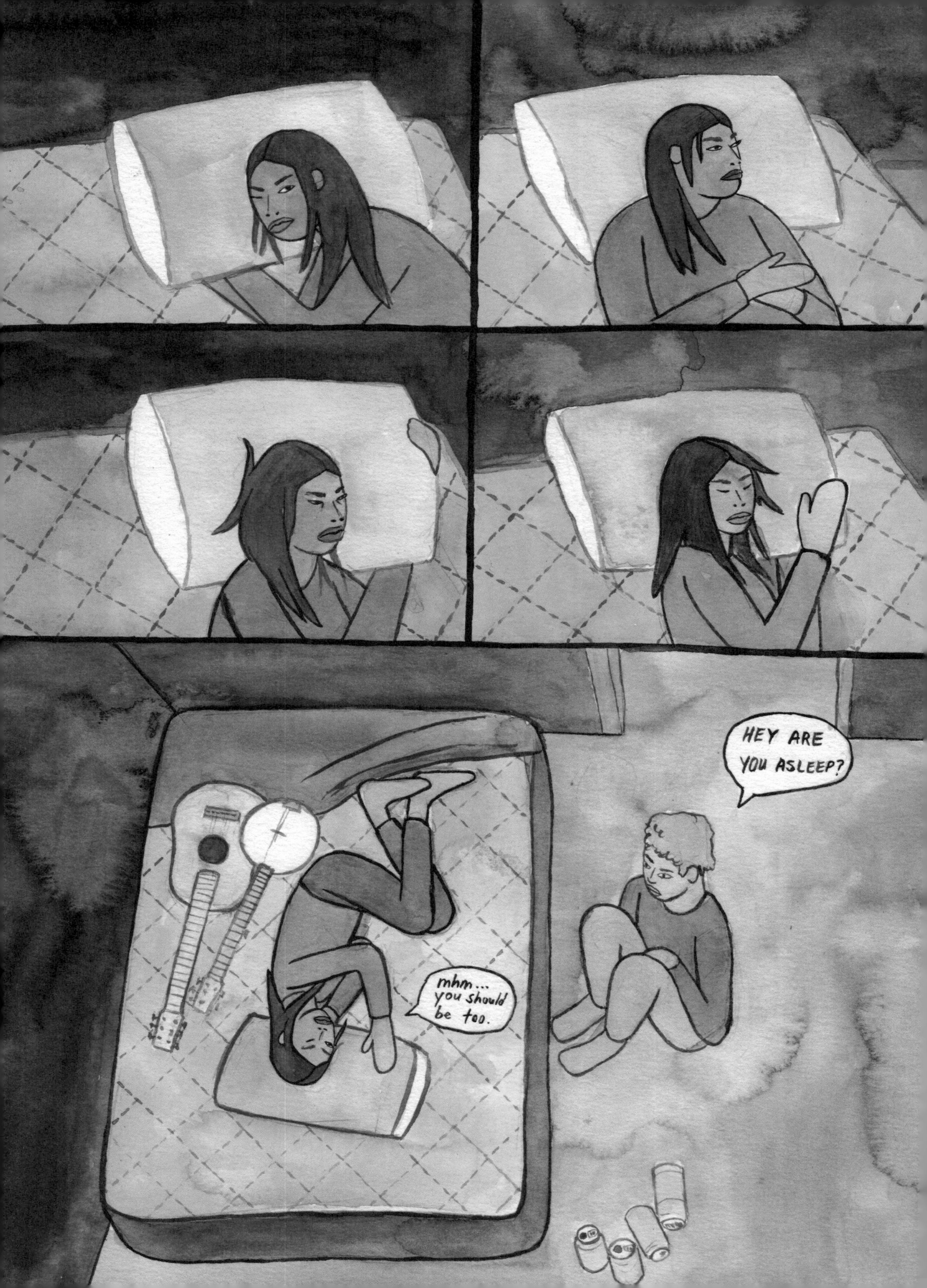
HEY ARE YOU ASLEEP?
mhm... you should be too.

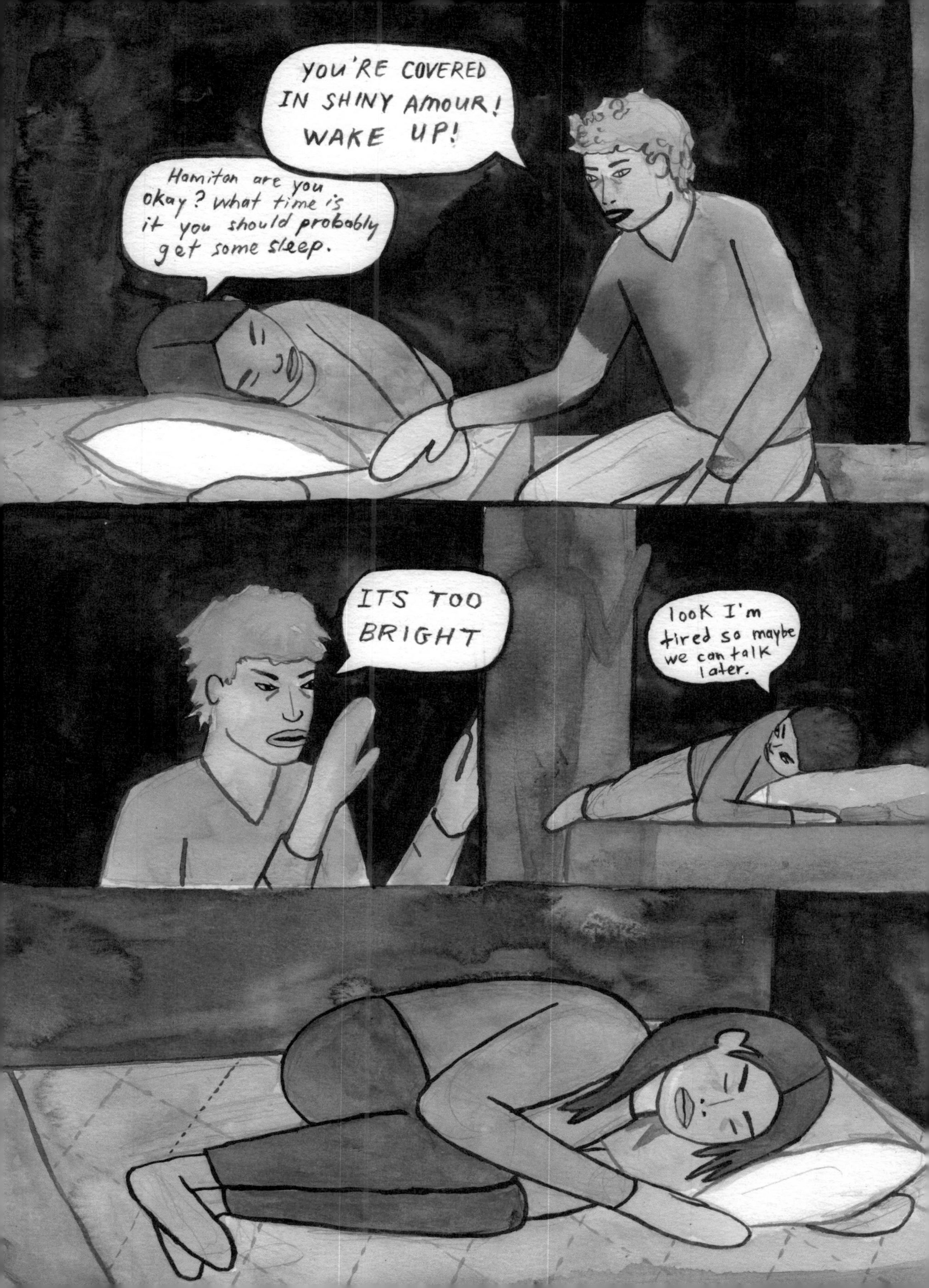
YOU'RE COVERED IN SHINY AMOUR! WAKE UP!
Hamiton are you okay? what time is it you should probably get some sleep.
ITS TOO BRIGHT
look I'm tired so maybe we can talk later.

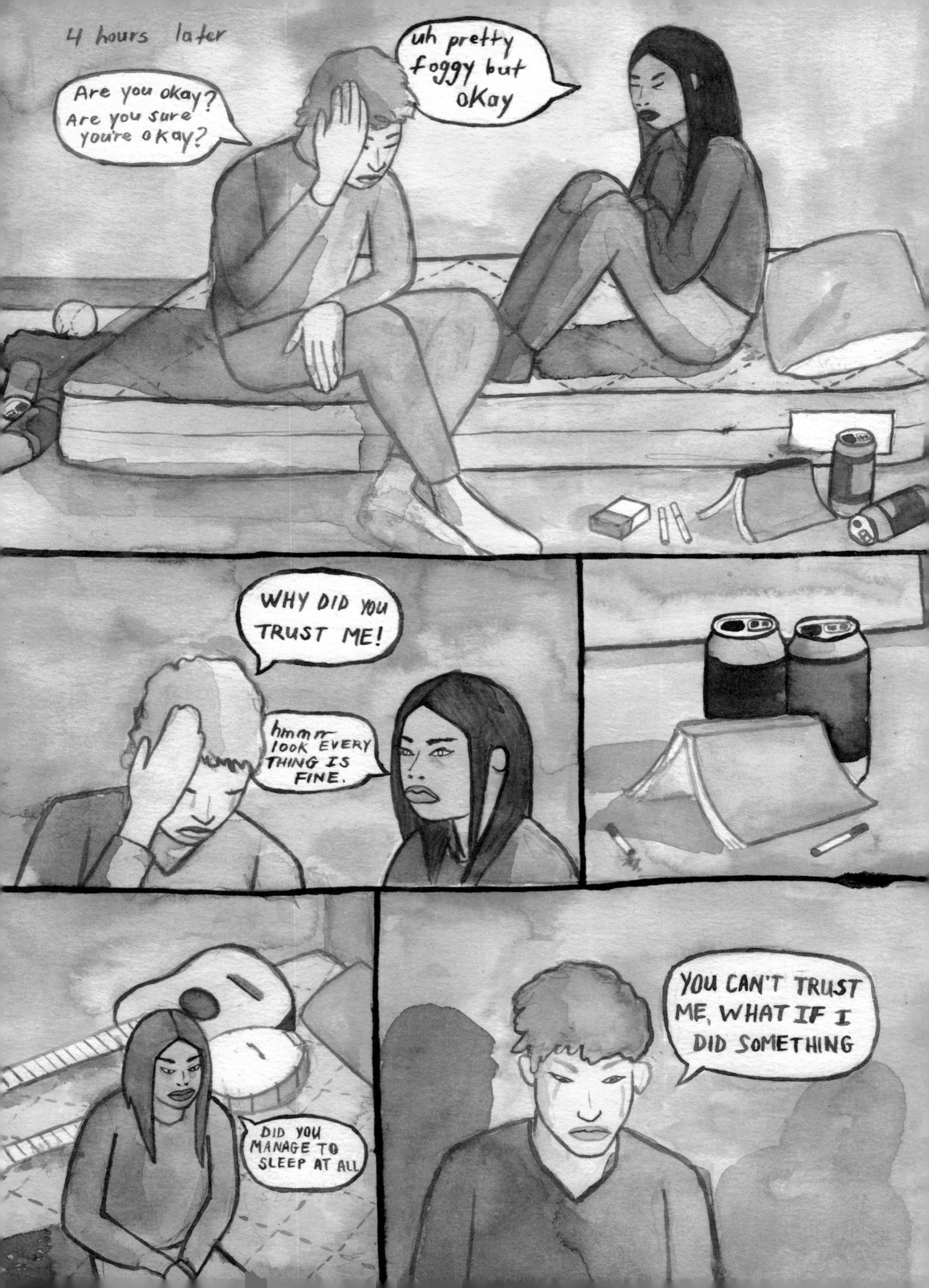
4 hours later
Are you okay? Are you sure you're okay?
uh pretty foggy but okay
WHY DID YOU TRUST ME!
hmmm look EVERY THING IS FINE.
DID YOU MANAGE TO SLEEP AT ALL
YOU CAN'T TRUST ME, WHAT IF I DID SOMETHING

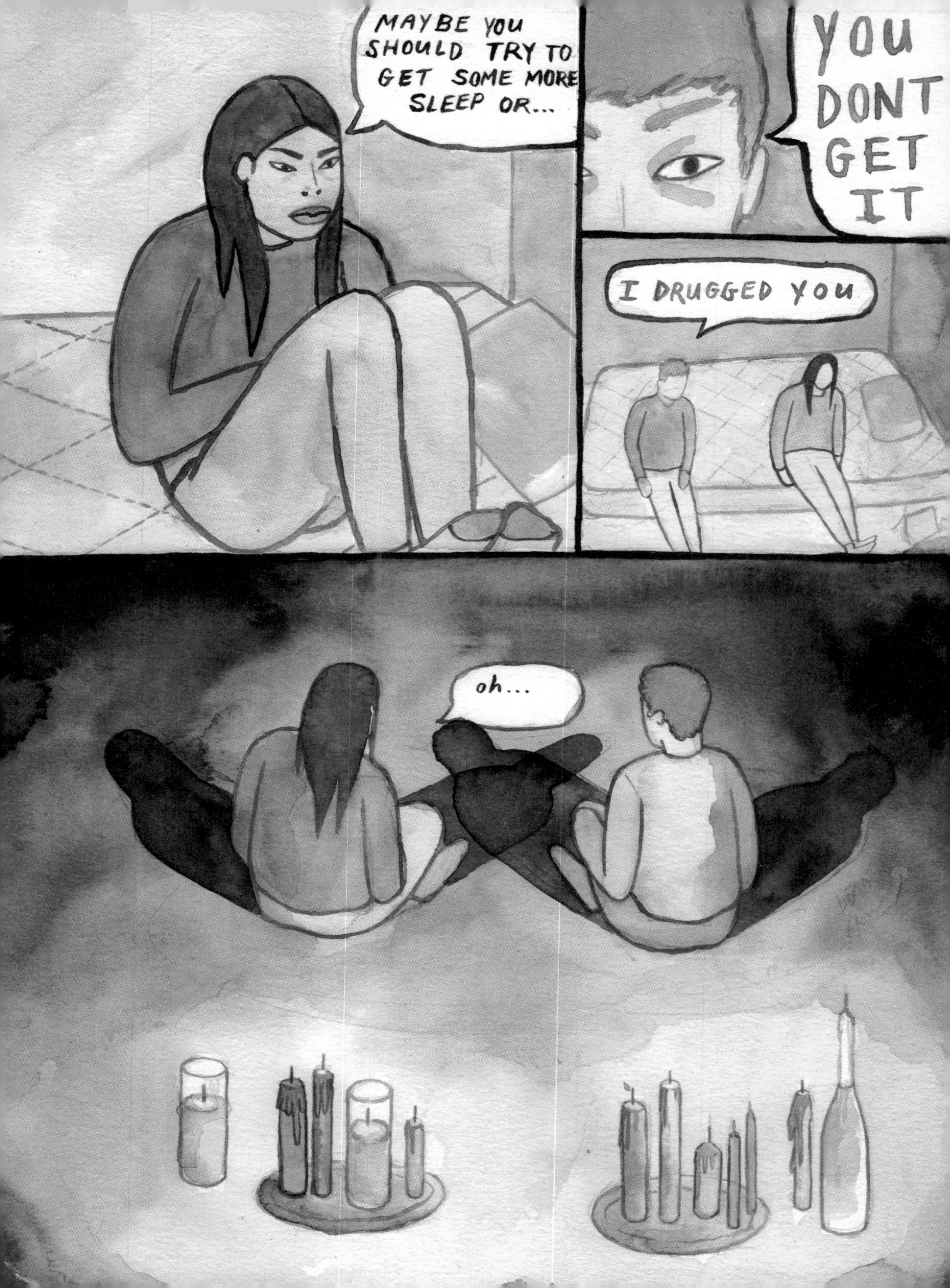
MAYBE YOU SHOULD TRY TO GET SOME MORE SLEEP OR...
YOU DONT GET IT
I DRUGGED YOU
oh...

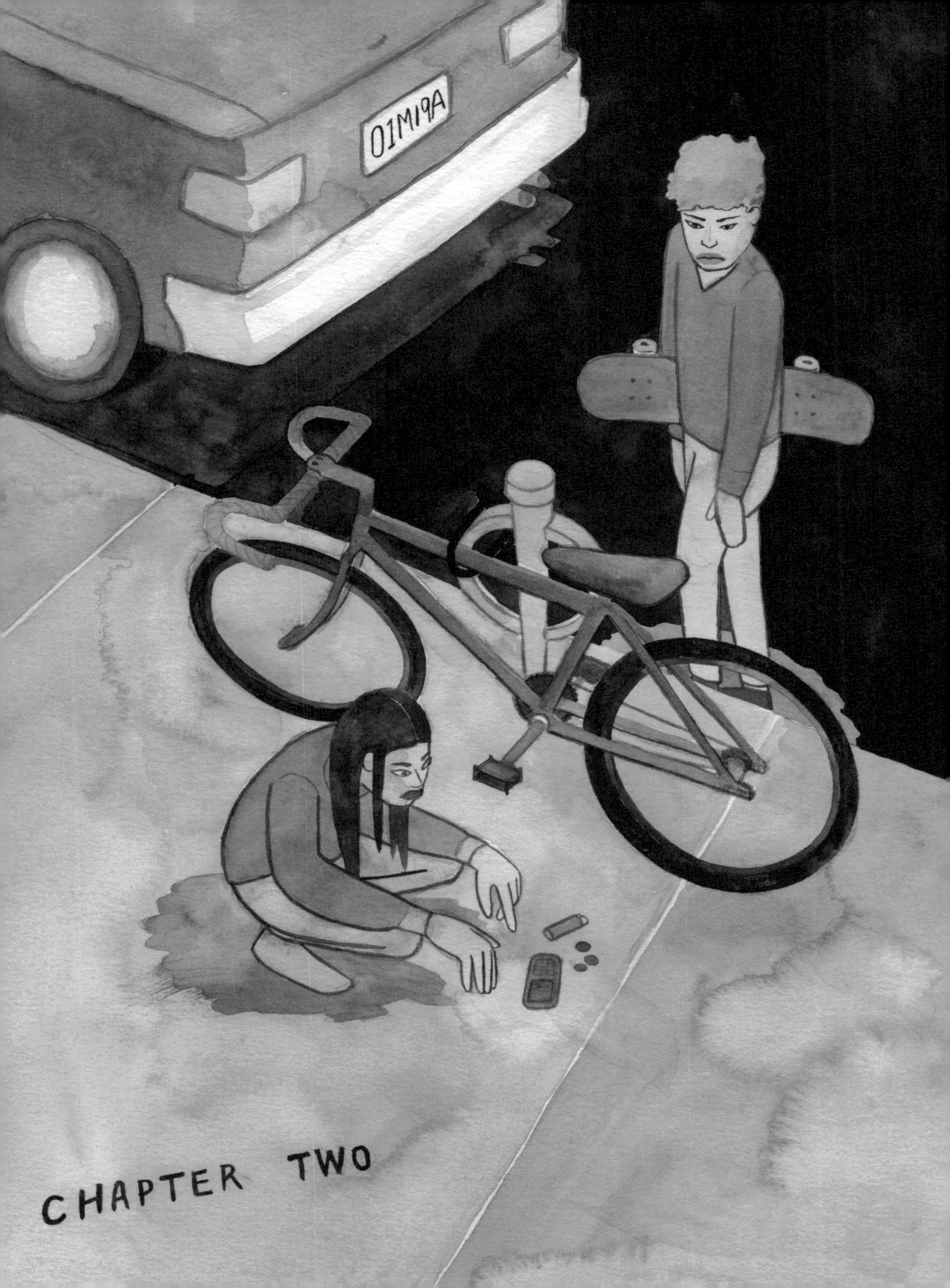
01M19A
CHAPTER TWO

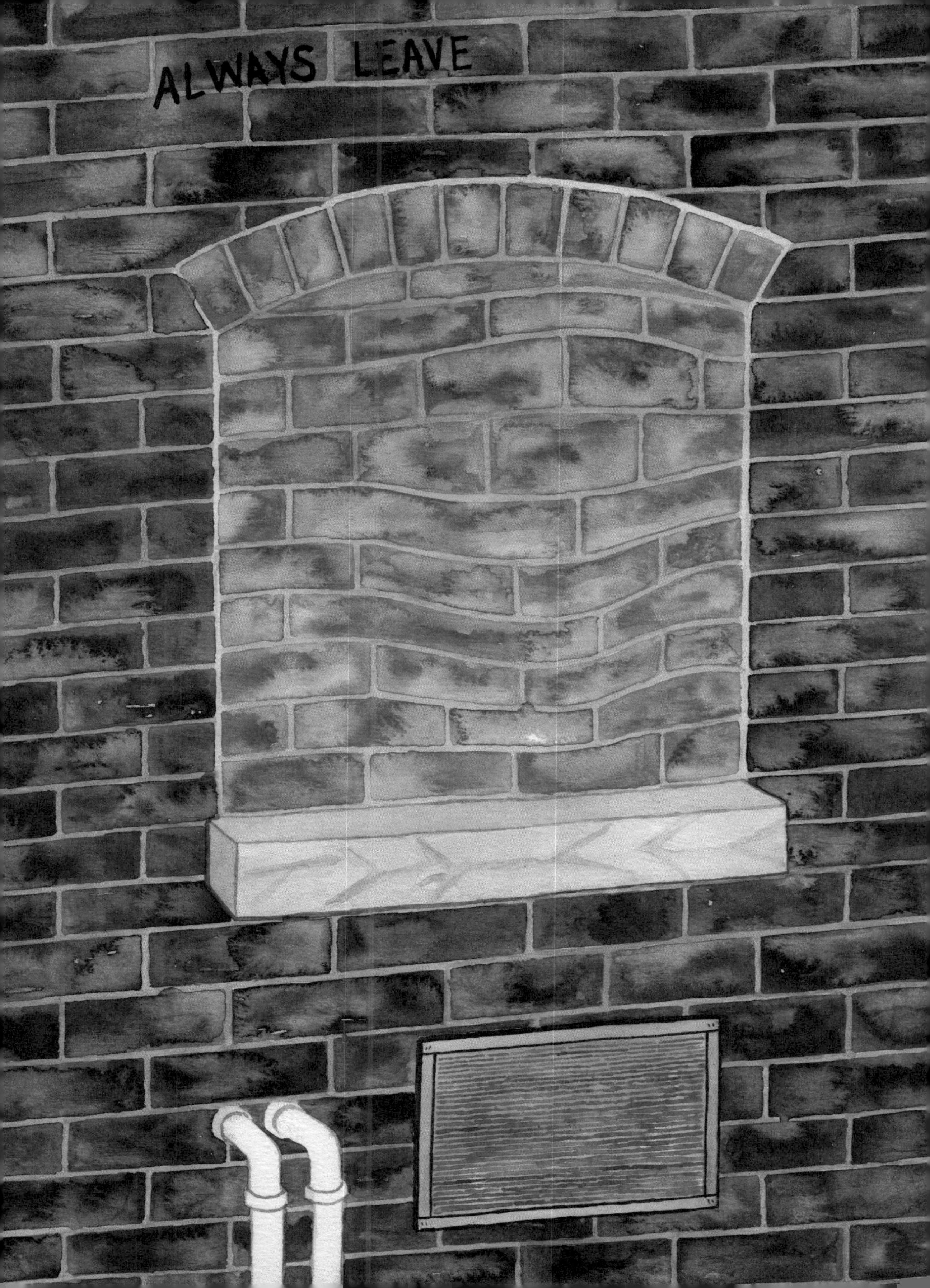
ALWAYS LEAVE

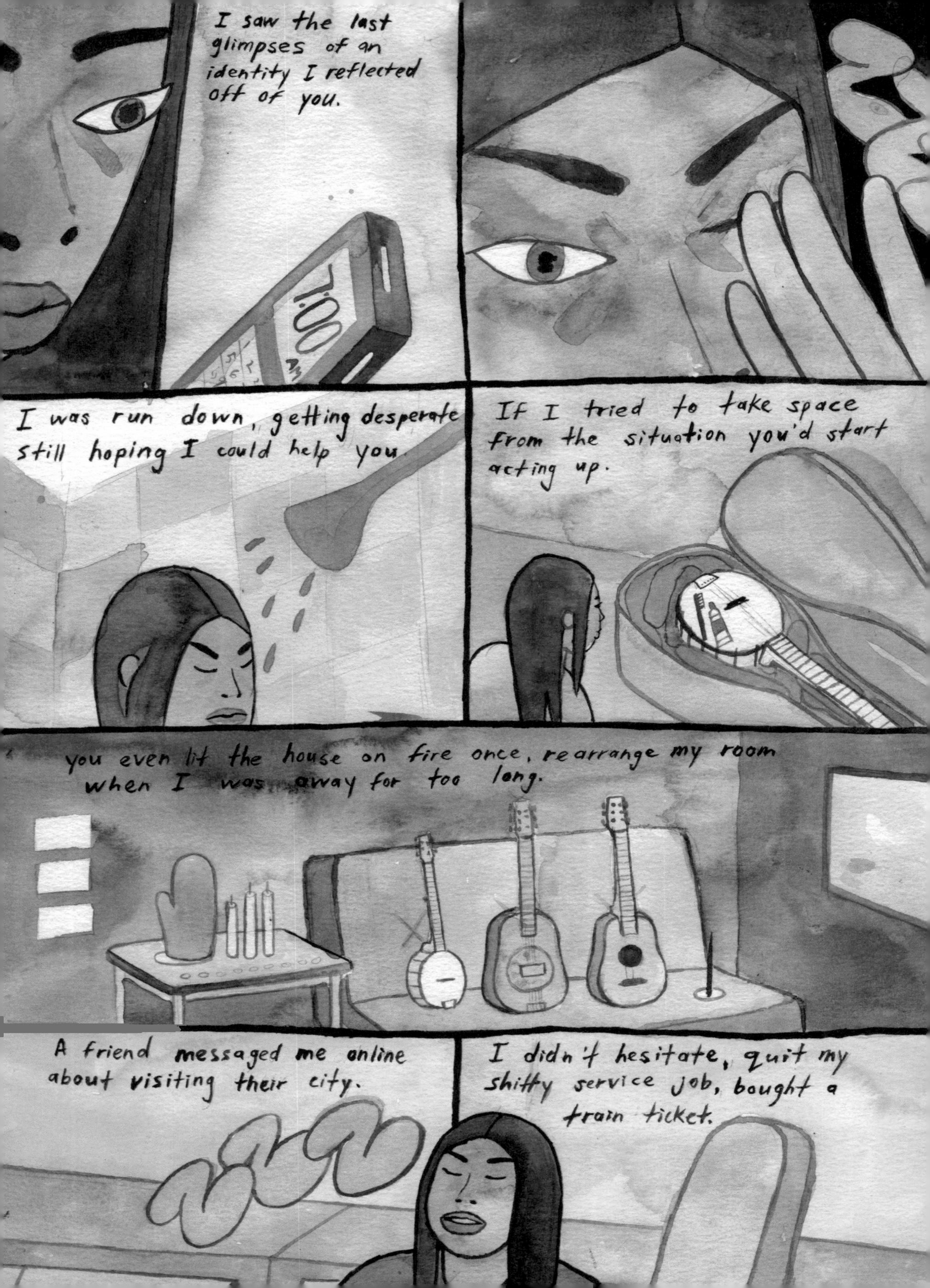
I saw the last glimpses of an identity I reflected off of you.
1:00
I was run down, getting desperate still hoping I could help you.
If I tried to take space from the situation you'd start acting up.
you even lit the house on fire once, rearrange my room when I was away for too long.
A friend messaged me online about visiting their city.
I didn't hesitate, quit my shitty service job, bought a train ticket.

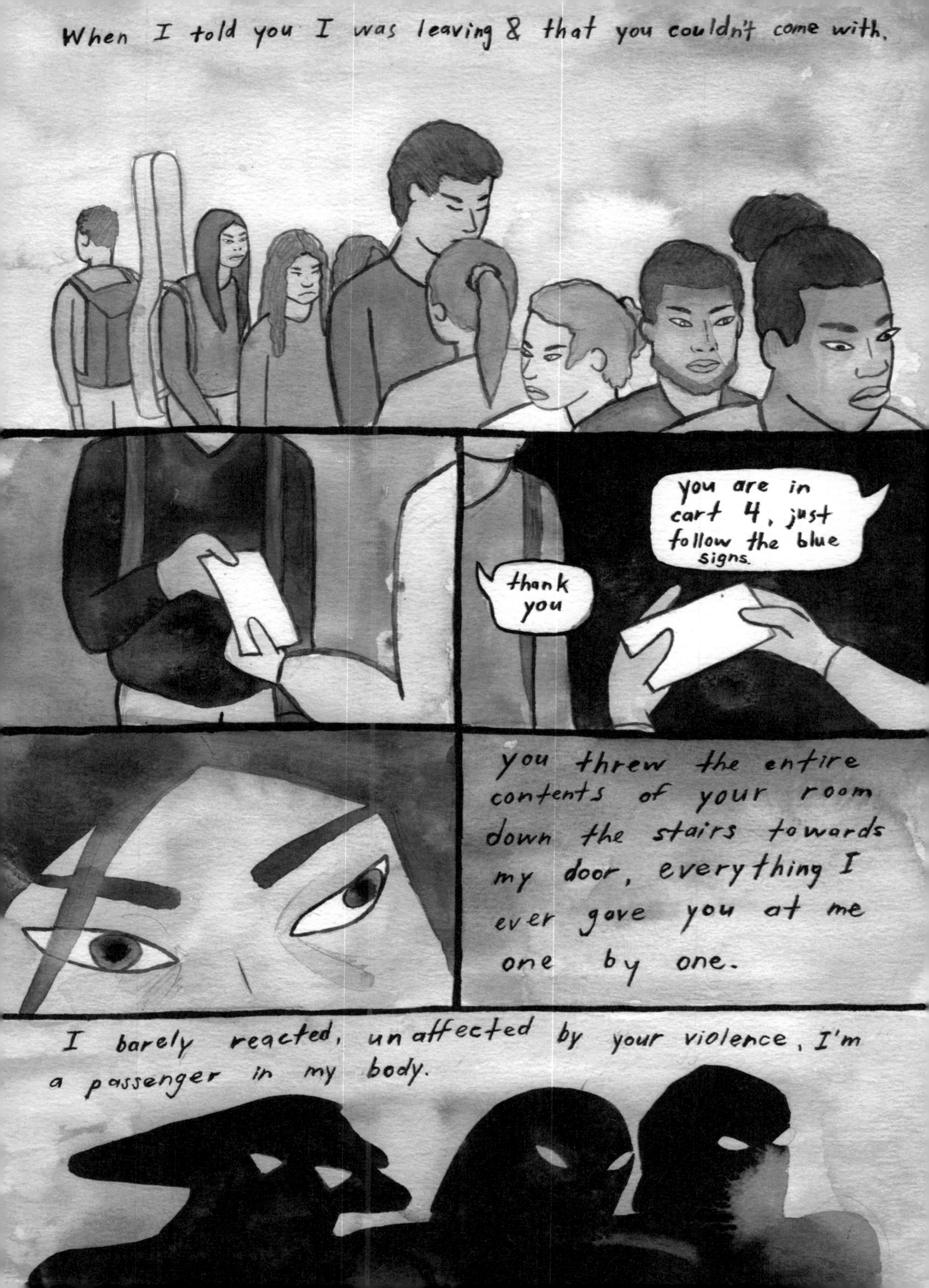
When I told you I was leaving & that you couldn't come with,
you are in cart 4, just follow the blue signs.
thank you
you threw the entire contents of your room down the stairs towards my door, everything I ever gave you at me one by one.
I barely reacted, unaffected by your violence, I'm a passenger in my body.

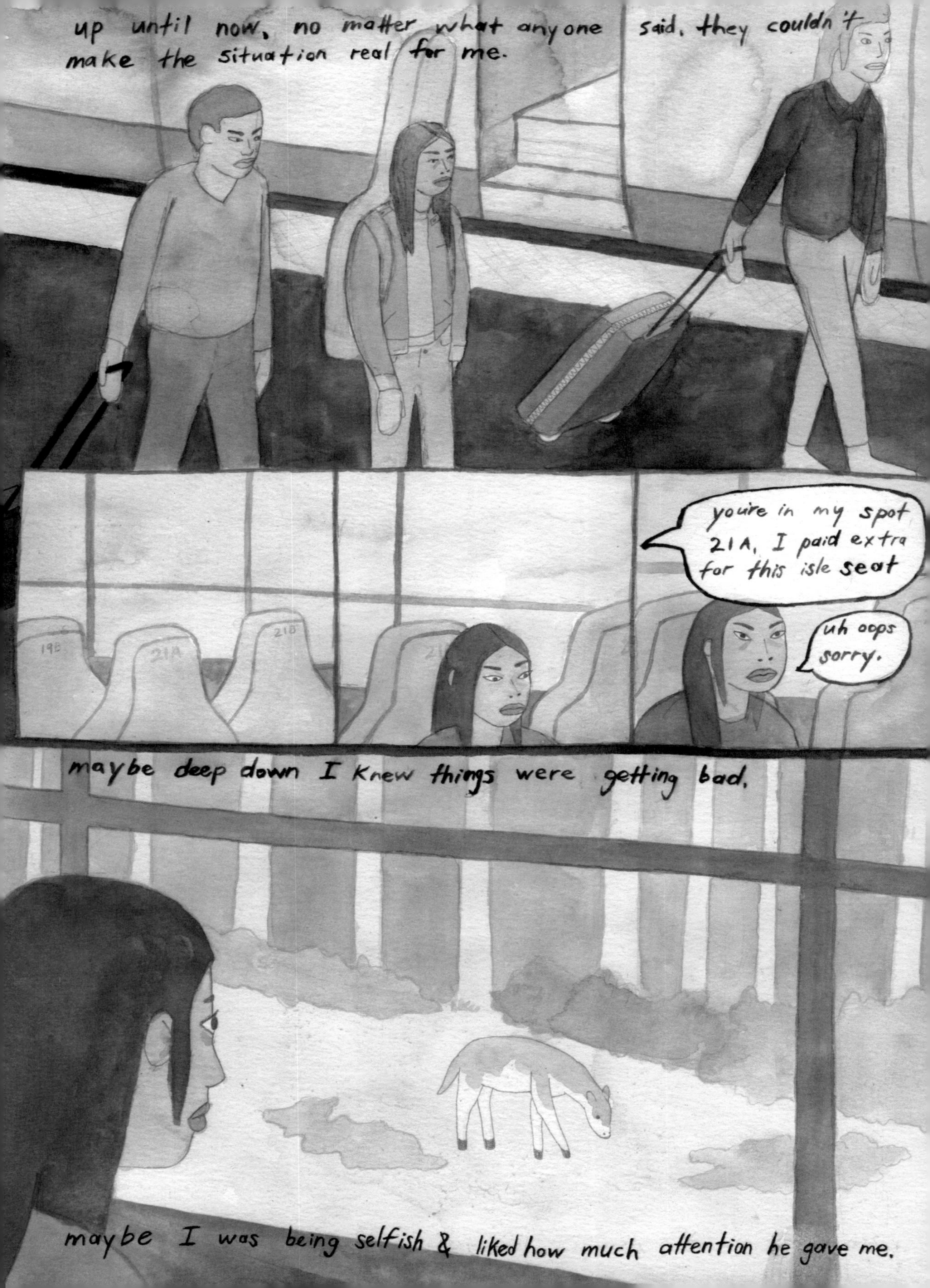
up until now, no matter what anyone said, they couldn't make the situation real for me.
19B
21A
21B
youire in my spot 21A, I paid extra for this isle seat
uh oops sorry.
maybe deep down I knew things were getting bad.
maybe I was being selfish & liked how much attention he gave me.

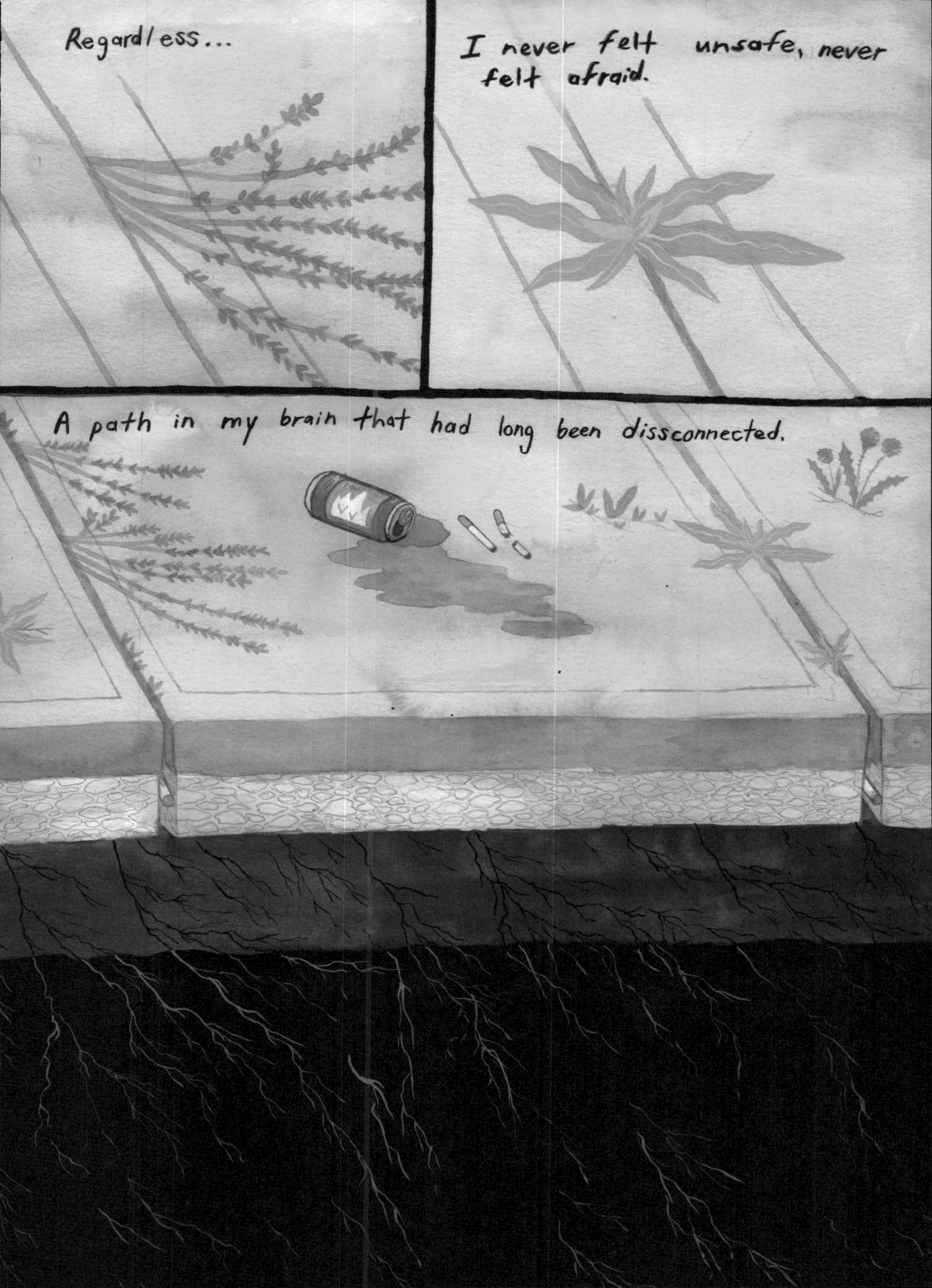
Regardless...
I never felt unsafe, never felt afraid.
A path in my brain that had long been dissconnected.

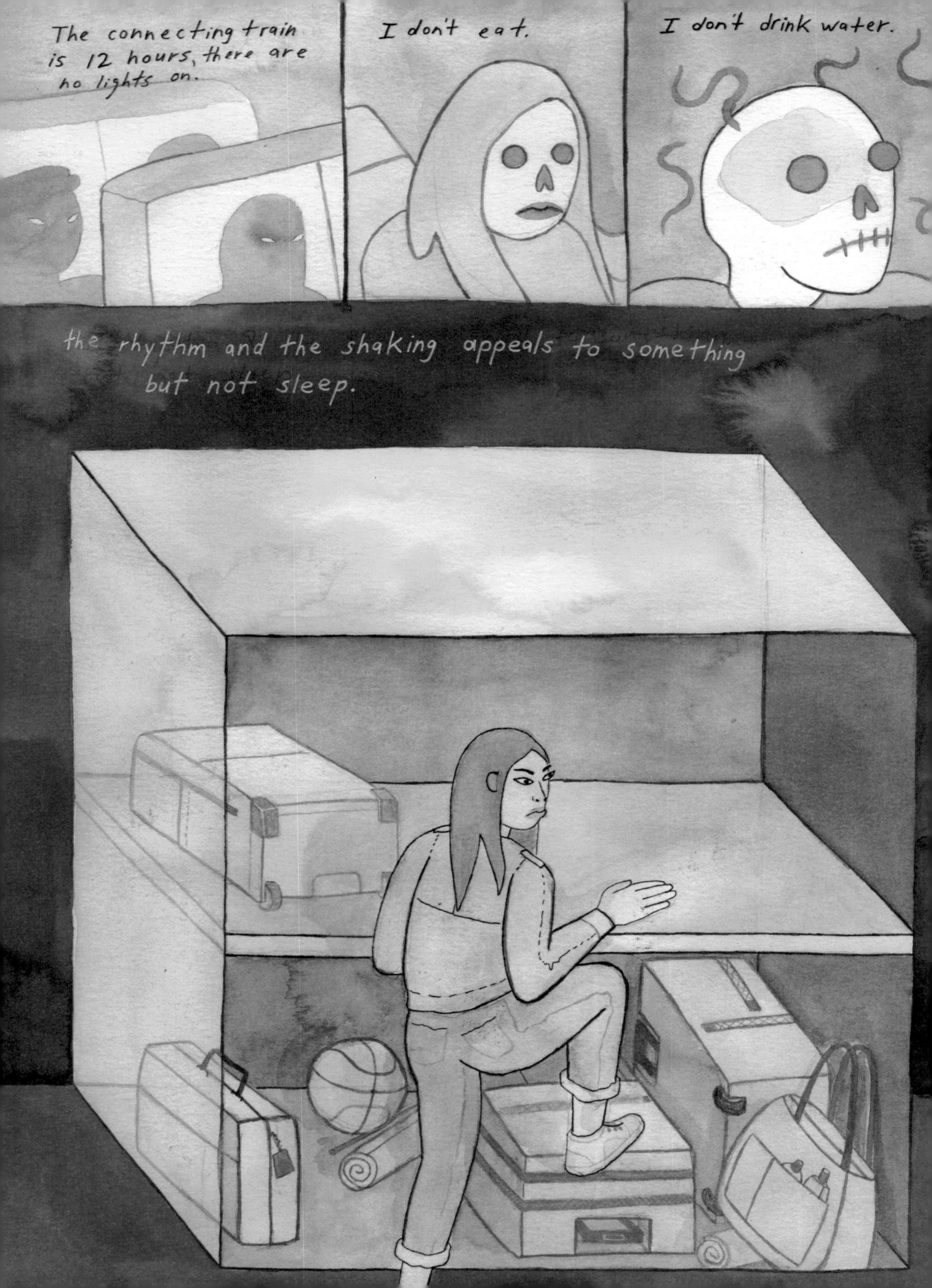
The connecting train is 12 hours, there are no lights on.
I don't eat.
I don't drink water.
the rhythm and the shaking appeals to something but not sleep.

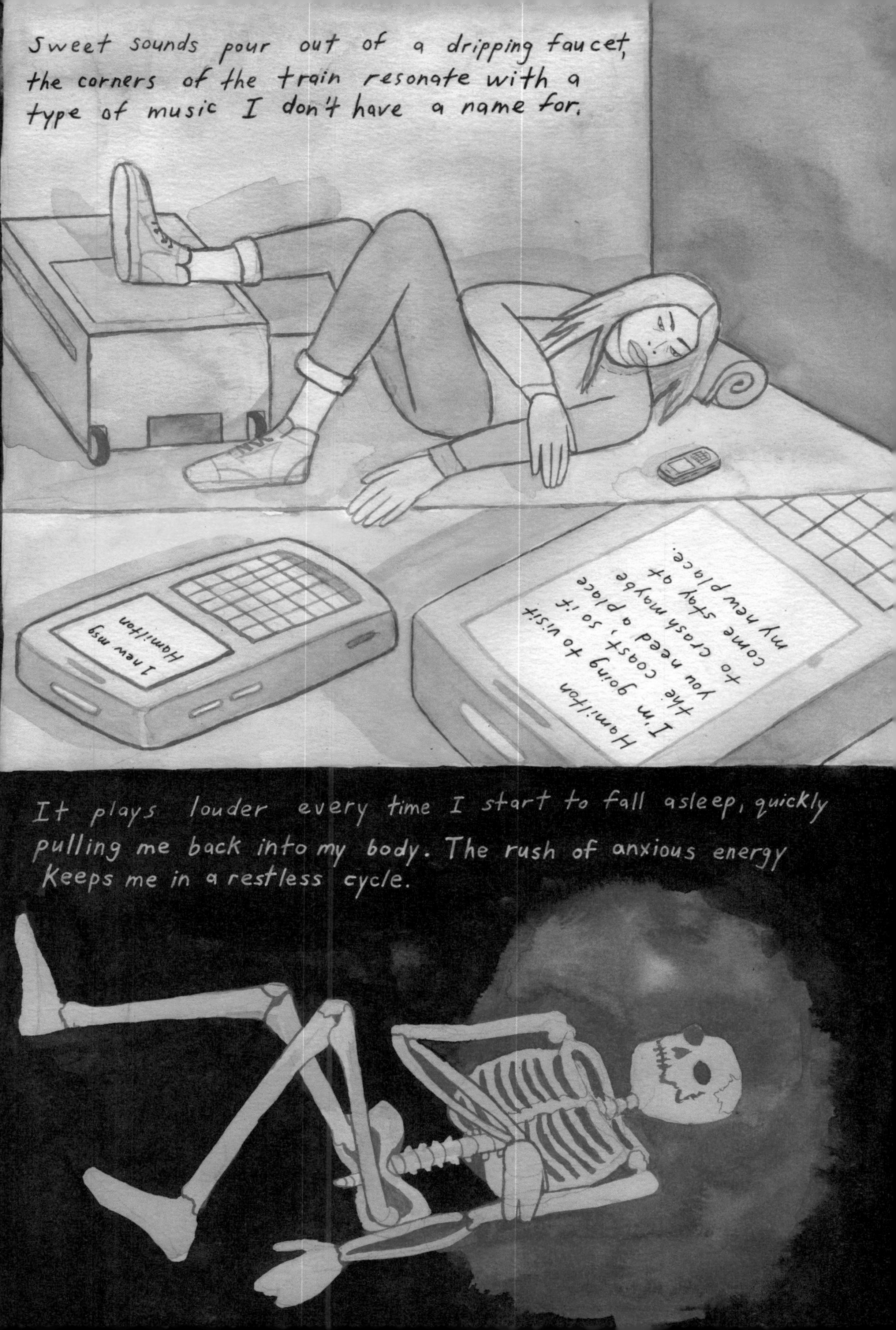
Sweet sounds pour out of a dripping faucet, the corners of the train resonate with a type of music I don't have a name for.
1 new msg
Hamilton
Hamilton
I'm going to the coast, so if you need a place to crash maybe come stay at my new place.
It plays louder every time I start to fall asleep, quickly pulling me back into my body. The rush of anxious energy keeps me in a restless cycle.

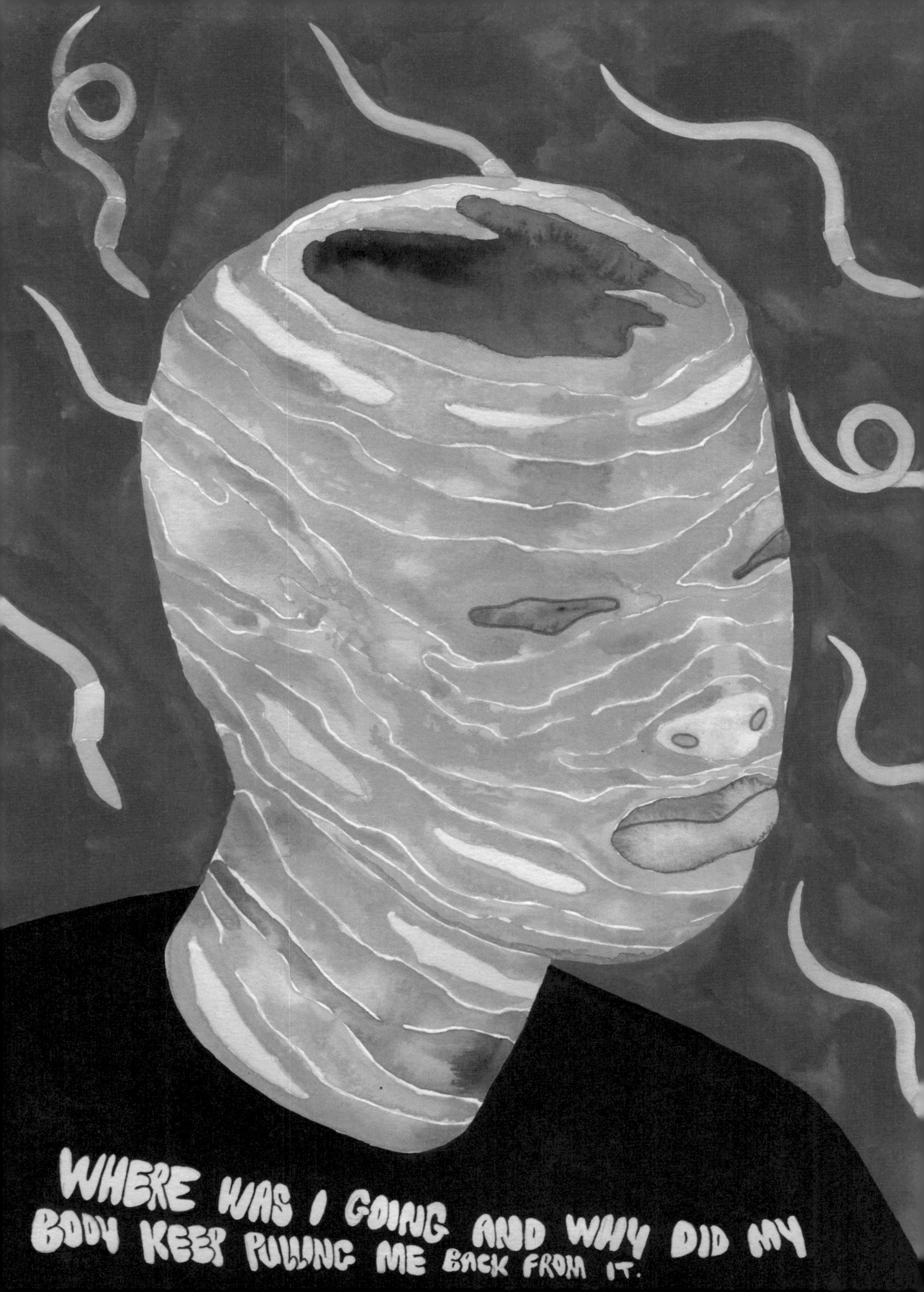
WHERE WAS I GOING AND WHY DID MY BODY KEEP PULLING ME BACK FROM IT.

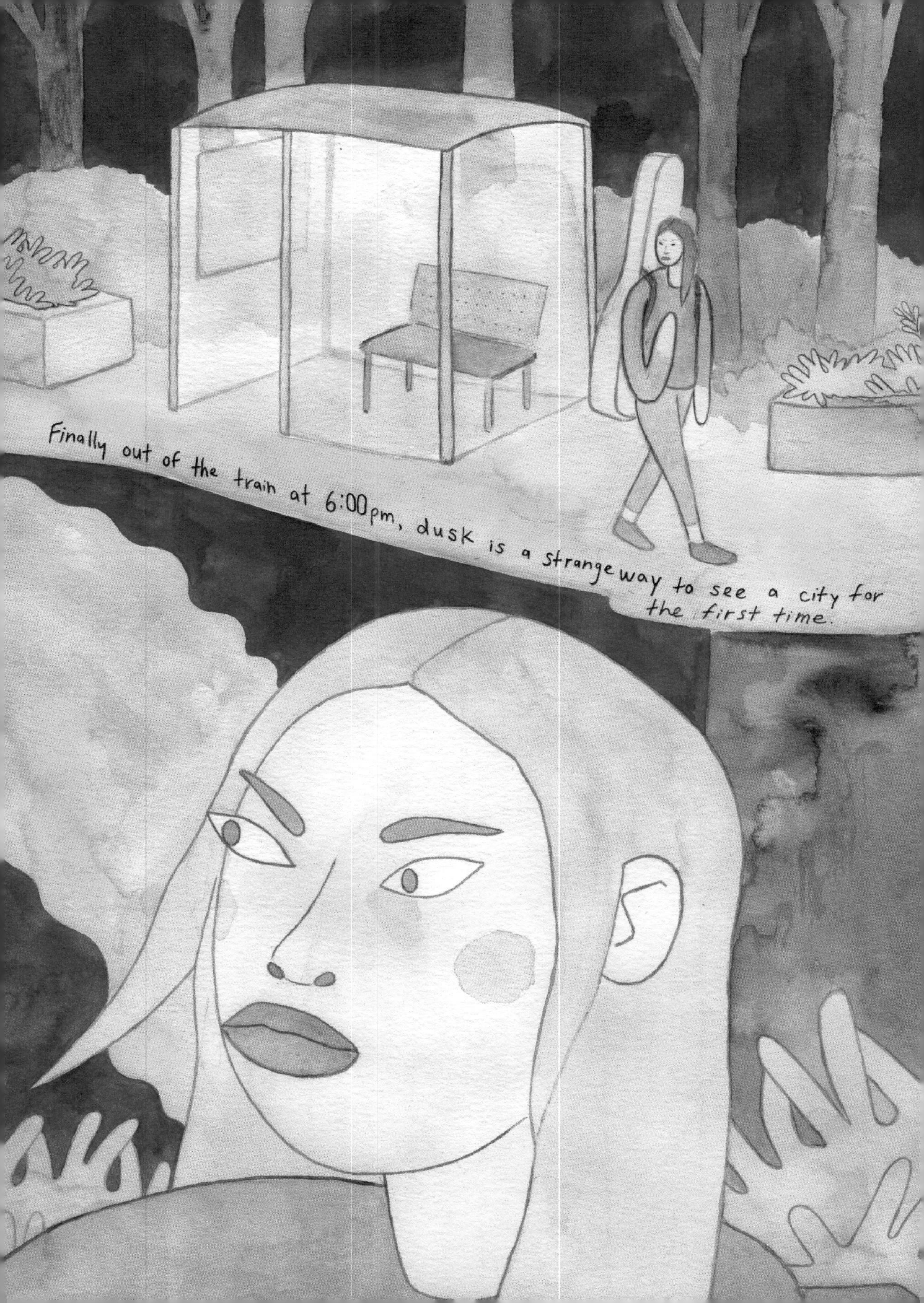
Finally out of the train at 6:00pm, dusk is a strange way to see a city for the first time.

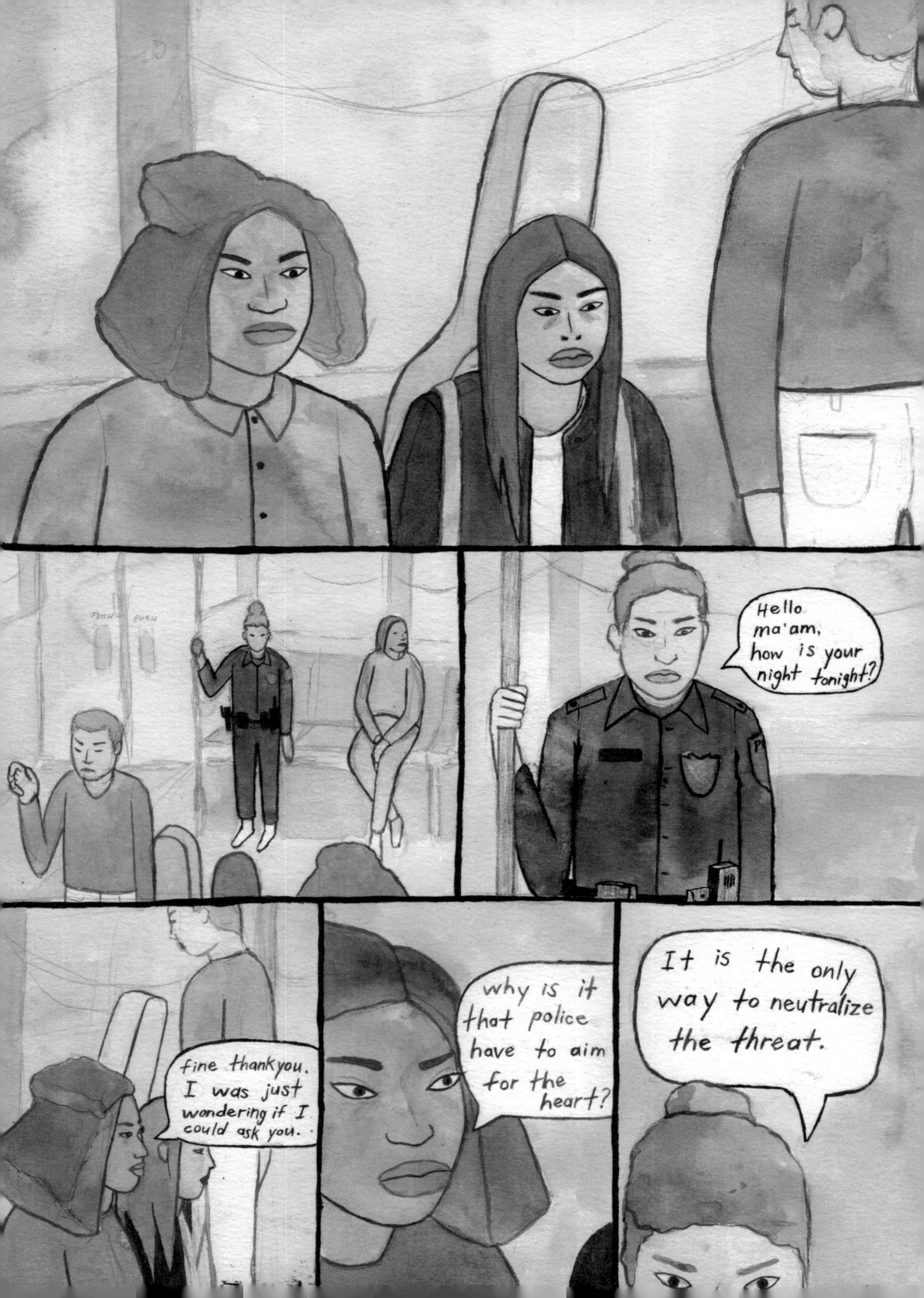
PUSH
PUSH
Hello ma'am, how is your night tonight?
fine thankyou. I was just wondering if I could ask you.
why is it that police have to aim for the heart?
It is the only way to neutralize the threat.

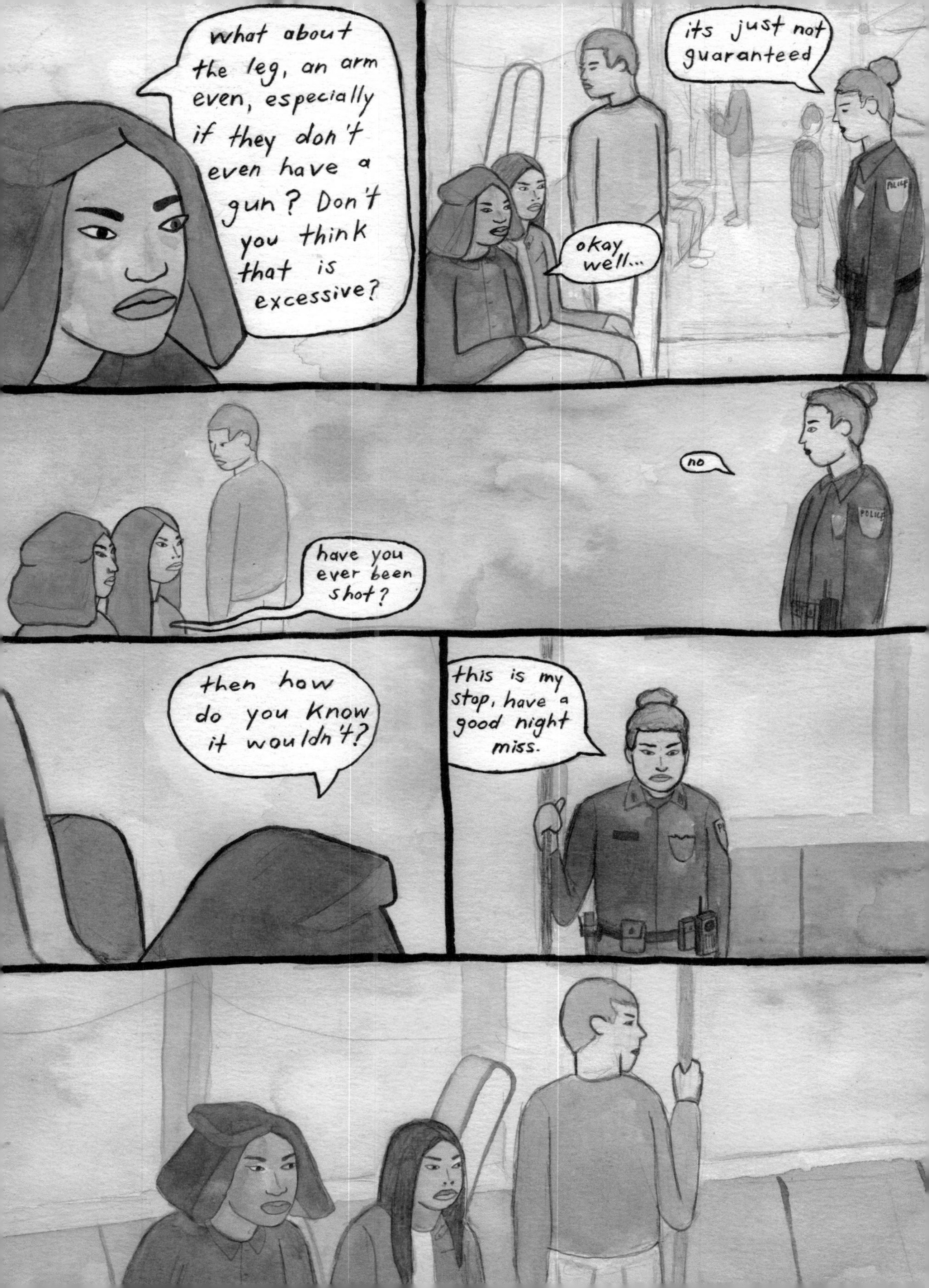
what about the leg, an arm even, especially if they don't even have a gun? Don't you think that is excessive?
its just not guaranteed
okay well...
no
have you ever been shot?
then how do you know it wouldn't?
this is my stop, have a good night miss.
POLICE
POLICE

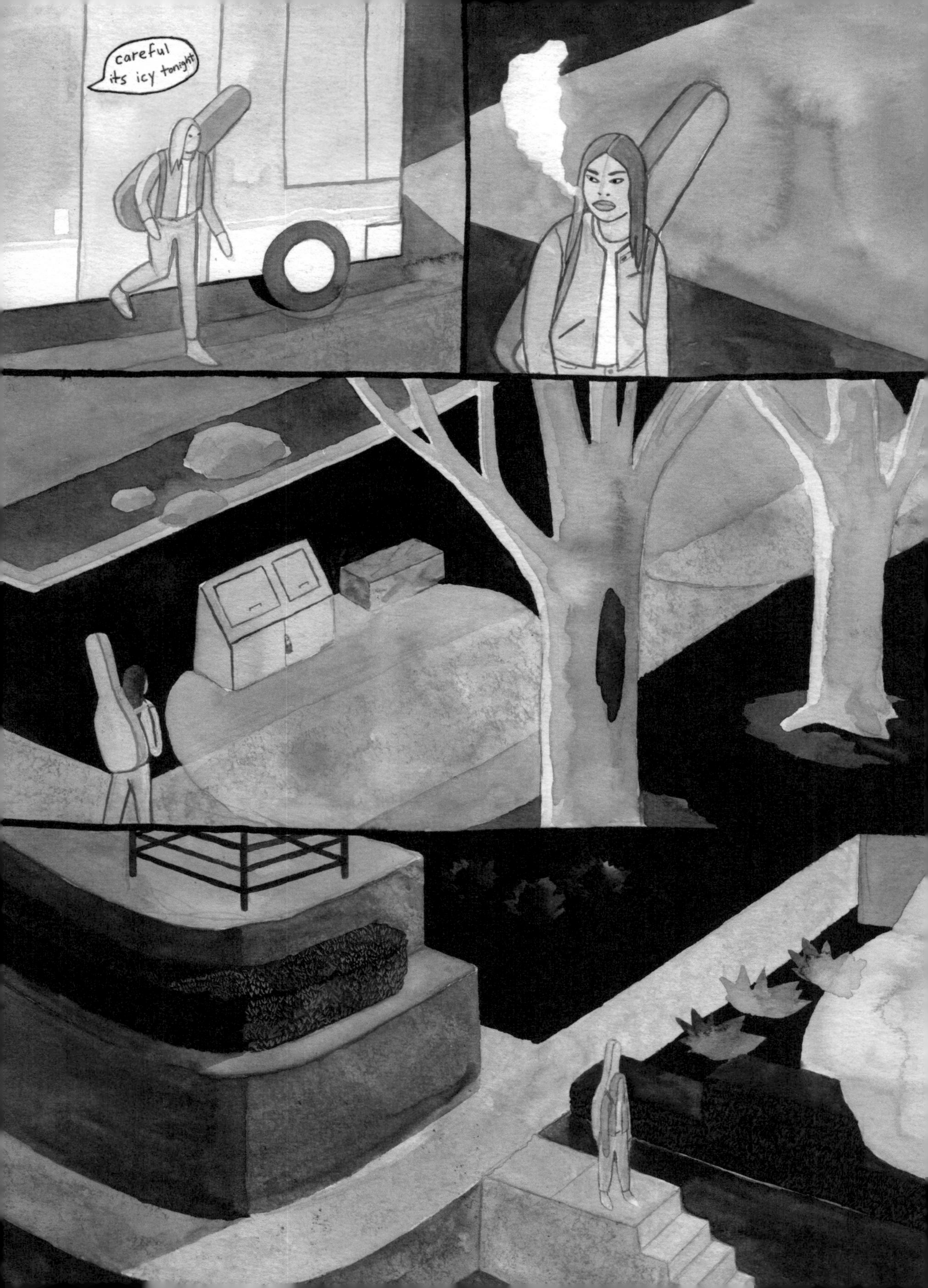
careful
its icy tonight

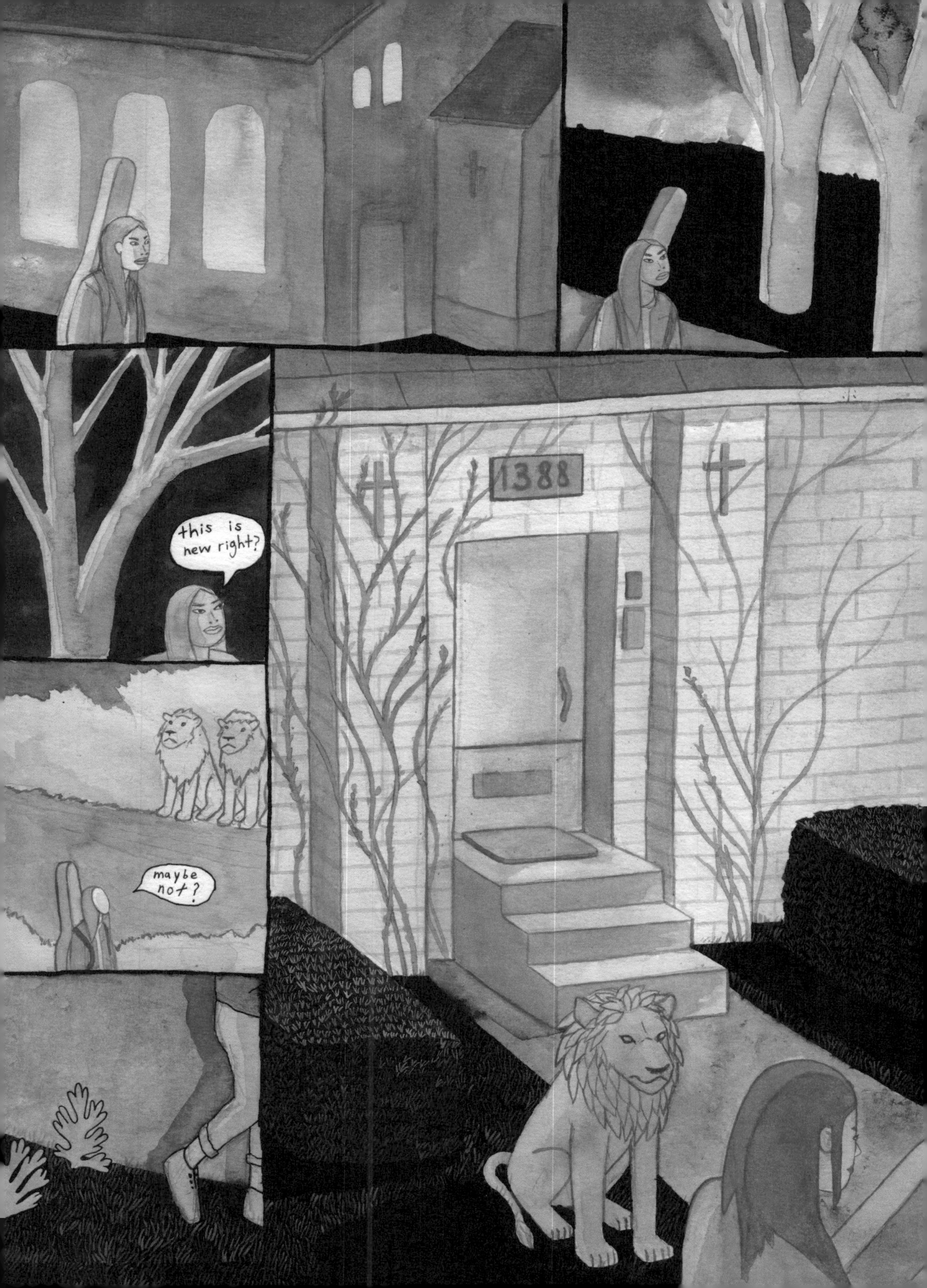
this is new right?
maybe not?
1388

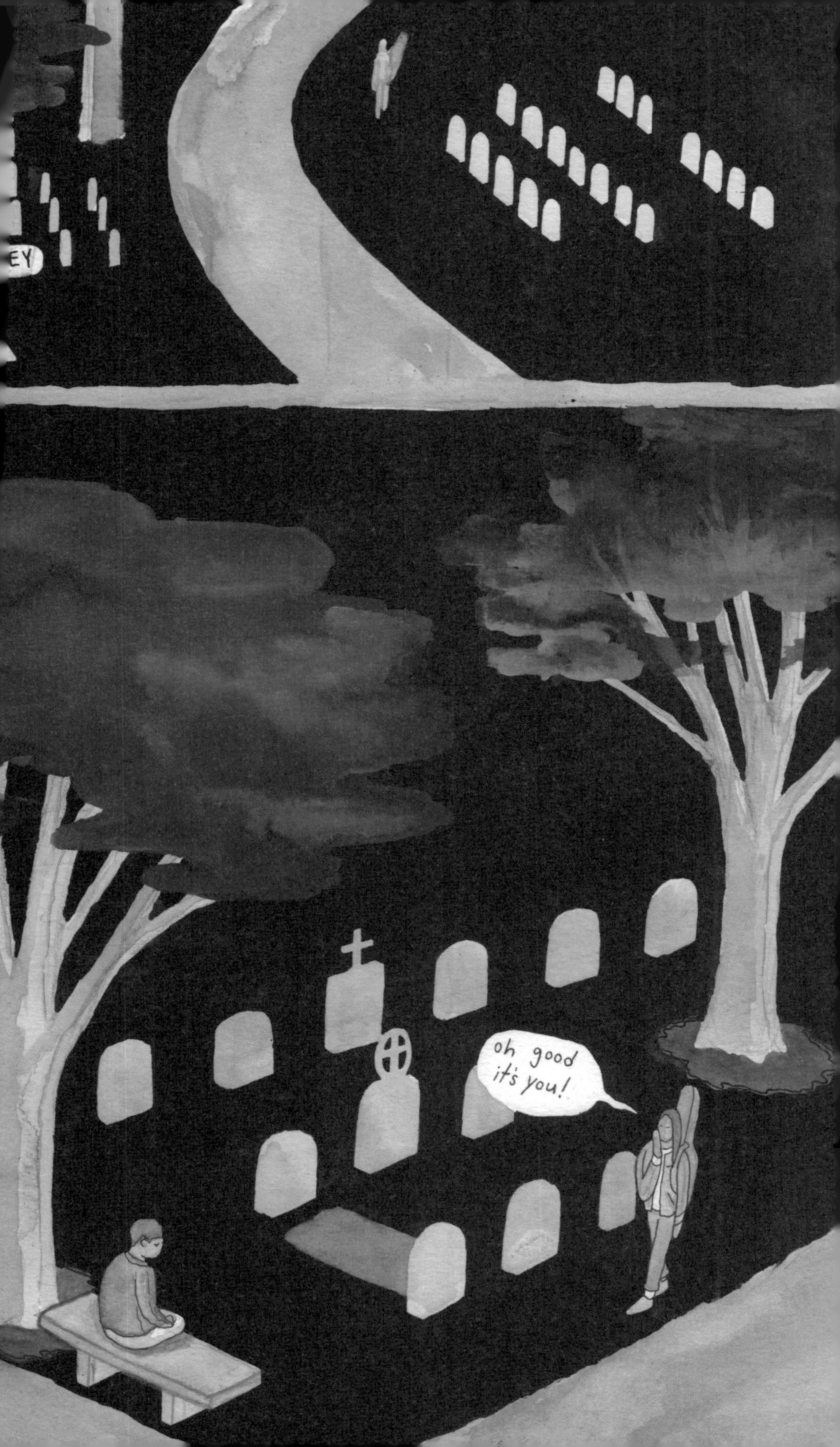
oh good it's you!

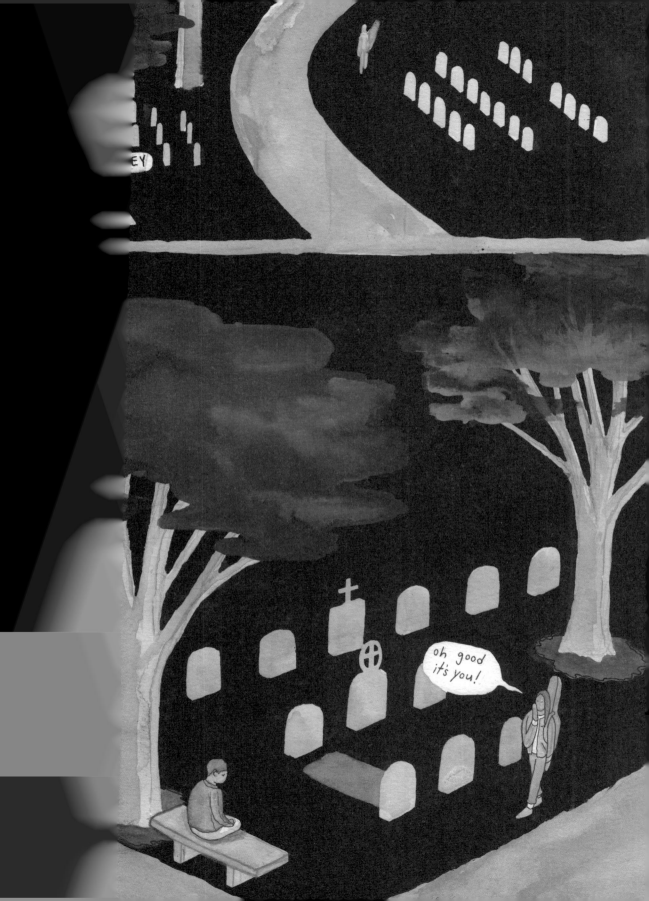

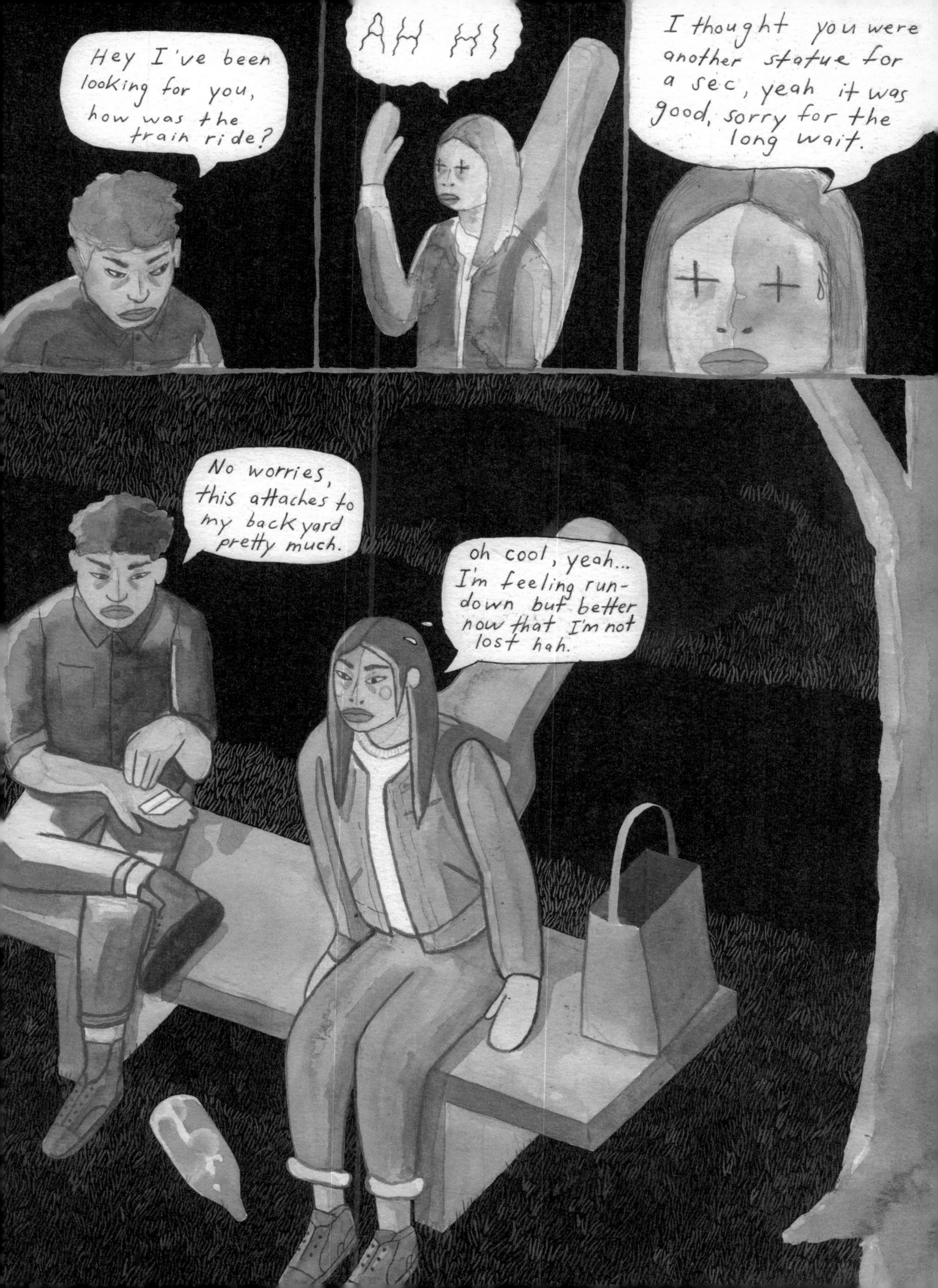
Hey I've been looking for you, how was the train ride?
AH HI
I thought you were another statue for a sec, yeah it was good, sorry for the long wait.
No worries, this attaches to my backyard pretty much.
oh cool, yeah... I'm feeling run-down but better now that I'm not lost hah.

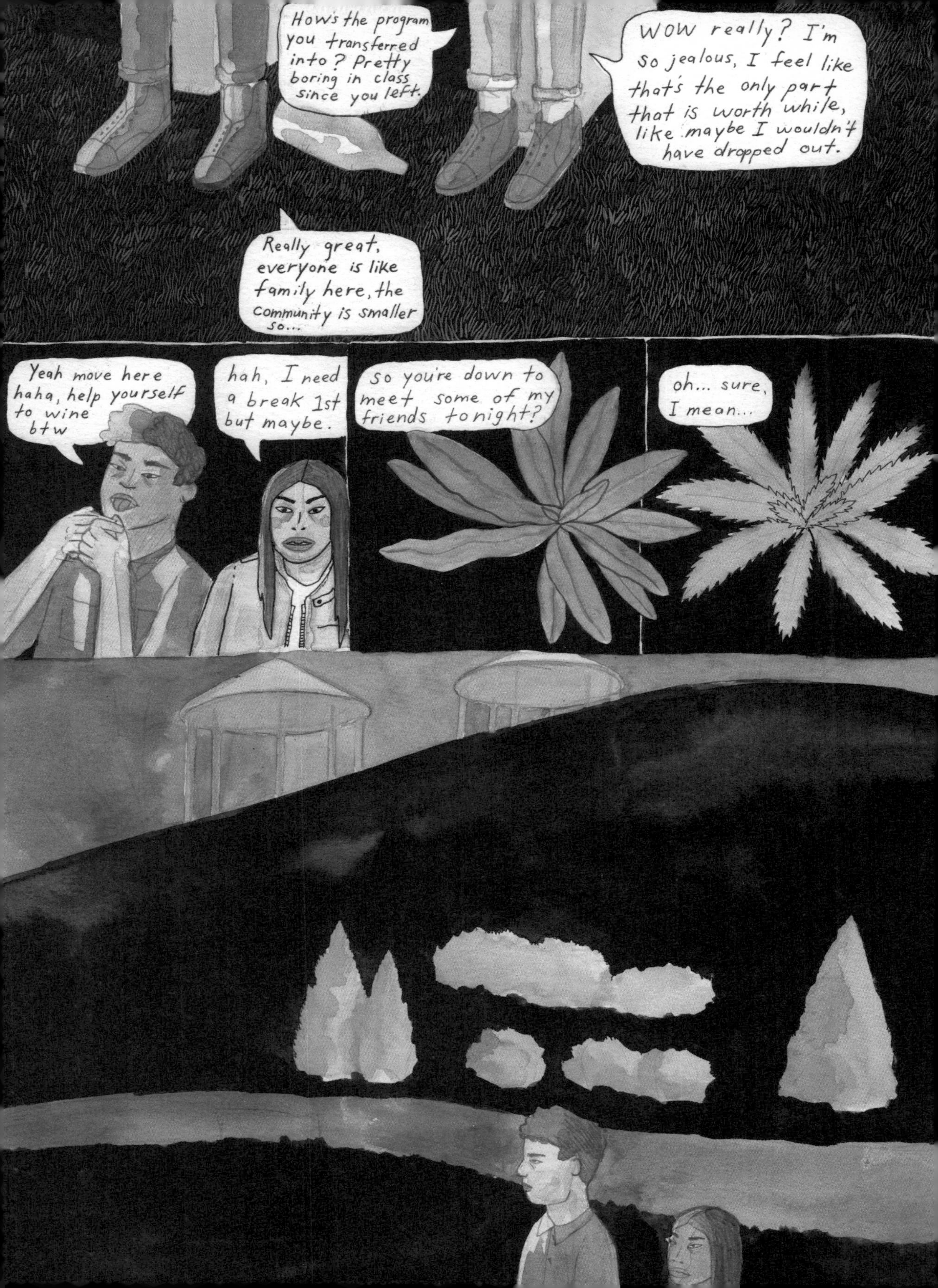
How's the program you transferred into? Pretty boring in class since you left.
WOW really? I'm so jealous, I feel like that's the only part that is worth while, like maybe I wouldn't have dropped out.
Really great, everyone is like family here, the community is smaller so...
Yeah move here haha, help yourself to wine btw
hah, I need a break 1st but maybe.
so you're down to meet some of my friends tonight?
oh... sure, I mean...

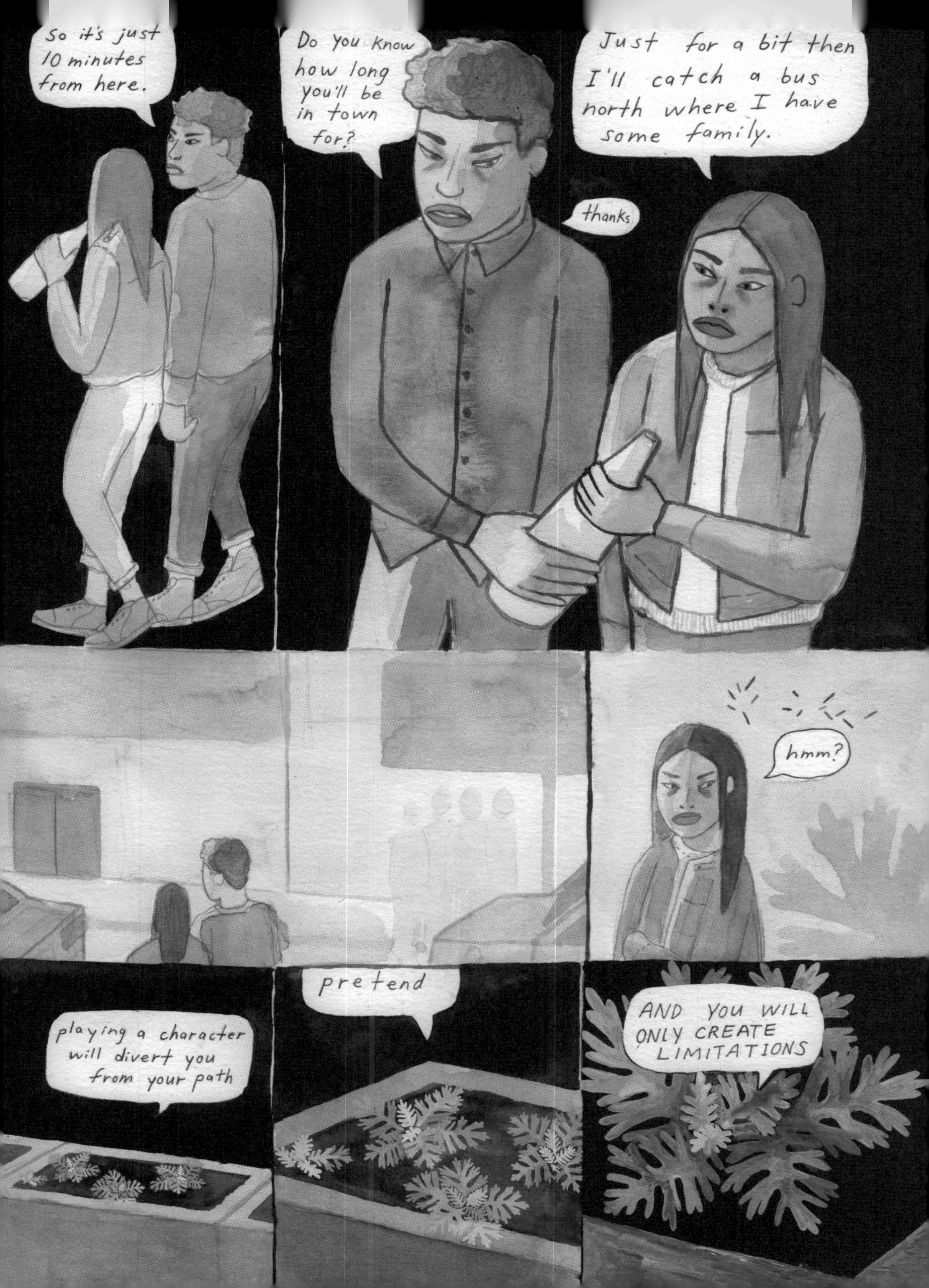
So it's just 10 minutes from here.
Do you know how long you'll be in town for?
Just for a bit then I'll catch a bus north where I have some family.
thanks
hmm?
playing a character will divert you from your path
pretend
AND YOU WILL ONLY CREATE LIMITATIONS

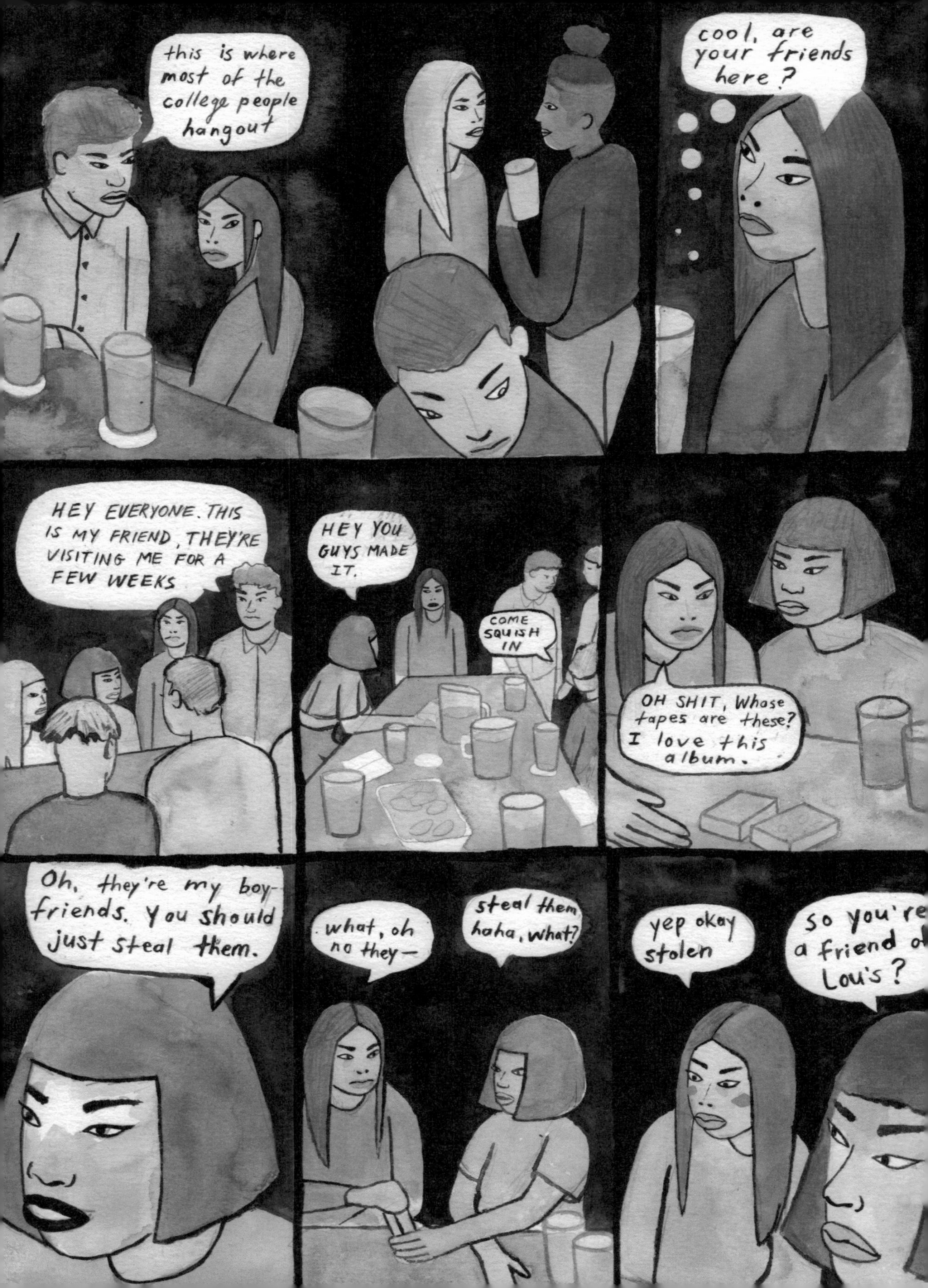
this is where most of the college people hangout
cool, are your friends here?
HEY EVERYONE. THIS IS MY FRIEND, THEY'RE VISITING ME FOR A FEW WEEKS
HEY YOU GUYS MADE IT.
COME SQUISH IN
OH SHIT, Whose tapes are these? I love this album.
Oh, they're my boy-friends. You should just steal them.
what, oh no they—
steal them haha, what?
yep okay stolen
so you're a friend of Lou's?

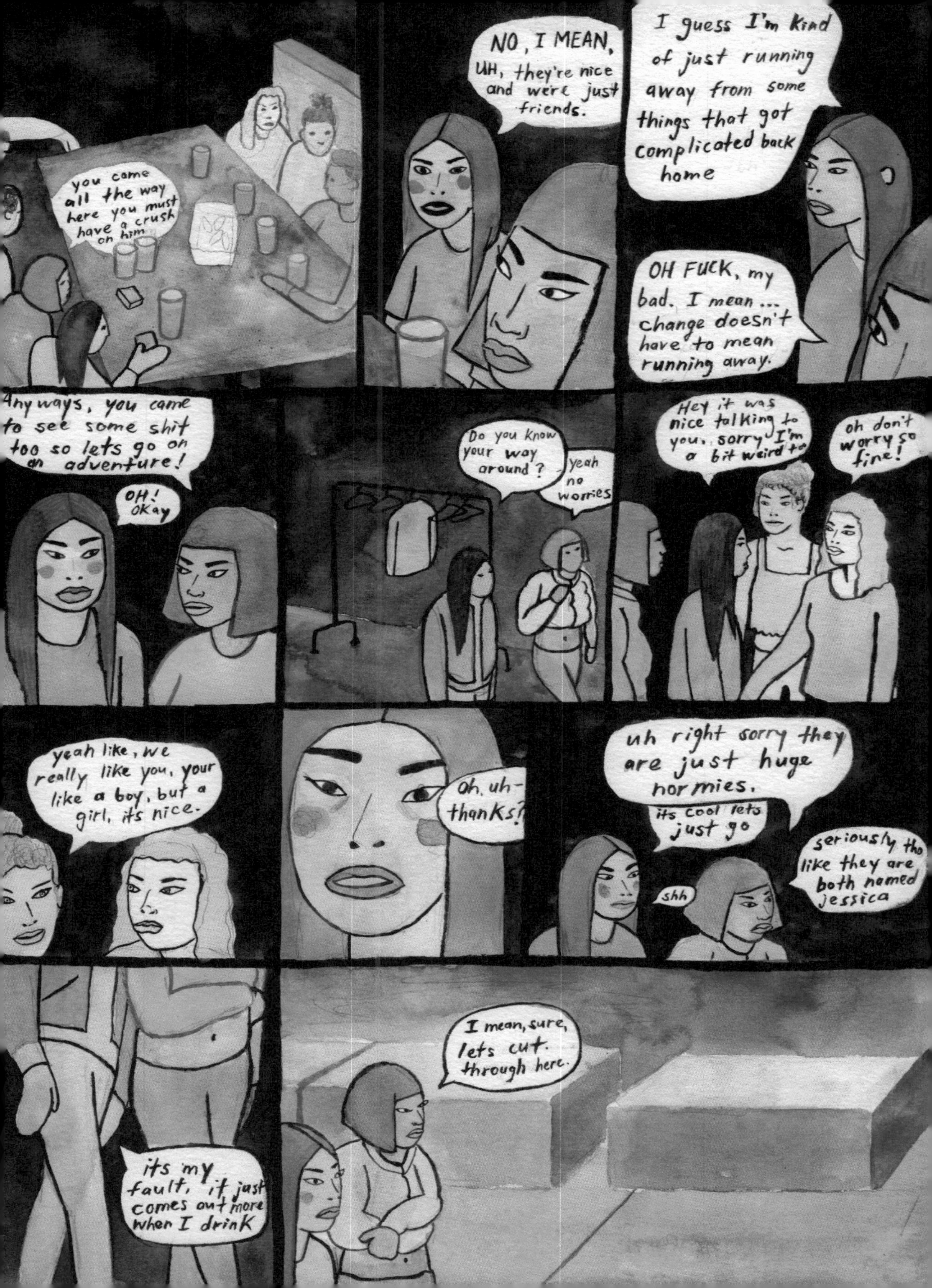
you came all the way here you must have a crush on him
NO, I MEAN, UH, they're nice and were just friends.
I guess I'm kind of just running away from some things that got complicated back home
OH FUCK, my bad. I mean ... change doesn't have to mean running away.
Any ways, you came to see some shit too so lets go on an adventure!
OH! Okay
Do you know your way around?
yeah no worries
Hey it was nice talking to you, sorry I'm a bit weird to
oh don't worry so fine!
yeah like, we really like you, your like a boy, but a girl, its nice.
Oh, uh- thanks?
uh right sorry they are just huge normies.
its cool lets just go
shh
seriously tho like they are both named jessica
its my fault, it just comes out more when I drink
I mean, sure, lets cut through here.

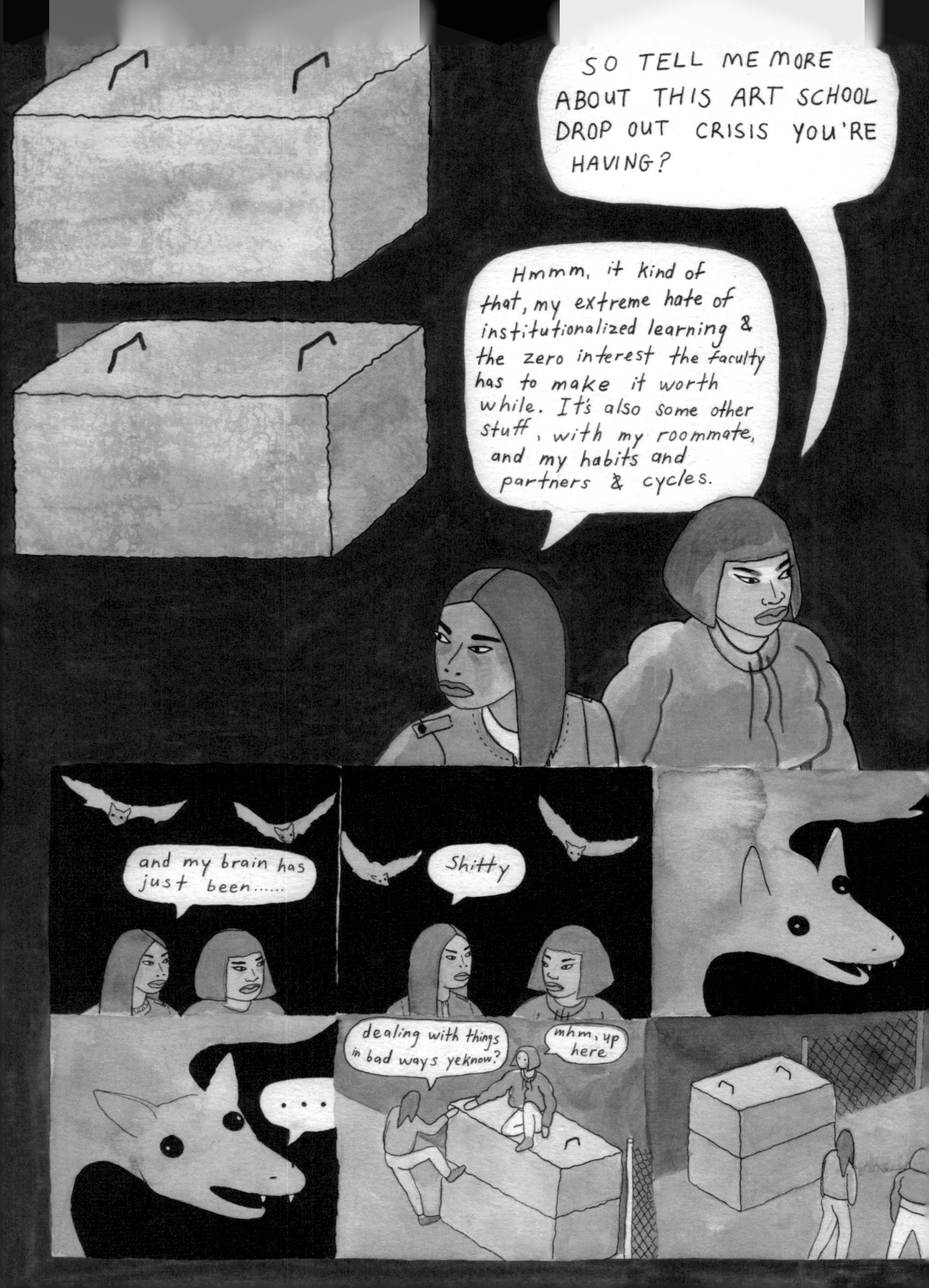
SO TELL ME MORE ABOUT THIS ART SCHOOL DROP OUT CRISIS YOU'RE HAVING?
Hmmm, it kind of that, my extreme hate of institutionalized learning & the zero interest the faculty has to make it worth while. It's also some other stuff, with my roommate, and my habits and partners & cycles.
and my brain has just been......
Shitty
...
dealing with things in bad ways yeknow?
mhm, up here

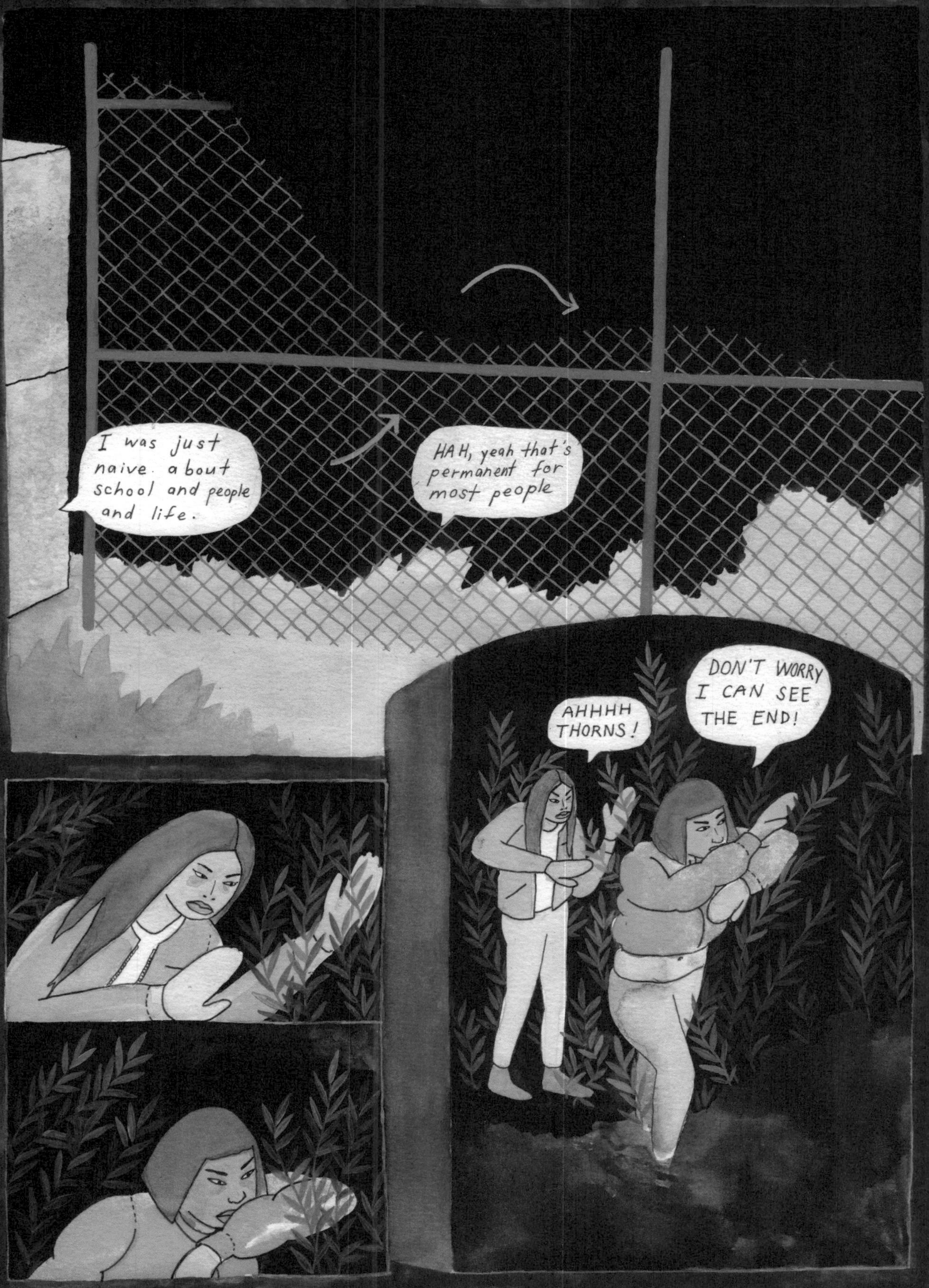
I was just naive about school and people and life.
HAH, yeah that's permanent for most people
AHHHH THORNS!
DON'T WORRY I CAN SEE THE END!

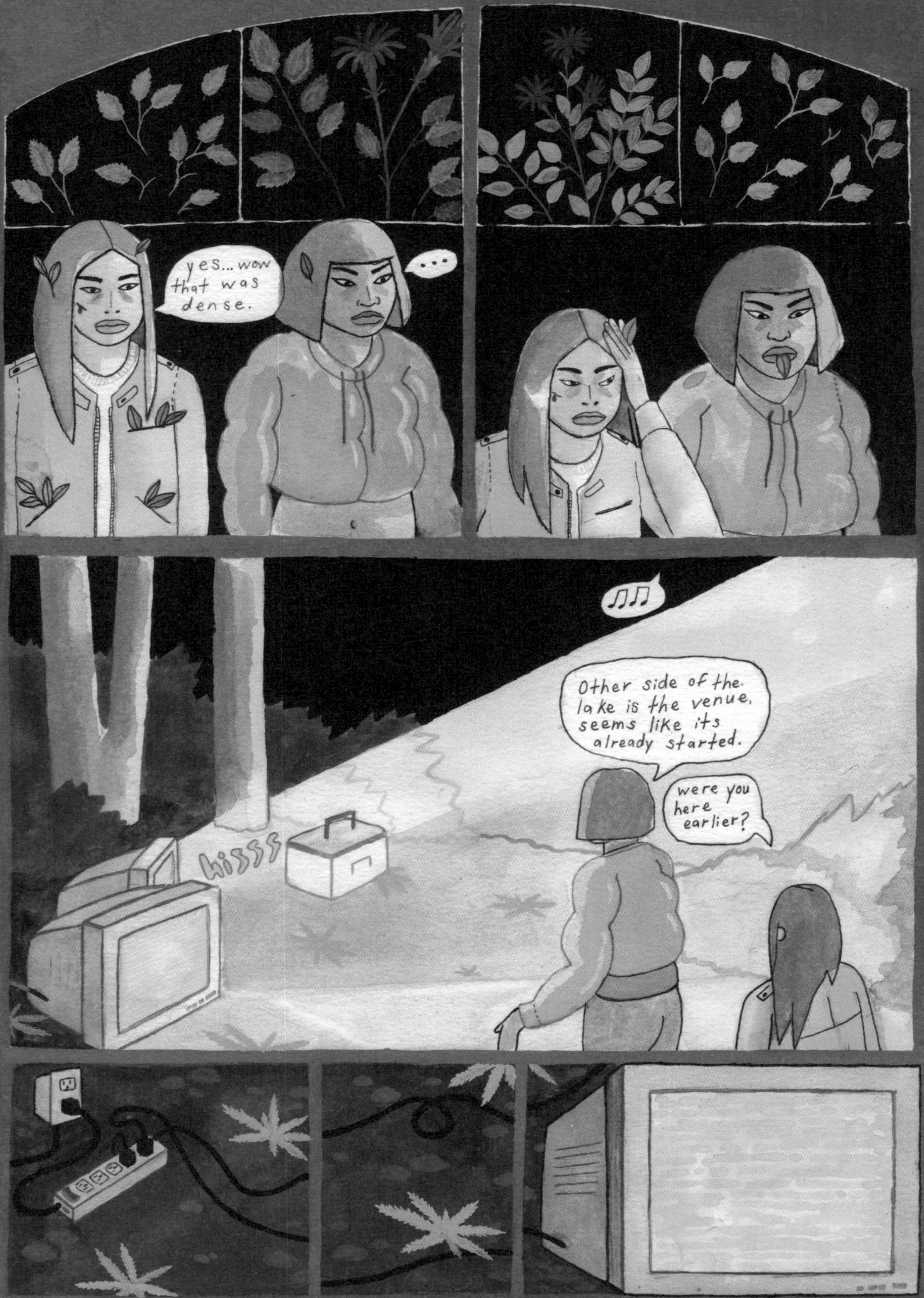
yes... wow that was dense.
...
♫♫
Other side of the lake is the venue, seems like its already started.
were you here earlier?
hisss

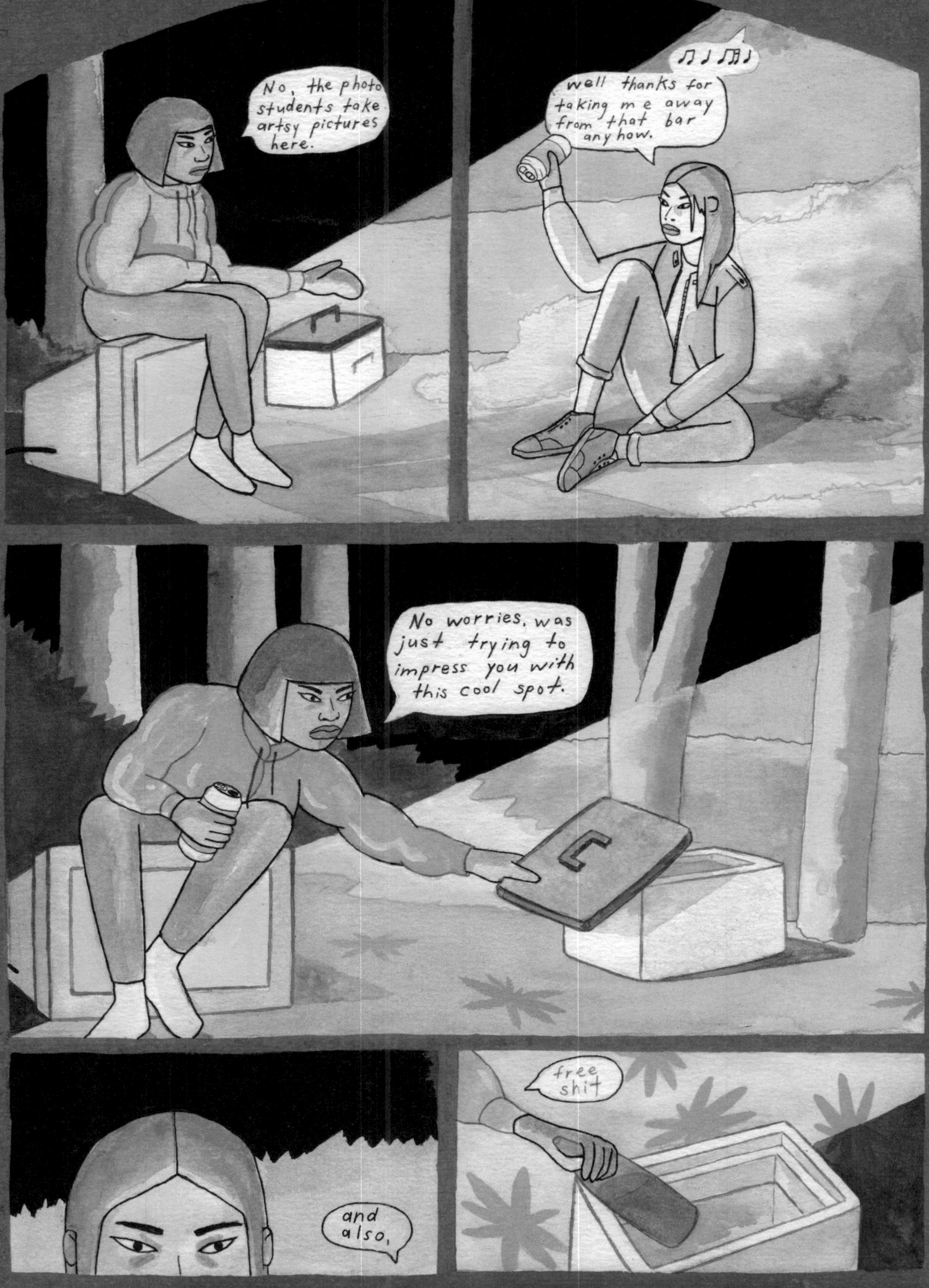
No, the photo students take artsy pictures here.
♫♩♫♬♩
well thanks for taking me away from that bar anyhow.
No worries, was just trying to impress you with this cool spot.
and also,
free shit

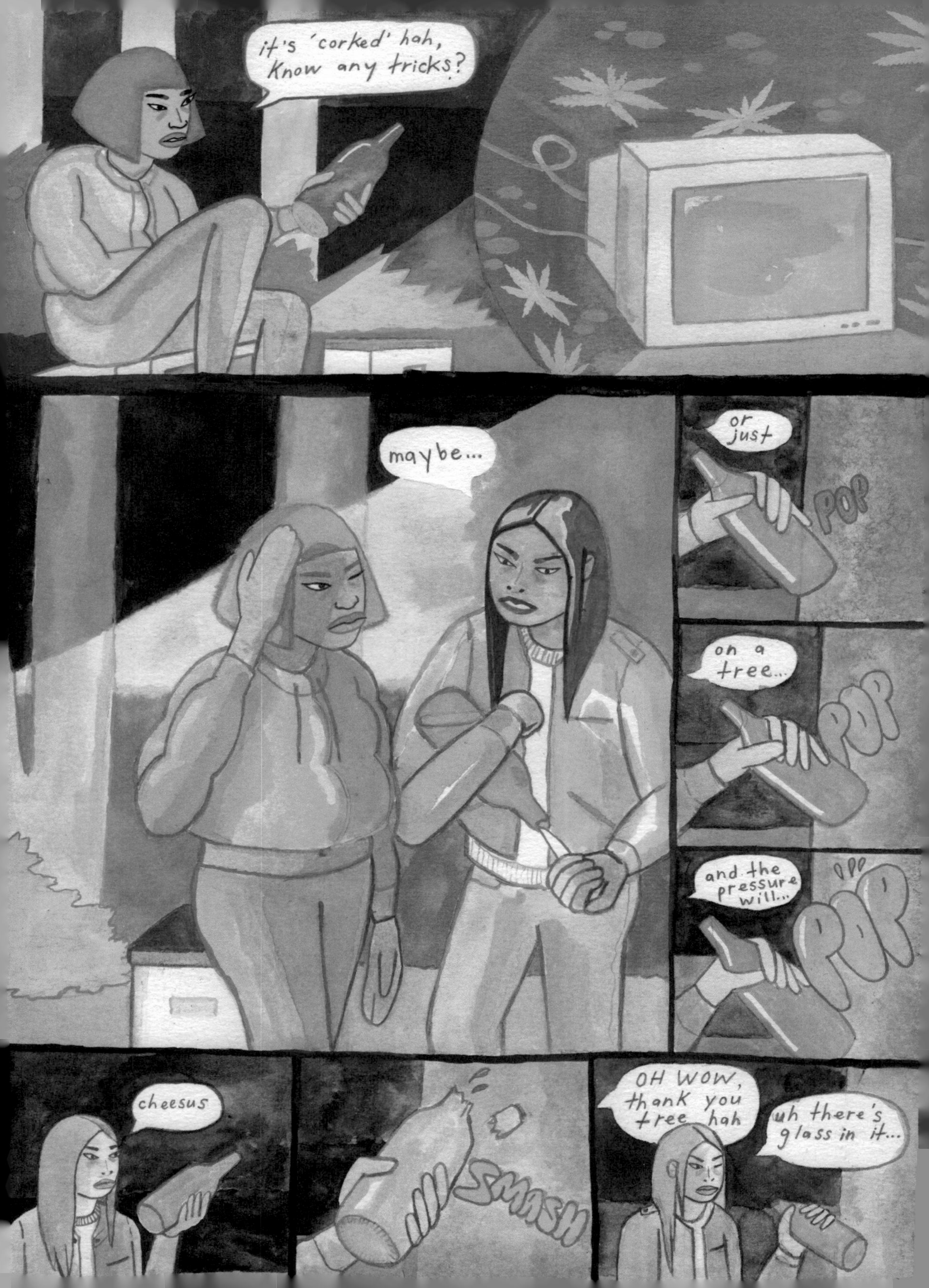
it's 'corked' hah, Know any tricks?
maybe...
or just
POP
on a tree...
POP
and the pressure will...
POP
cheesus
SMASH
OH WOW, thank you tree hah
uh there's glass in it...

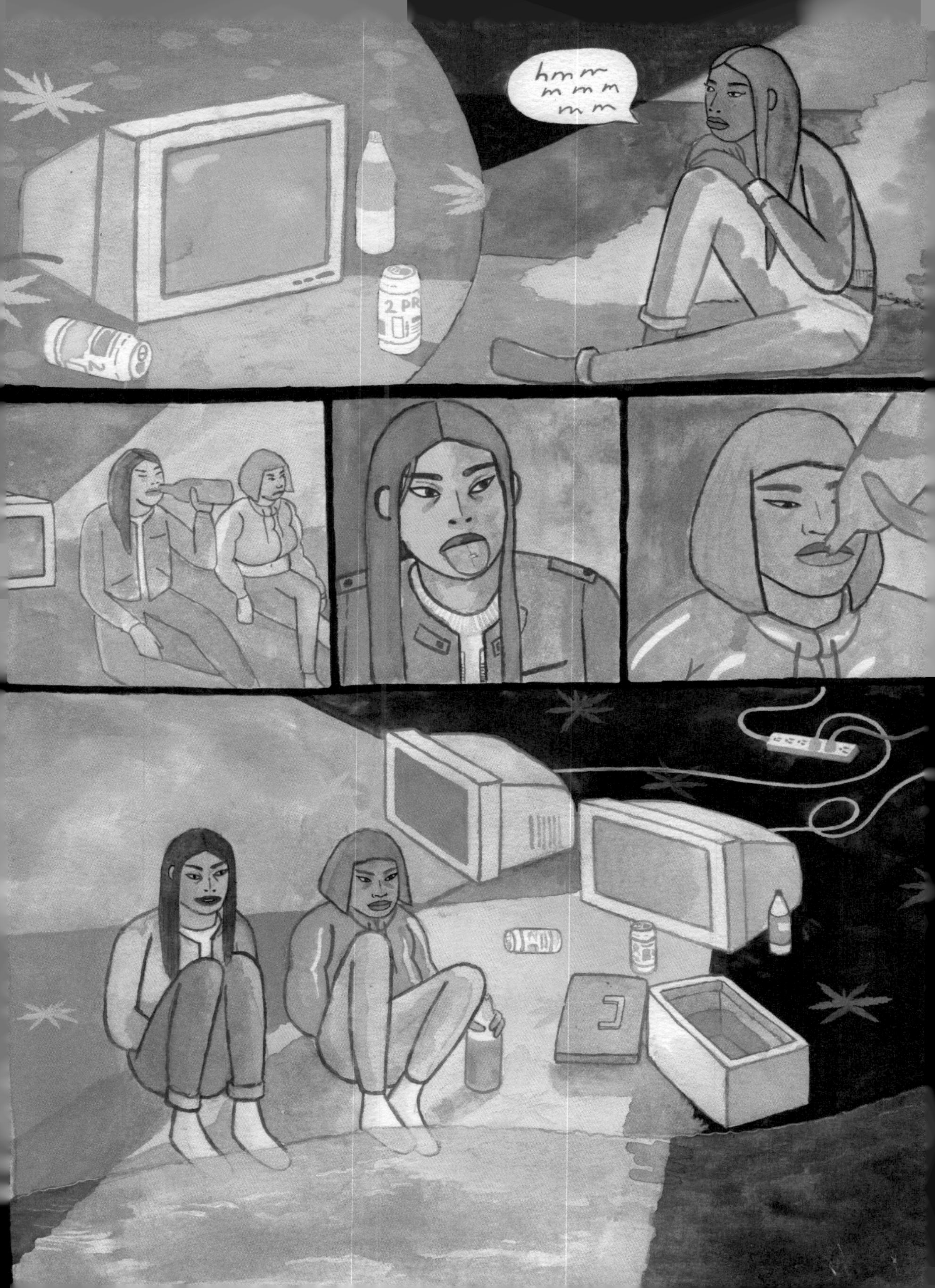

hmm mmm mm

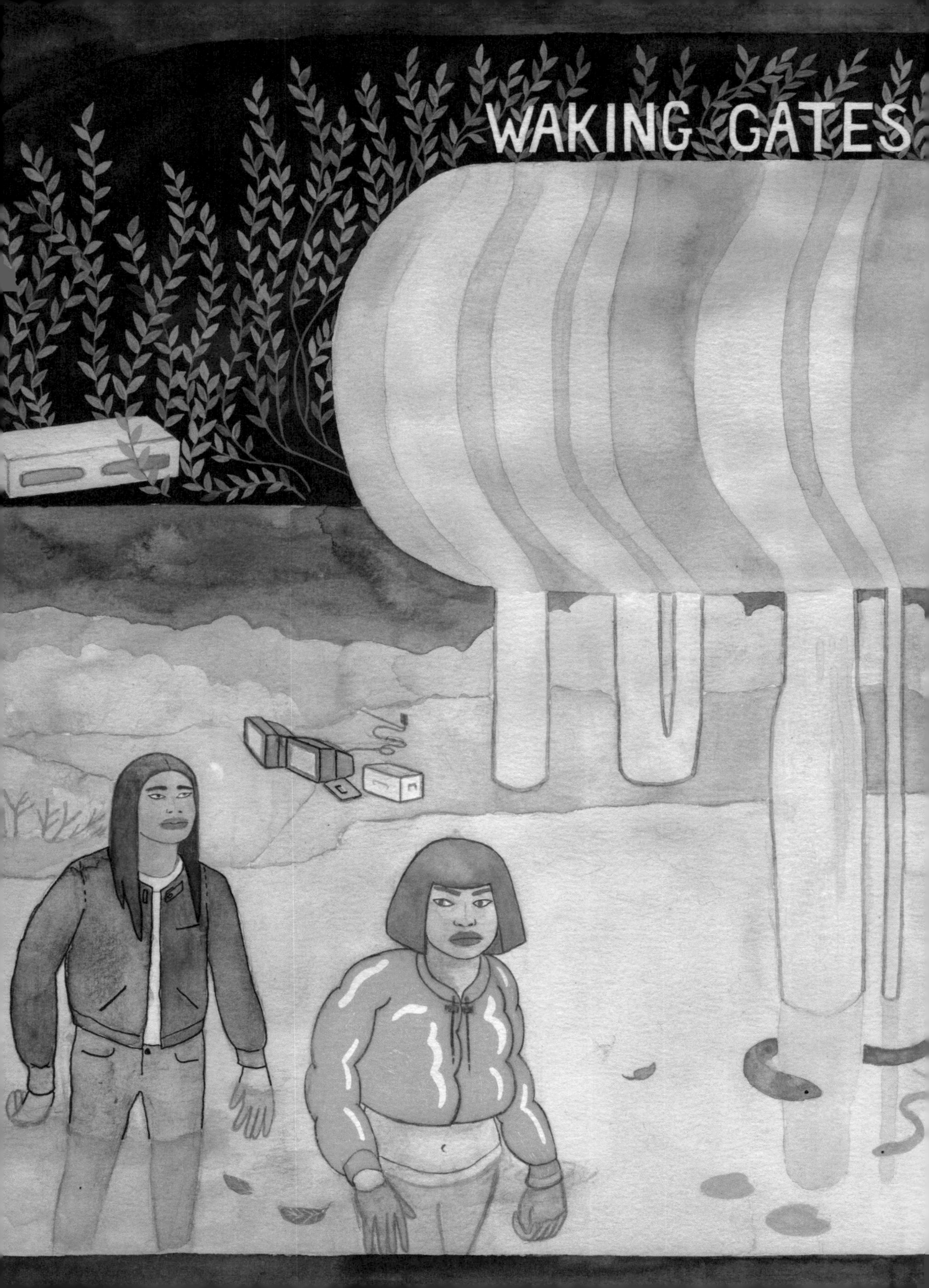
WAKING GATES

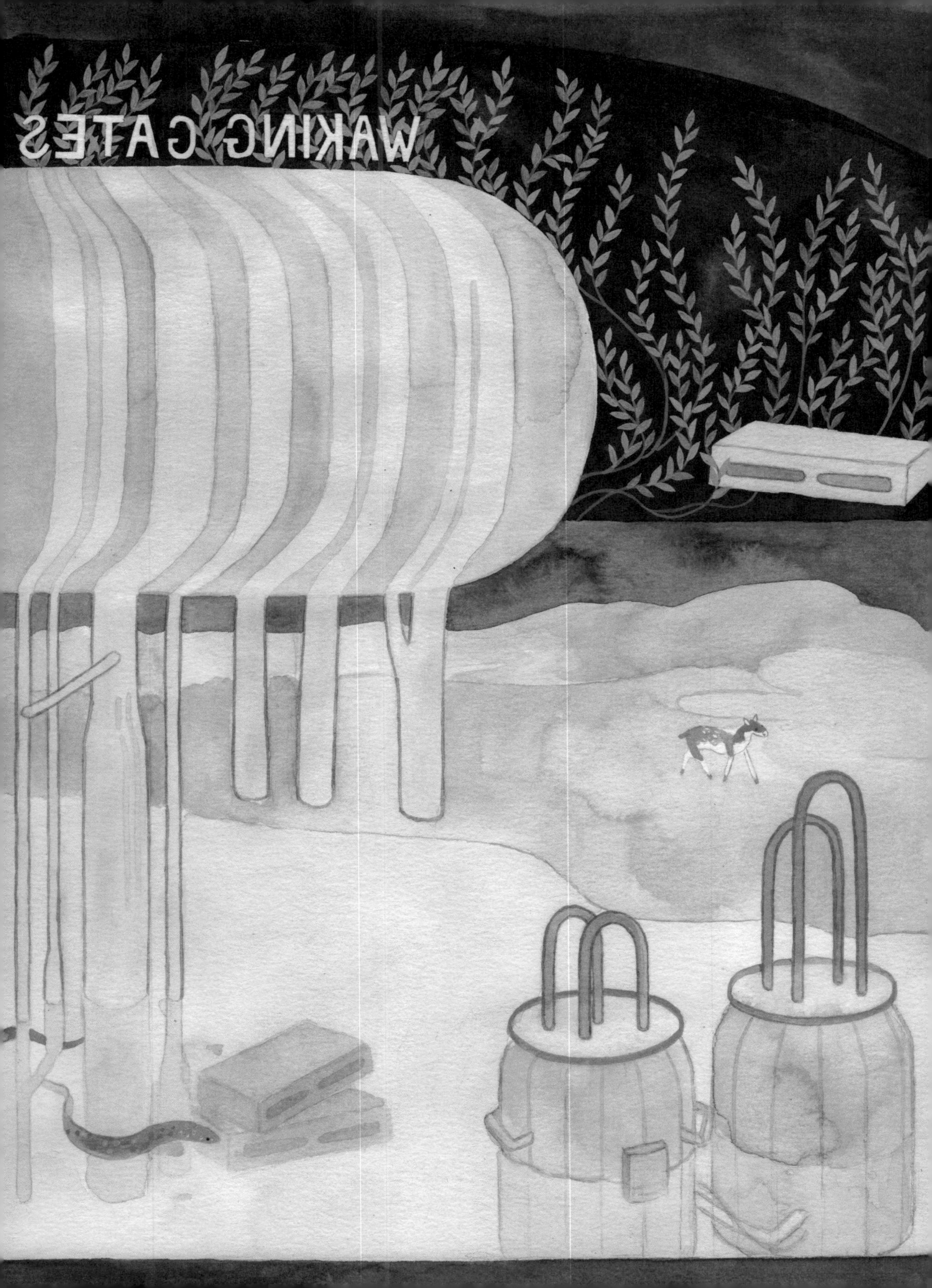
WAKING GATES

I COULD FEEL MYSELF MOVING TO

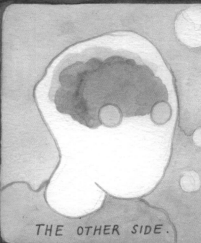

THE OTHER SIDE.

NO LONGER ON THE OUTSIDE, PAST THE SKIN, BUT THE LEGS KEEP MOVING.

AUTOPILOT, YOU'D NEVER NOTICE.

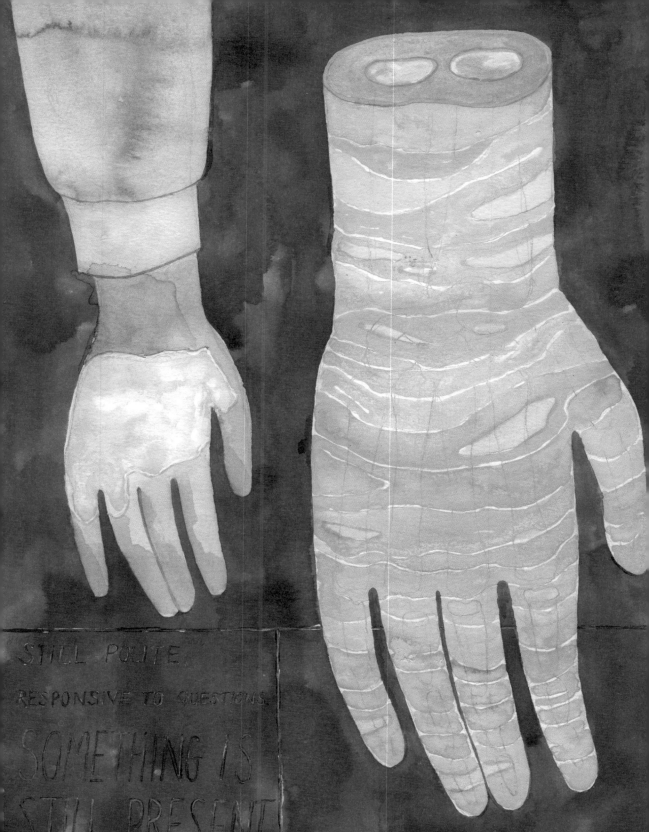

STILL POLITE,

RESPONSIVE TO QUESTIONS,

SOMETHING IS
STILL PRESENT

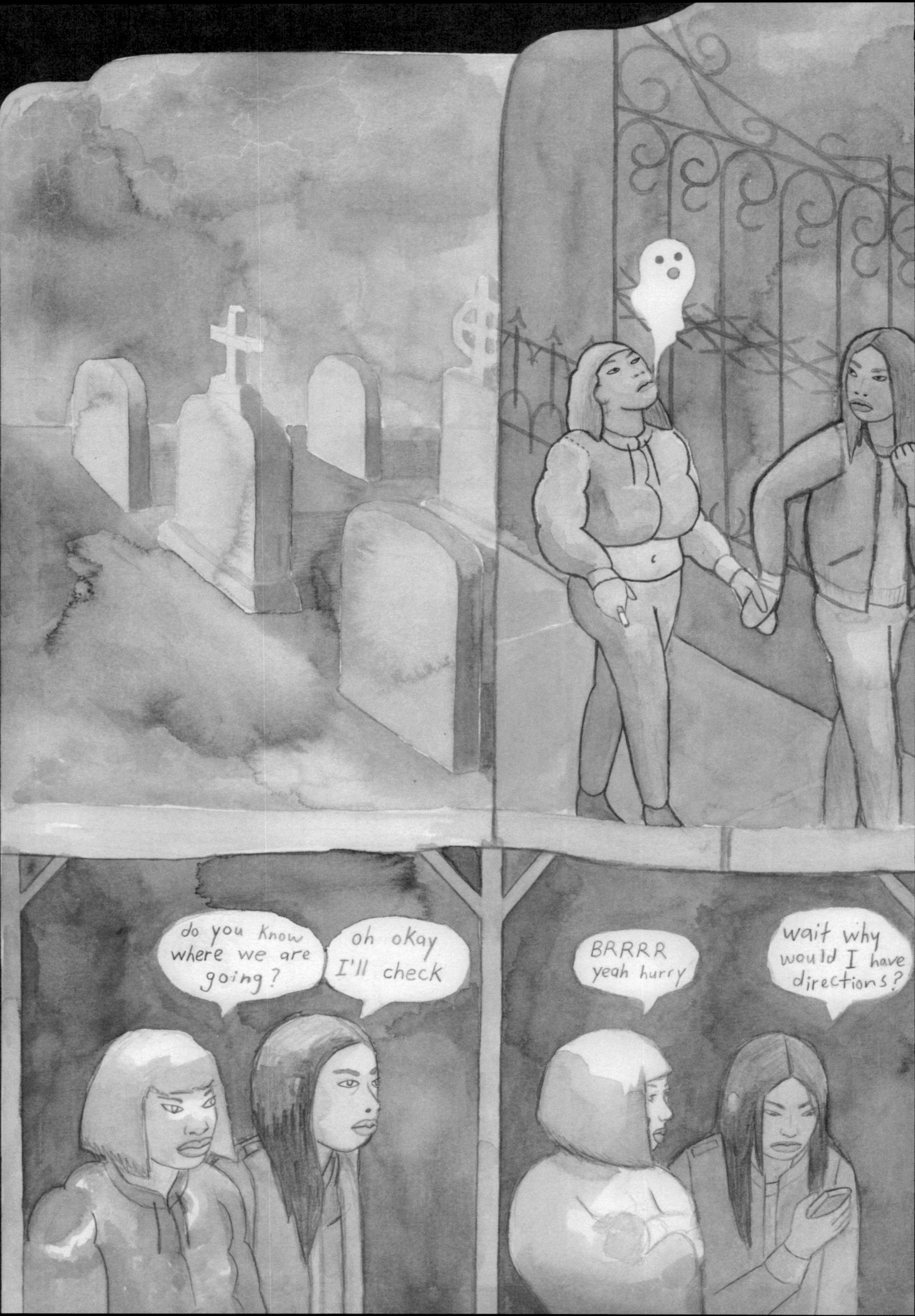
do you know where we are going?
oh okay I'll check
BRRRR yeah hurry
wait why would I have directions?

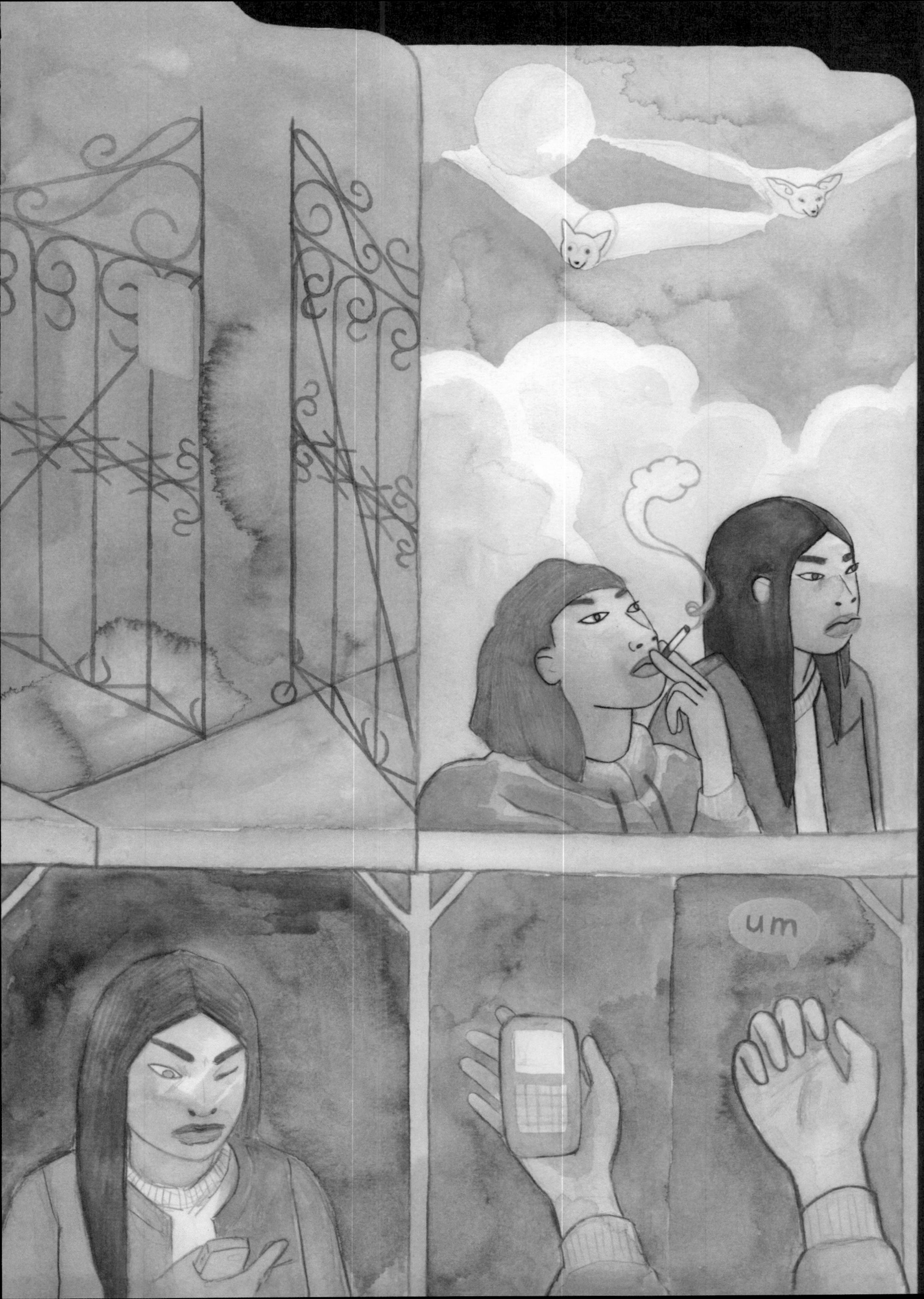
um

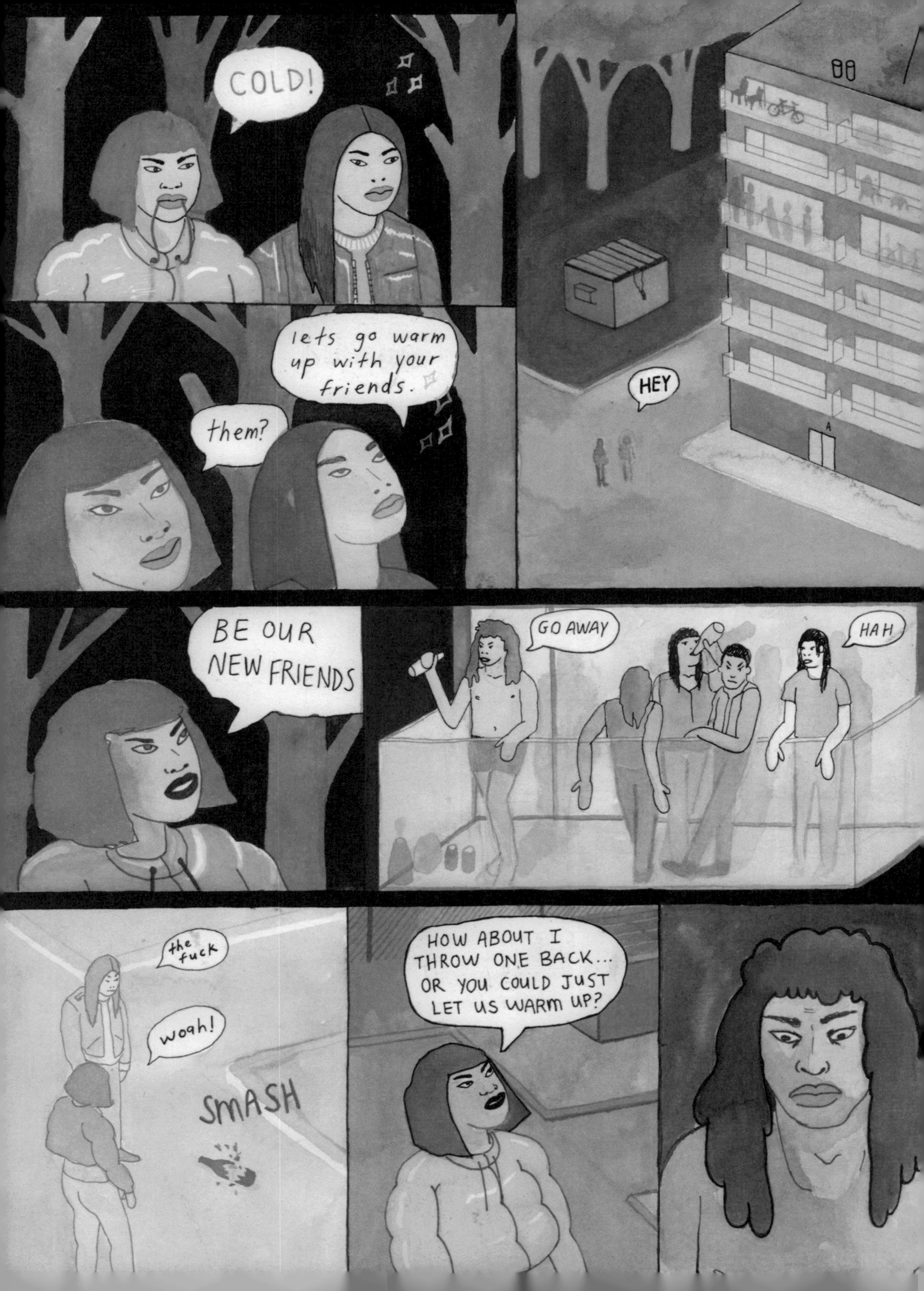
COLD!
lets go warm up with your friends.
them?
HEY
BE OUR NEW FRIENDS
GO AWAY
HAH
the fuck
woah!
SMASH
HOW ABOUT I THROW ONE BACK... OR YOU COULD JUST LET US WARM UP?

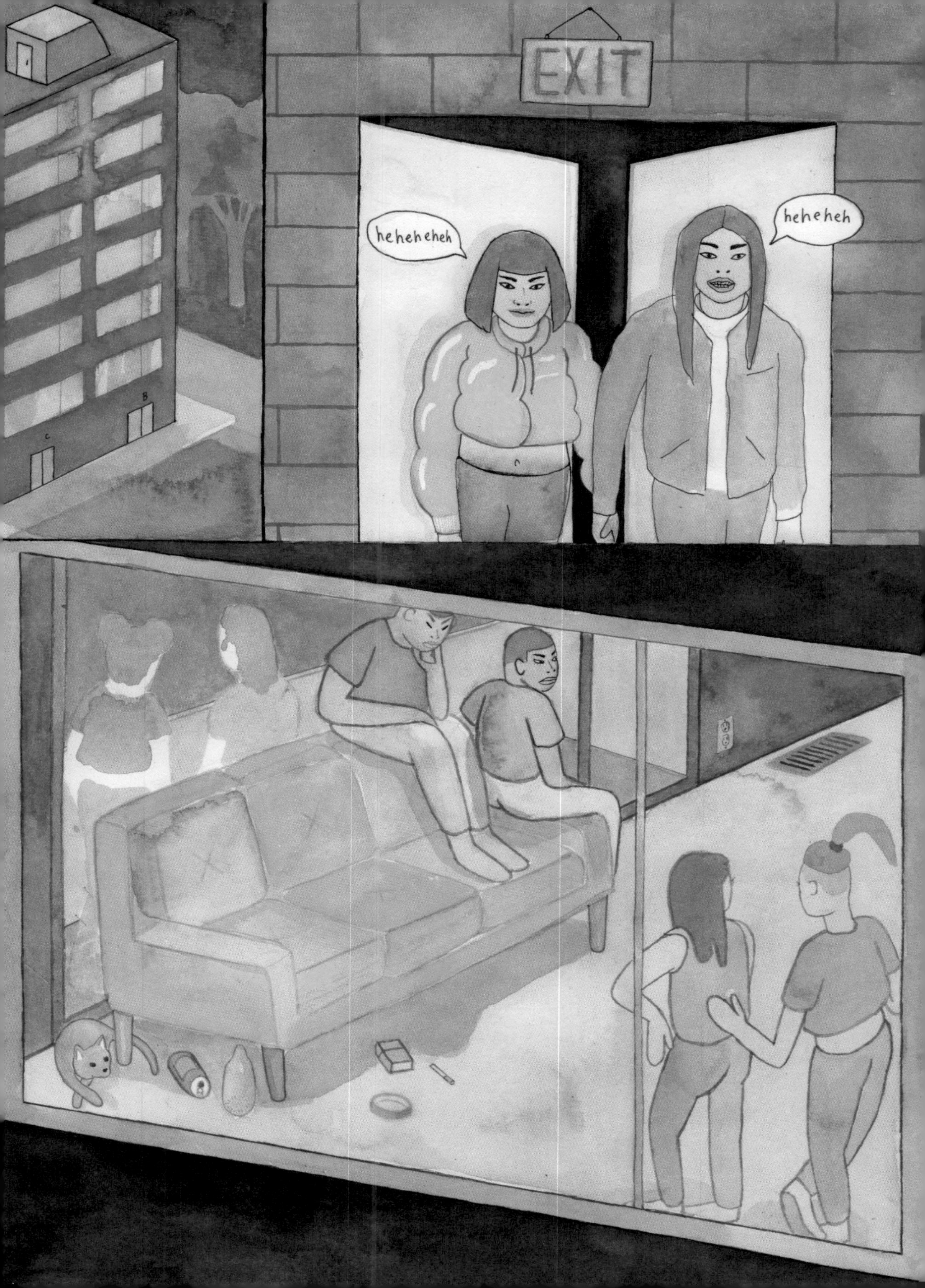
EXIT
heheheheh
heheheh

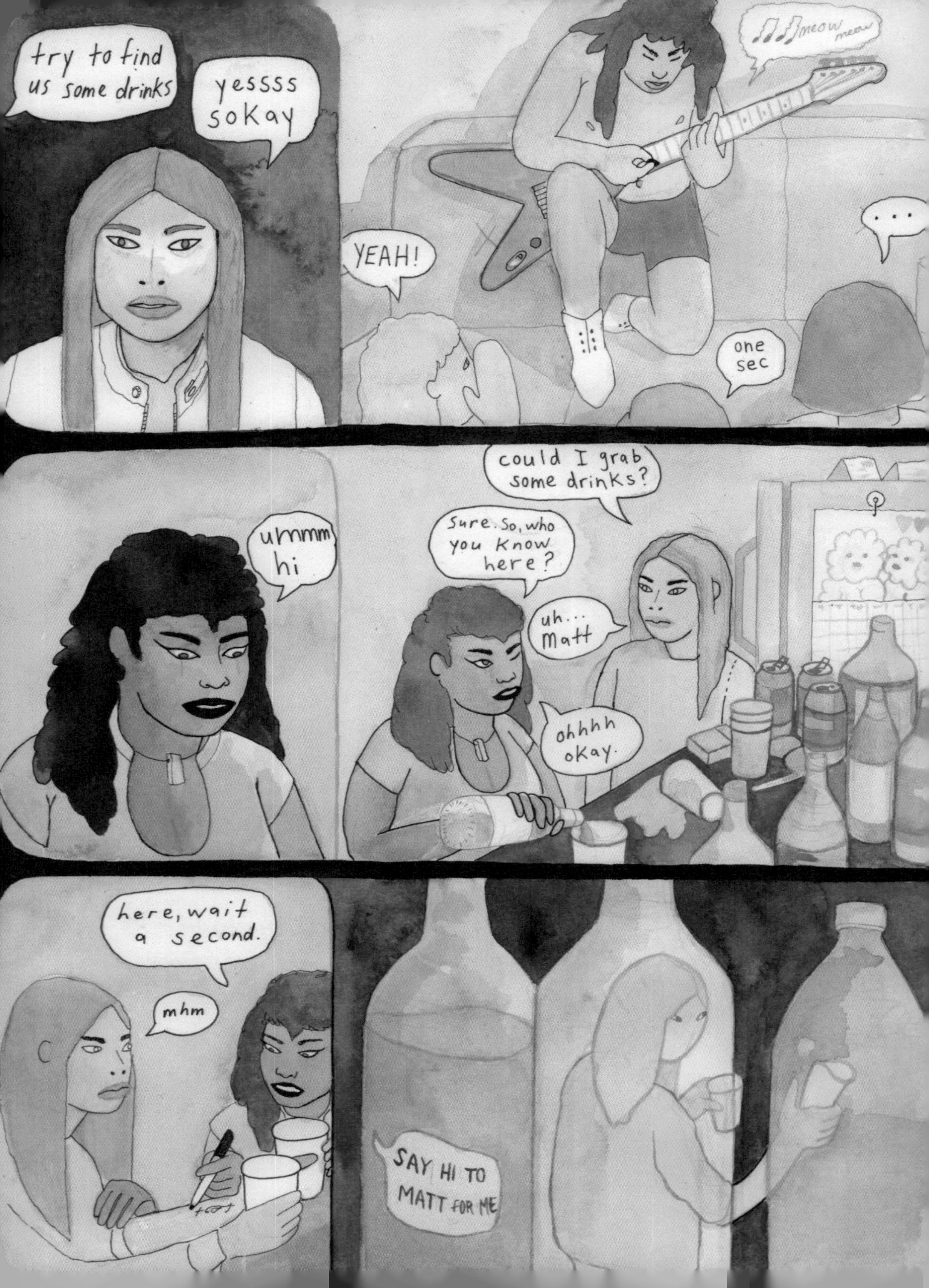

try to find us some drinks
yessss sokay
YEAH!
meow meow
...
one sec
ummm hi
could I grab some drinks?
Sure. So, who you know here?
uh... Matt
ohhhh okay.
here, wait a second.
mhm
SAY HI TO MATT FOR ME

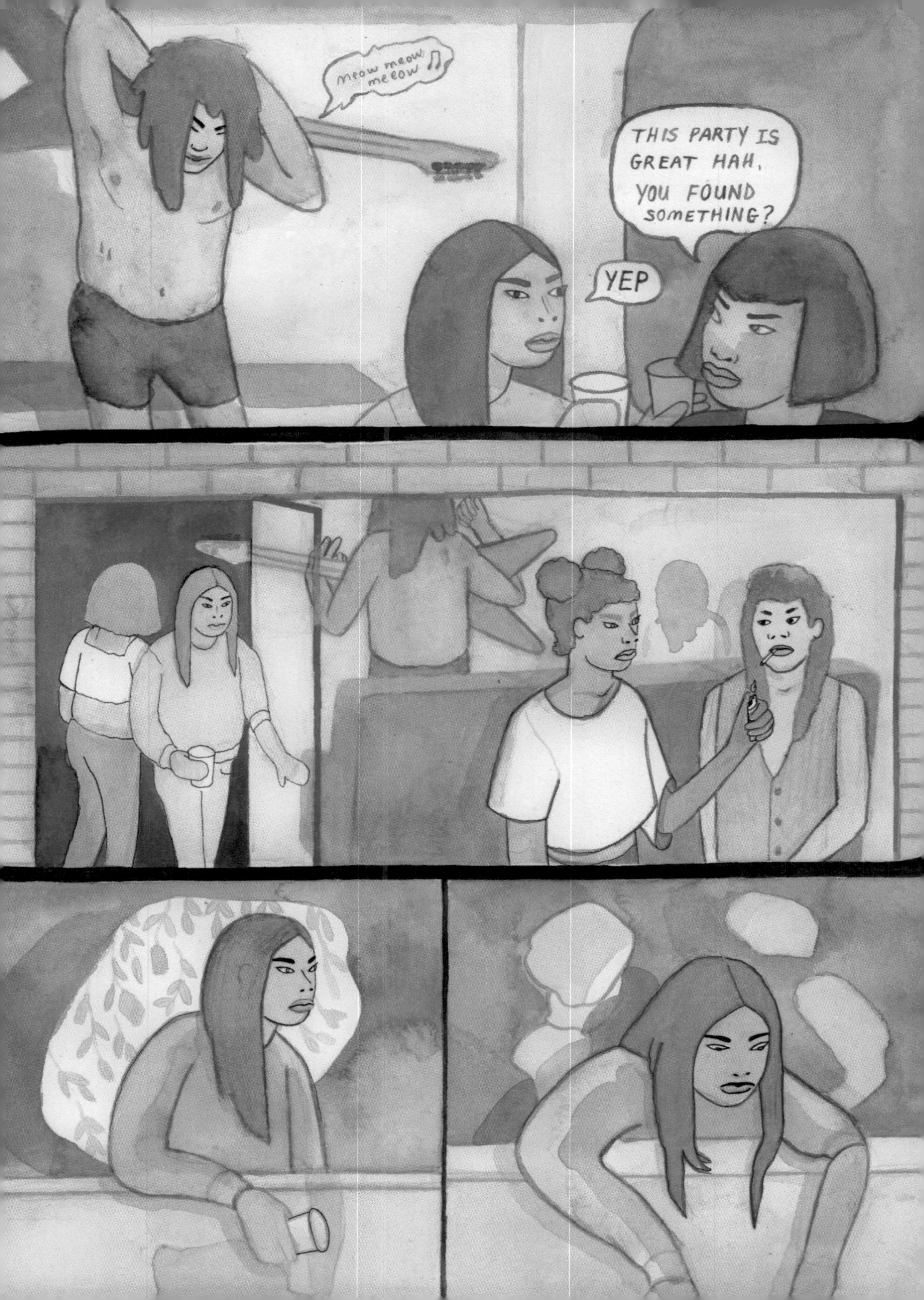
meow meow meeow ♫
THIS PARTY IS GREAT HAH, YOU FOUND SOMETHING?
YEP

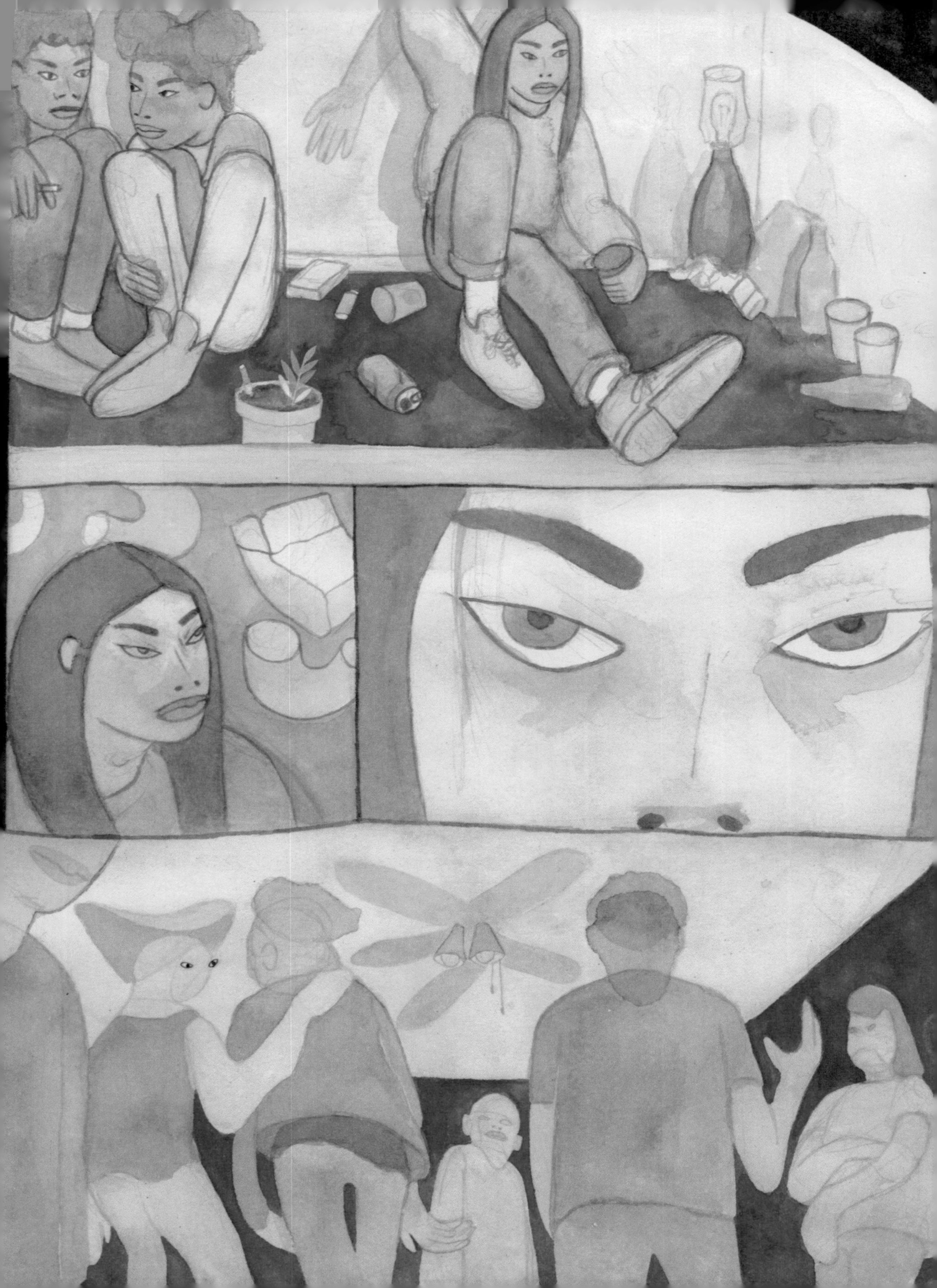

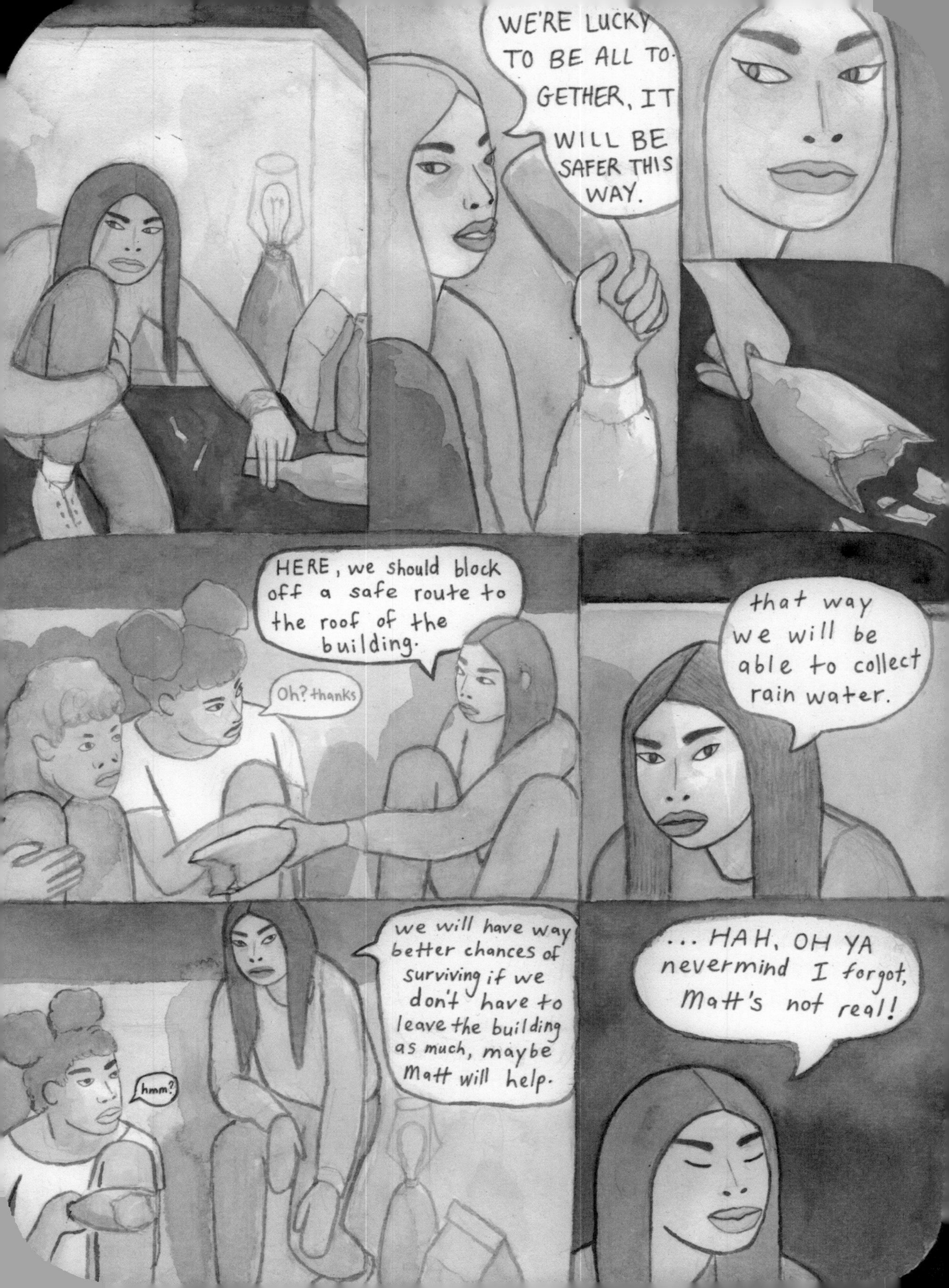
WE'RE LUCKY TO BE ALL TO-GETHER, IT WILL BE SAFER THIS WAY.
HERE, we should block off a safe route to the roof of the building.
Oh? thanks
that way we will be able to collect rain water.
we will have way better chances of surviving if we don't have to leave the building as much, maybe Matt will help.
hmm?
... HAH, OH YA nevermind I forgot, Matt's not real!

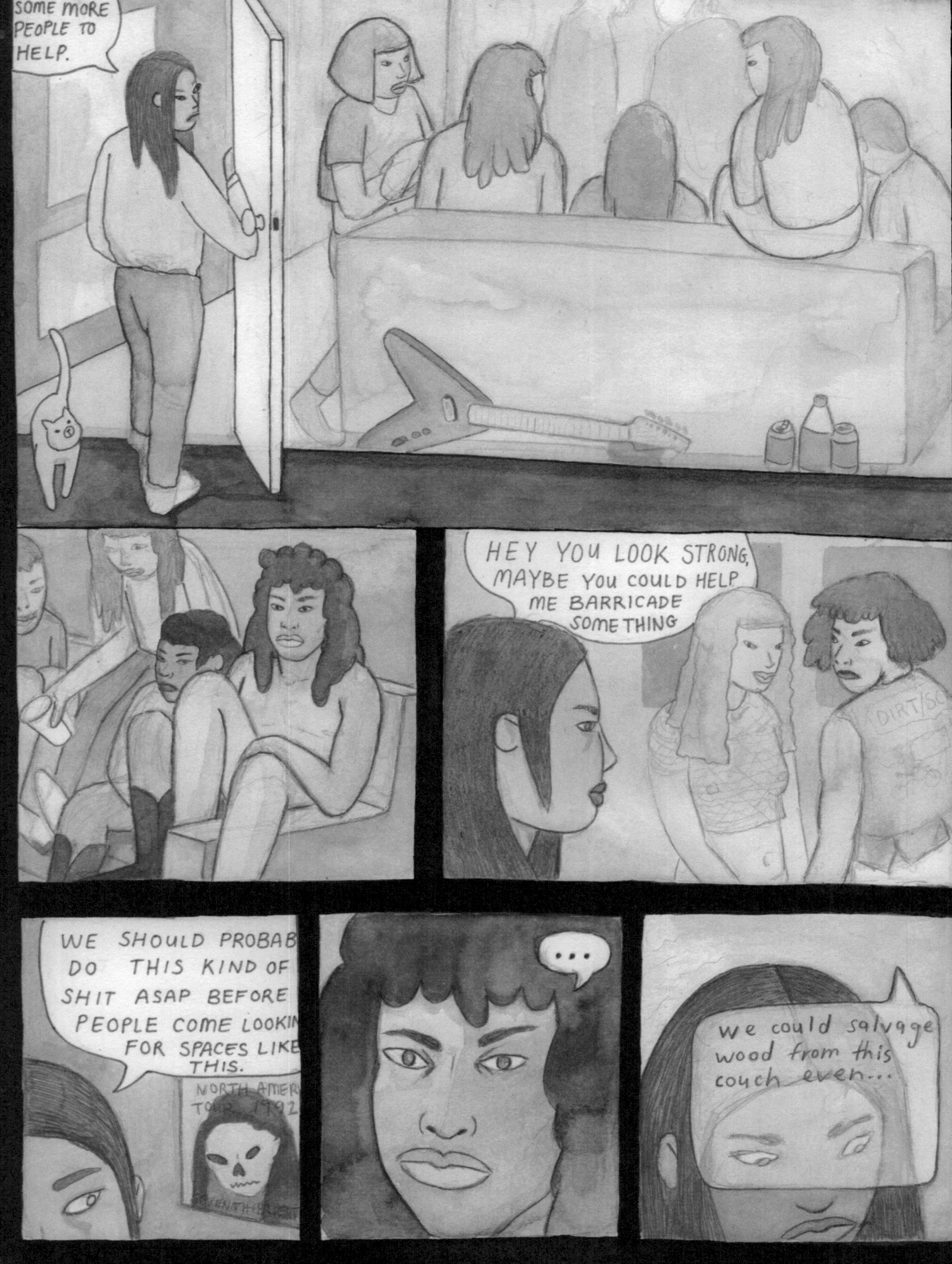
SOME MORE PEOPLE TO HELP.
HEY YOU LOOK STRONG, MAYBE YOU COULD HELP ME BARRICADE SOMETHING
DIRT/SC
WE SHOULD PROBAB DO THIS KIND OF SHIT ASAP BEFORE PEOPLE COME LOOKIN FOR SPACES LIKE THIS.
NORTH AMER TOUR 1992
...
we could salvage wood from this couch even...

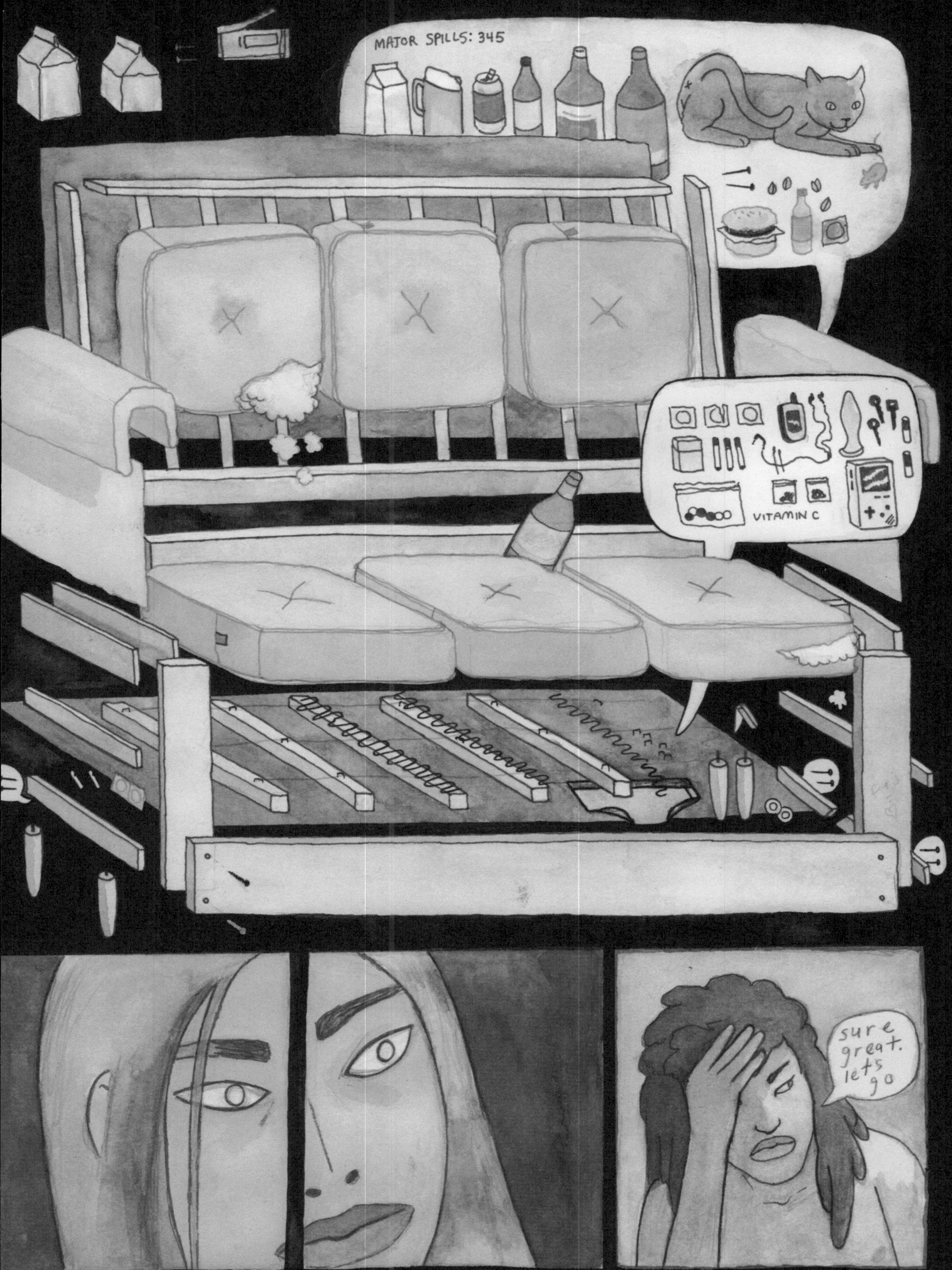
MAJOR SPILLS: 345
VITAMIN C
sure great. lets go

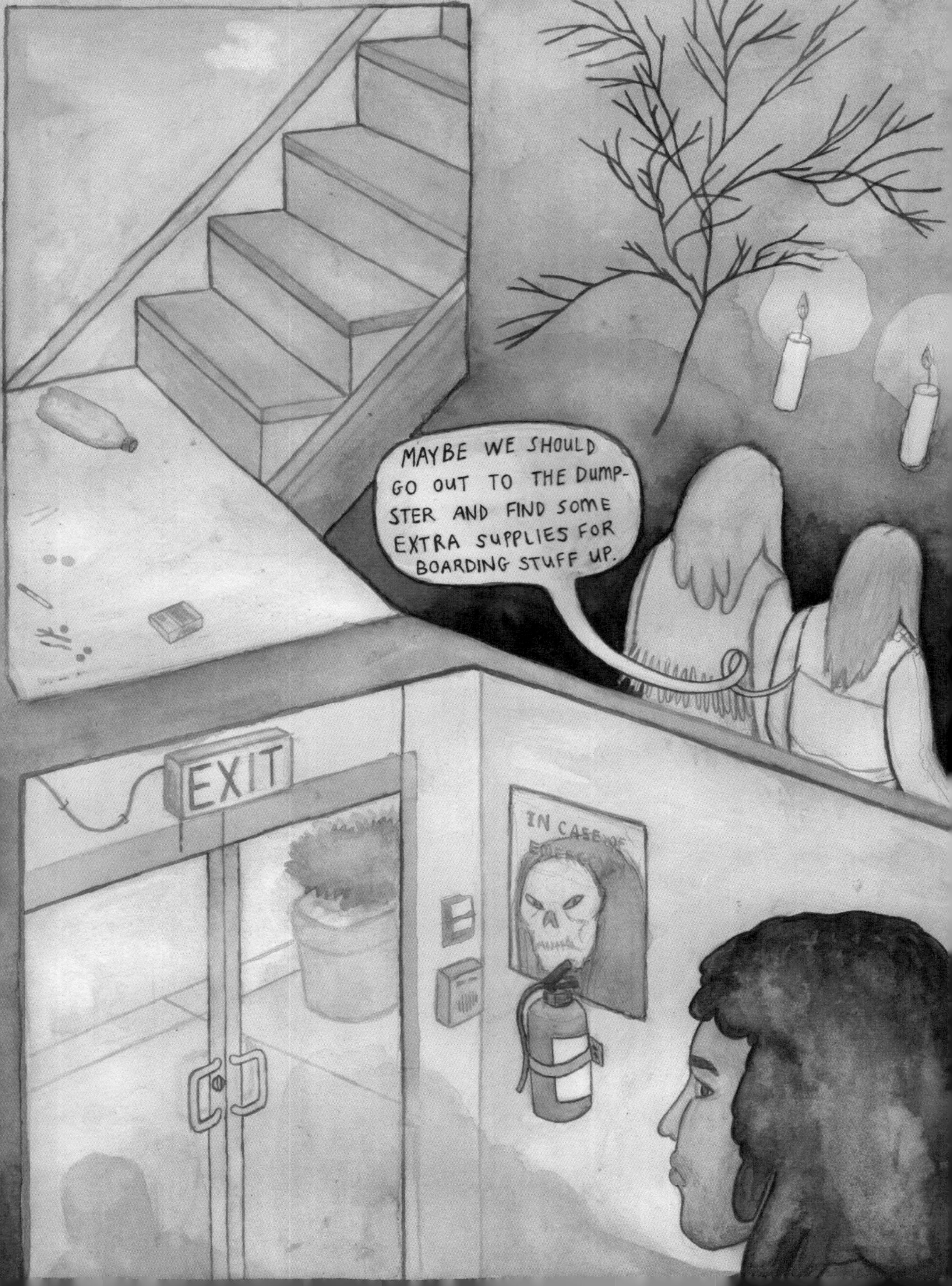
MAYBE WE SHOULD GO OUT TO THE DUMP-STER AND FIND SOME EXTRA SUPPLIES FOR BOARDING STUFF UP.
EXIT
IN CASE OF

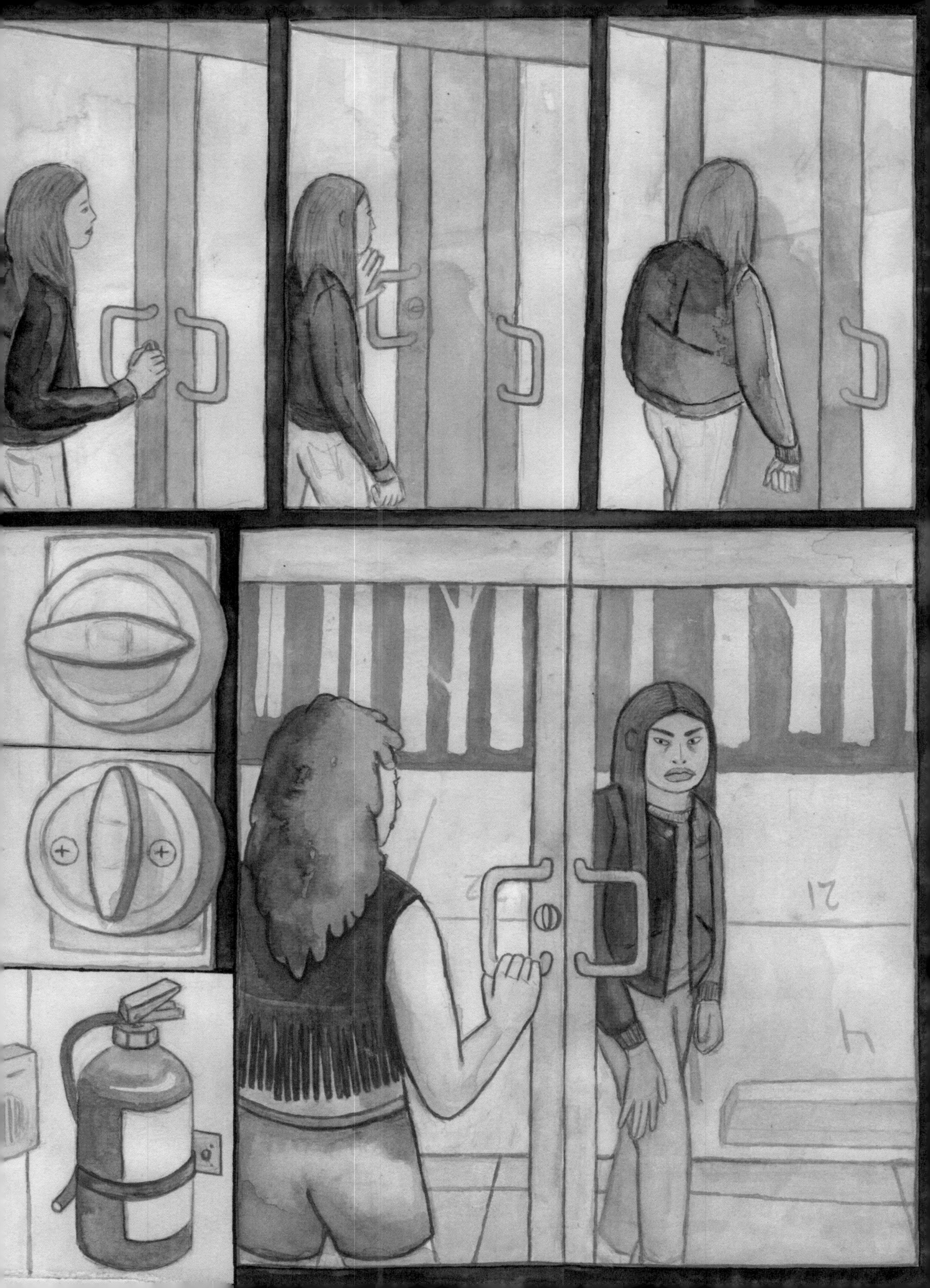

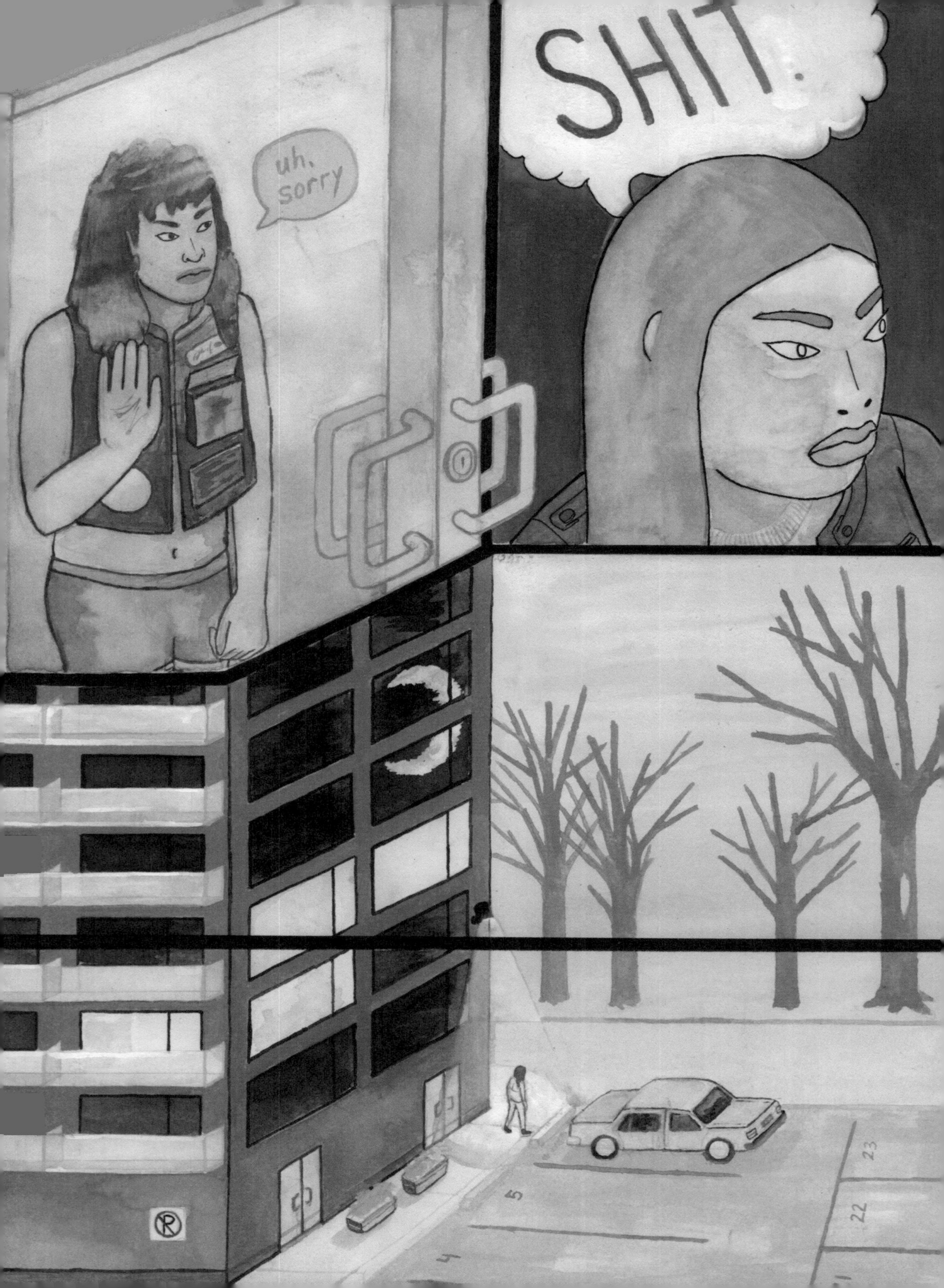
uh, sorry
SHIT.
5
4
23
22

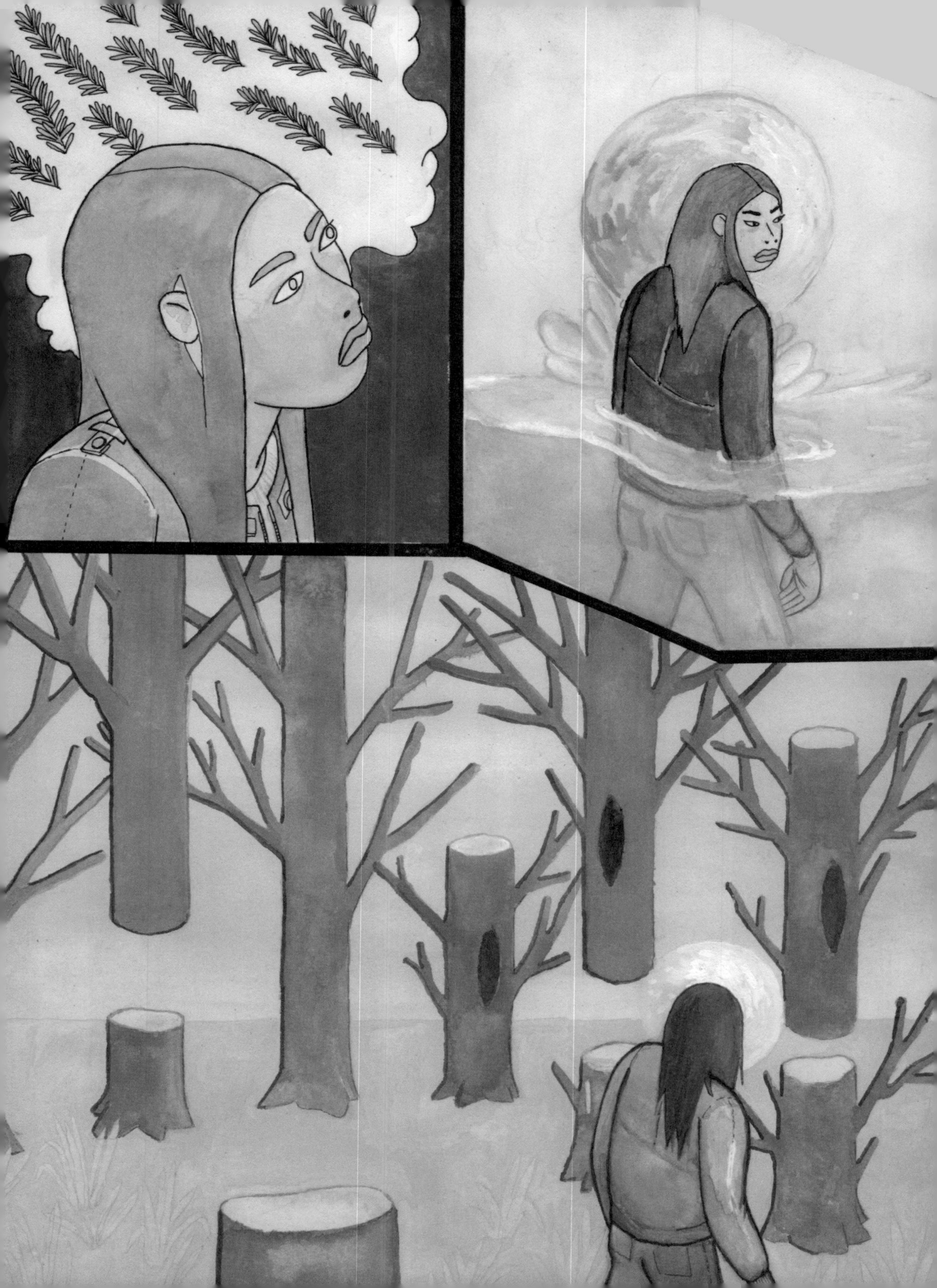

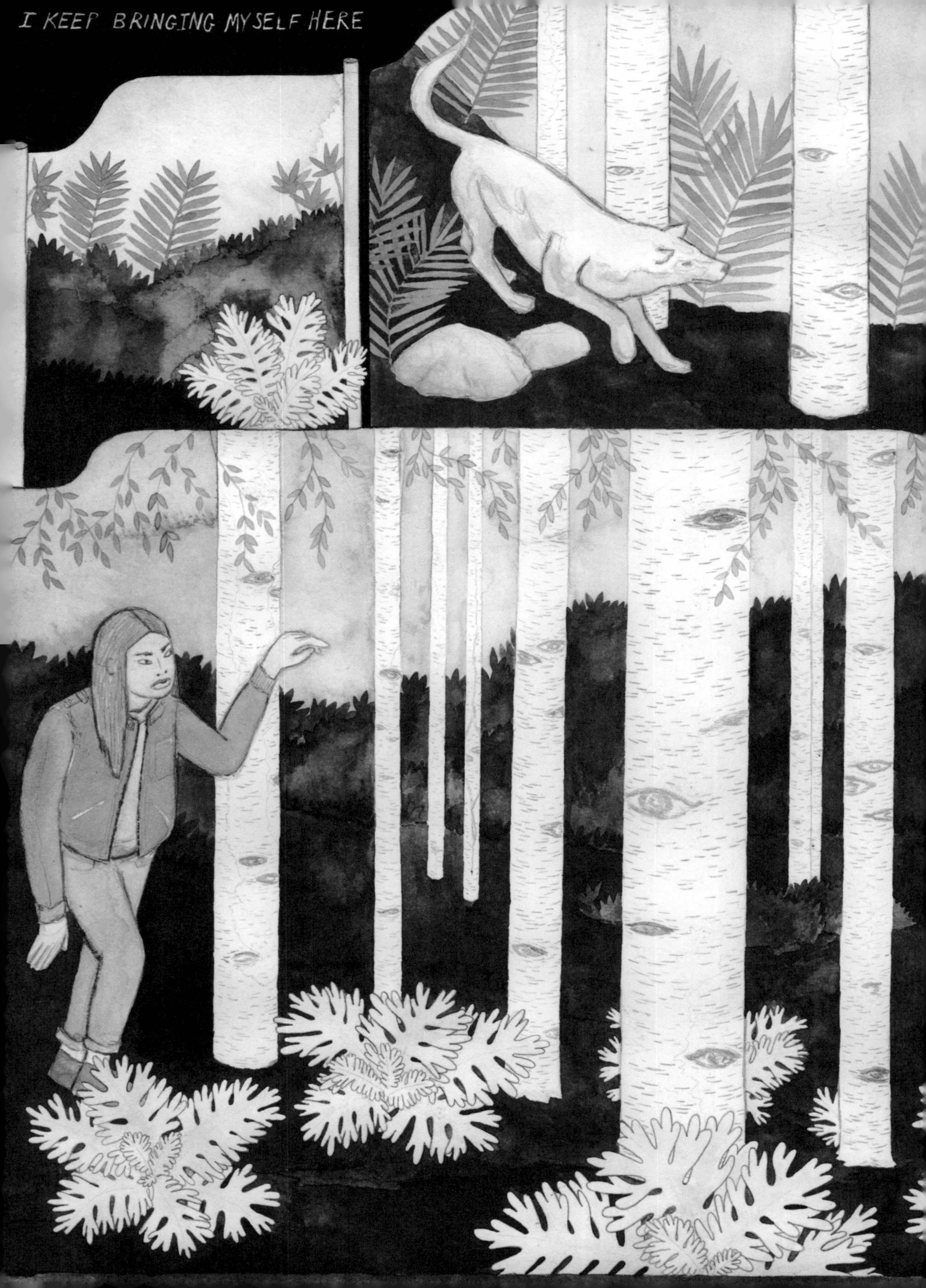
I KEEP BRINGING MYSELF HERE

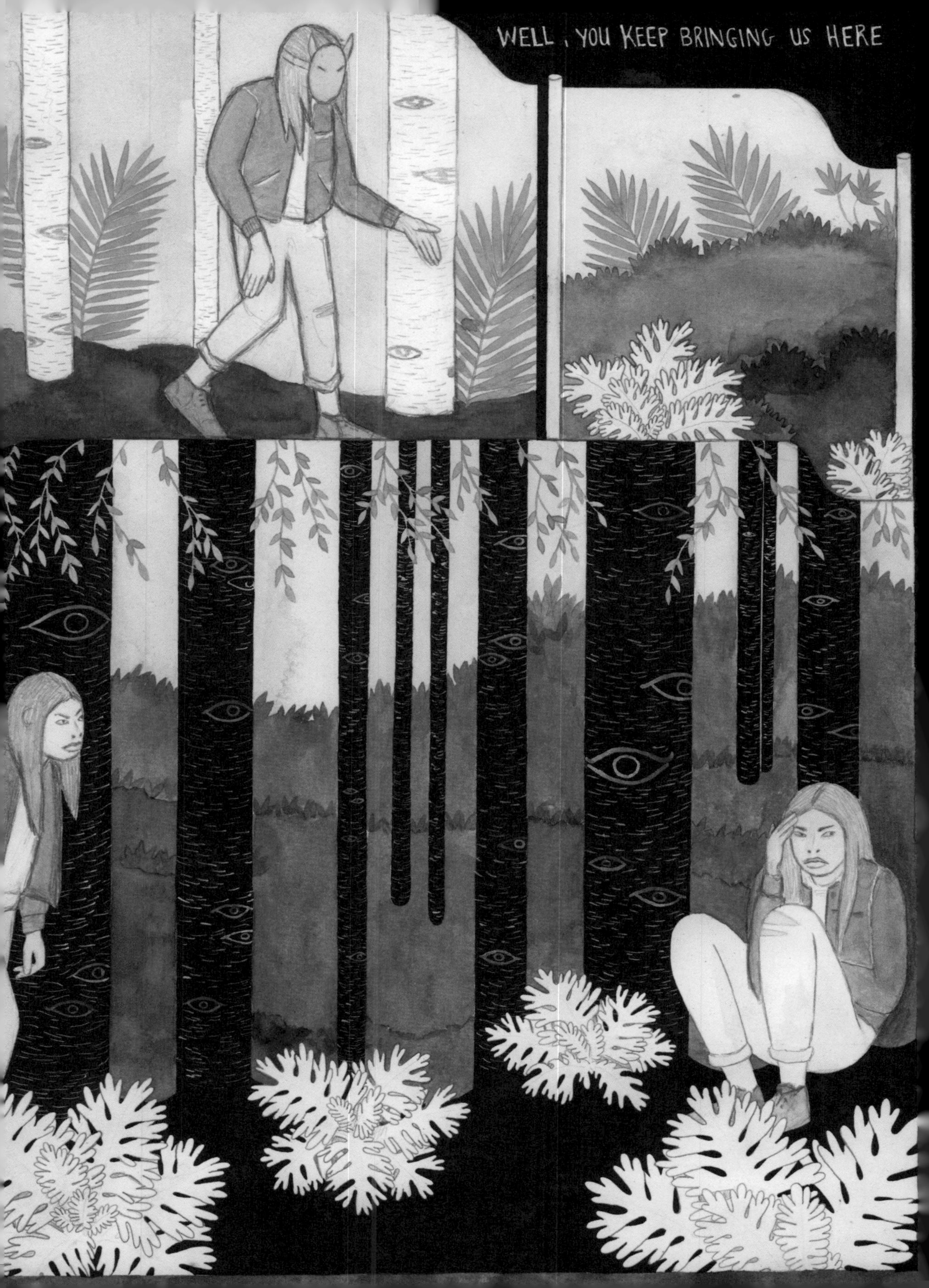
WELL, YOU KEEP BRINGING US HERE

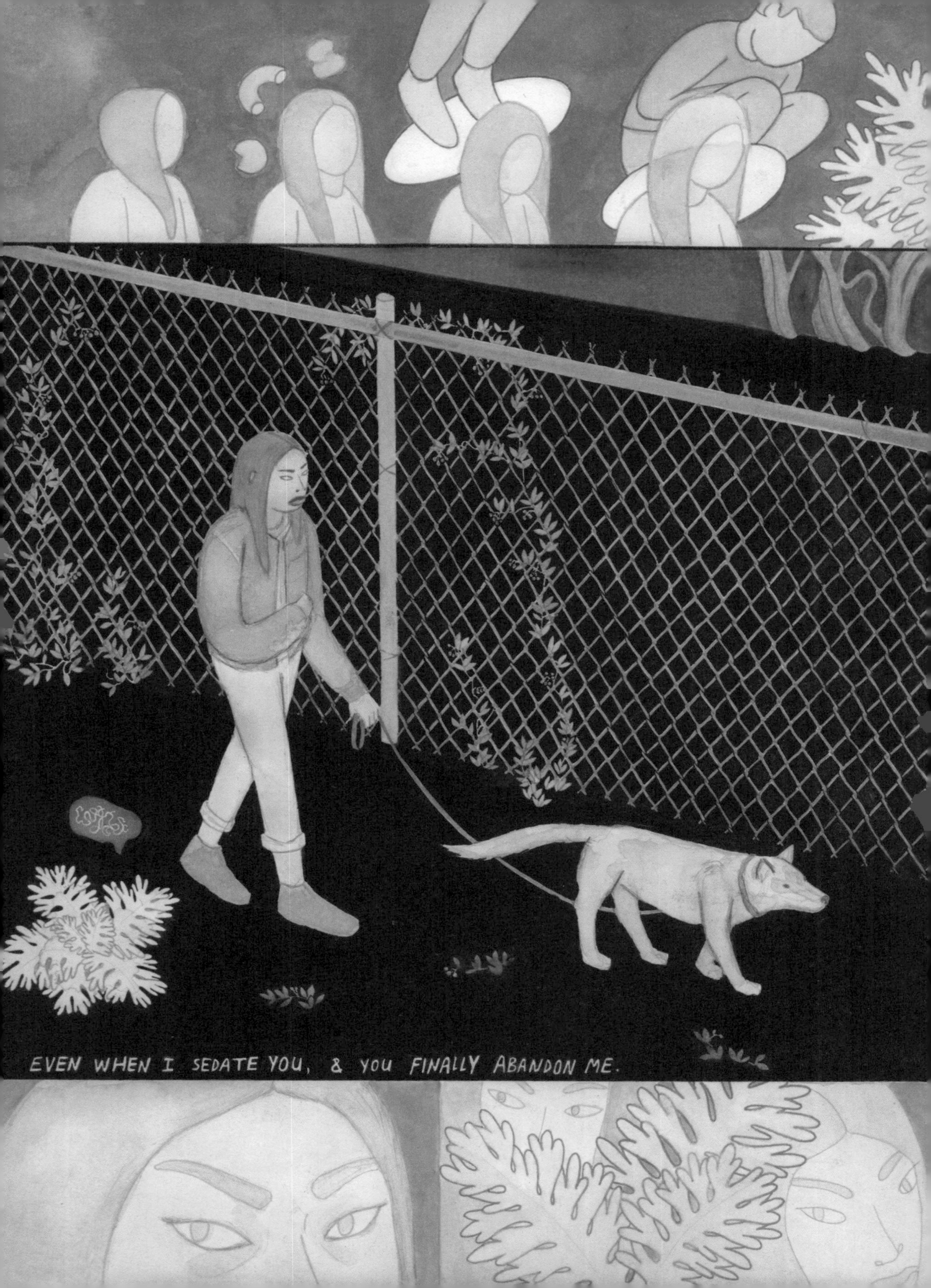
EVEN WHEN I SEDATE YOU, & YOU FINALLY ABANDON ME.

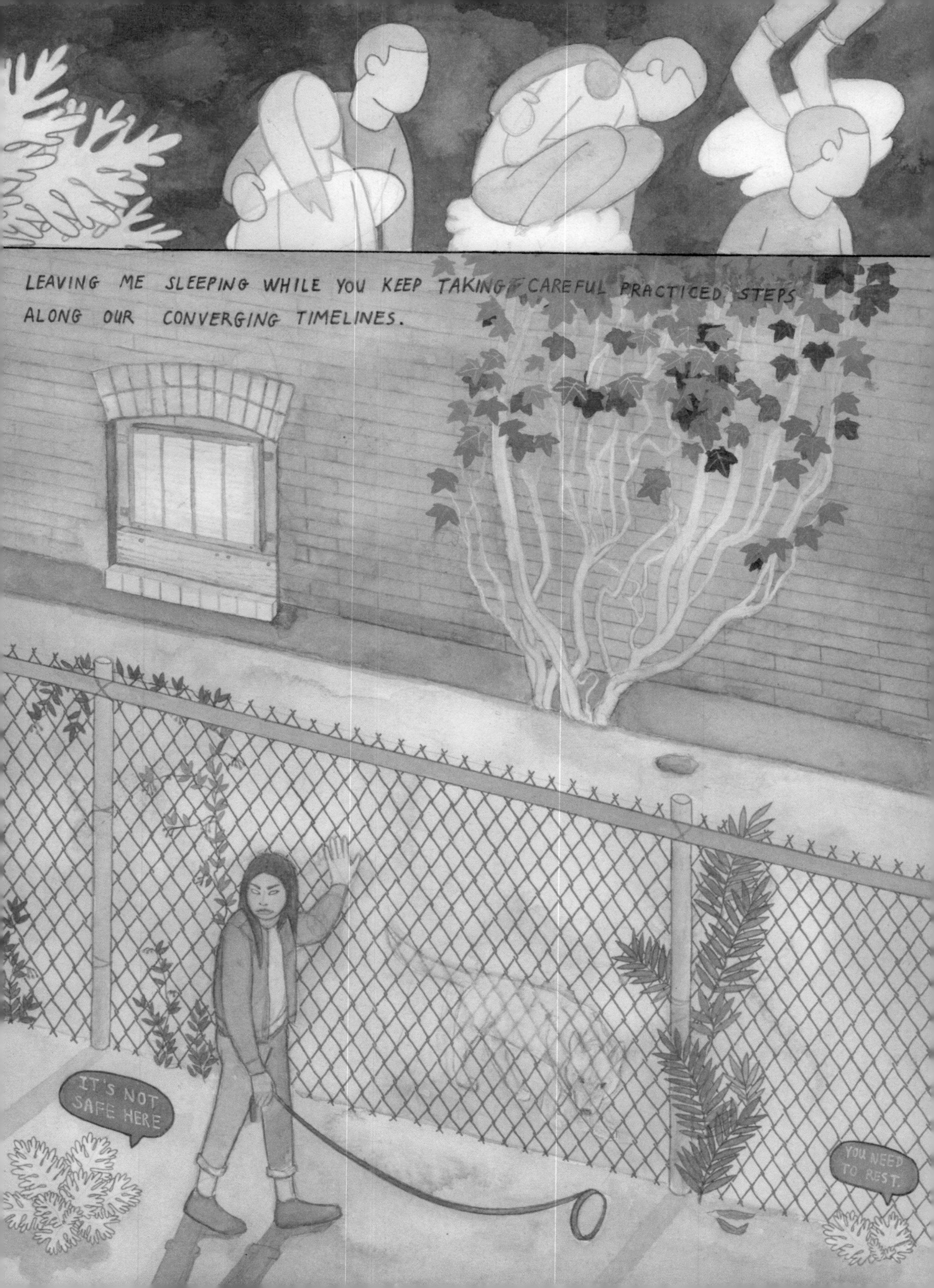
LEAVING ME SLEEPING WHILE YOU KEEP TAKING CAREFUL PRACTICED STEPS ALONG OUR CONVERGING TIMELINES.
IT'S NOT SAFE HERE
YOU NEED TO REST.

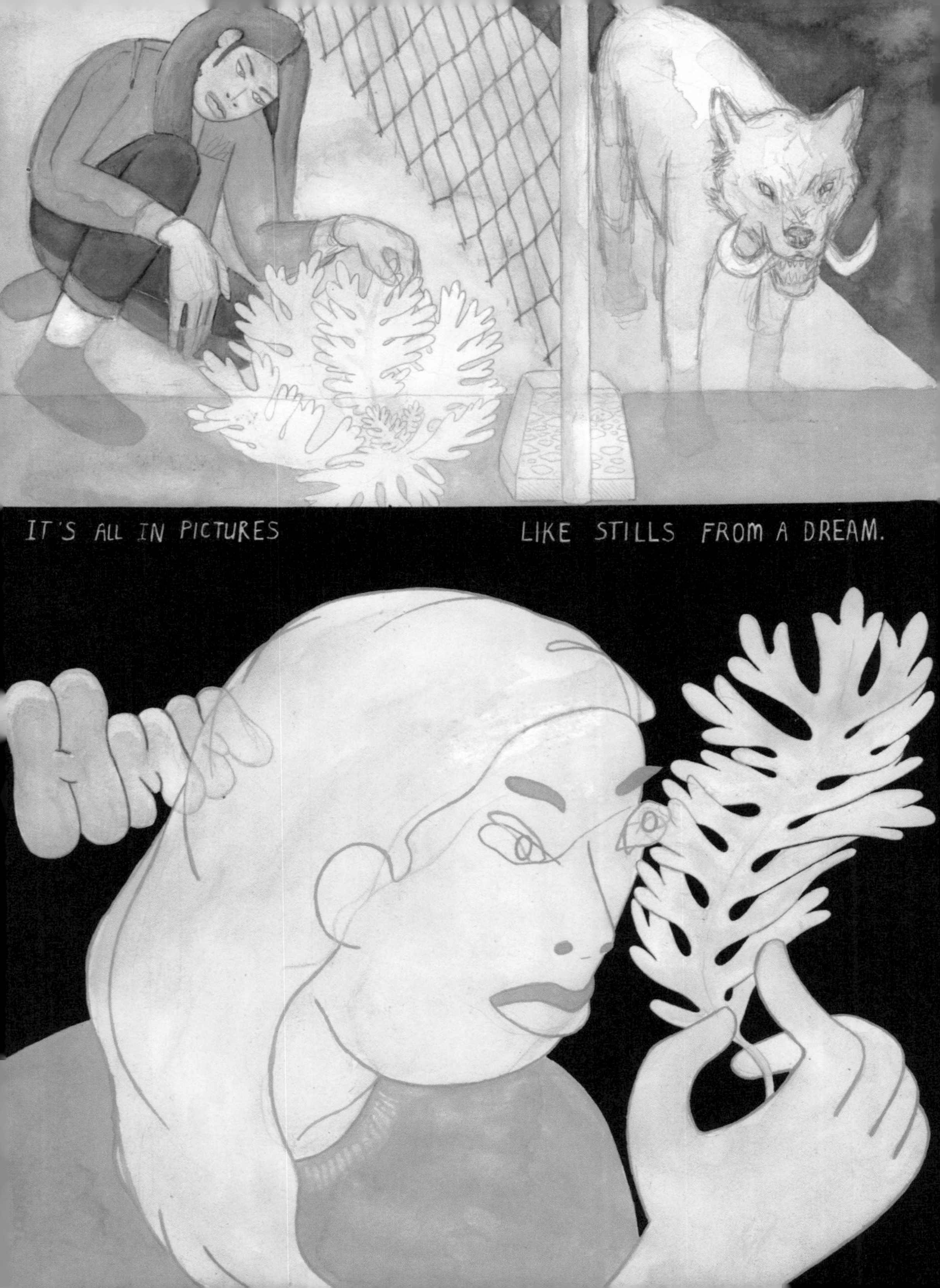
IT'S ALL IN PICTURES
LIKE STILLS FROM A DREAM.

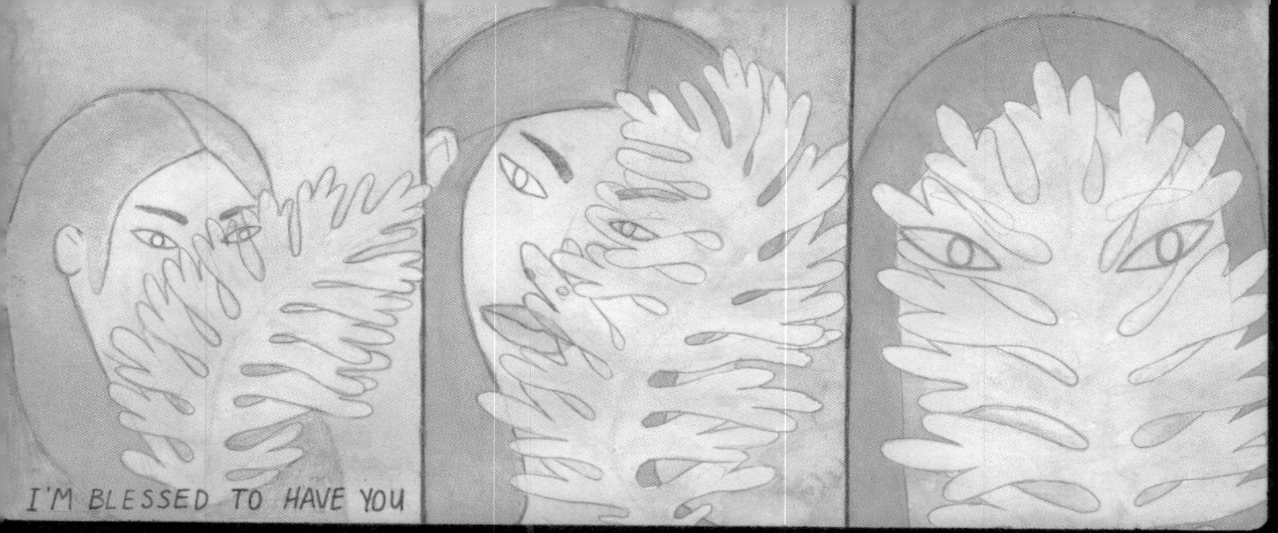
I'M BLESSED TO HAVE YOU

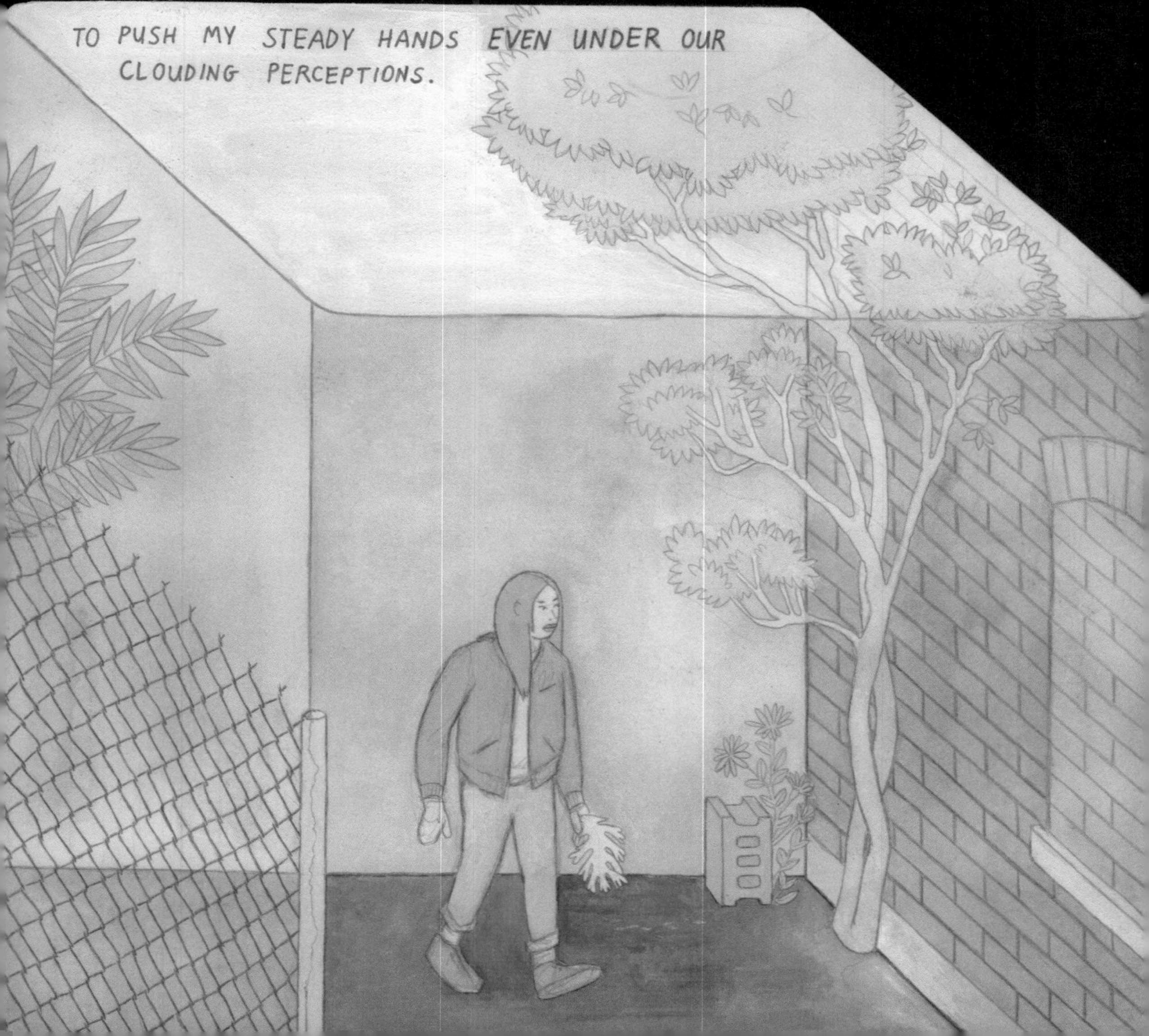
TO PUSH MY STEADY HANDS EVEN UNDER OUR CLOUDING PERCEPTIONS.

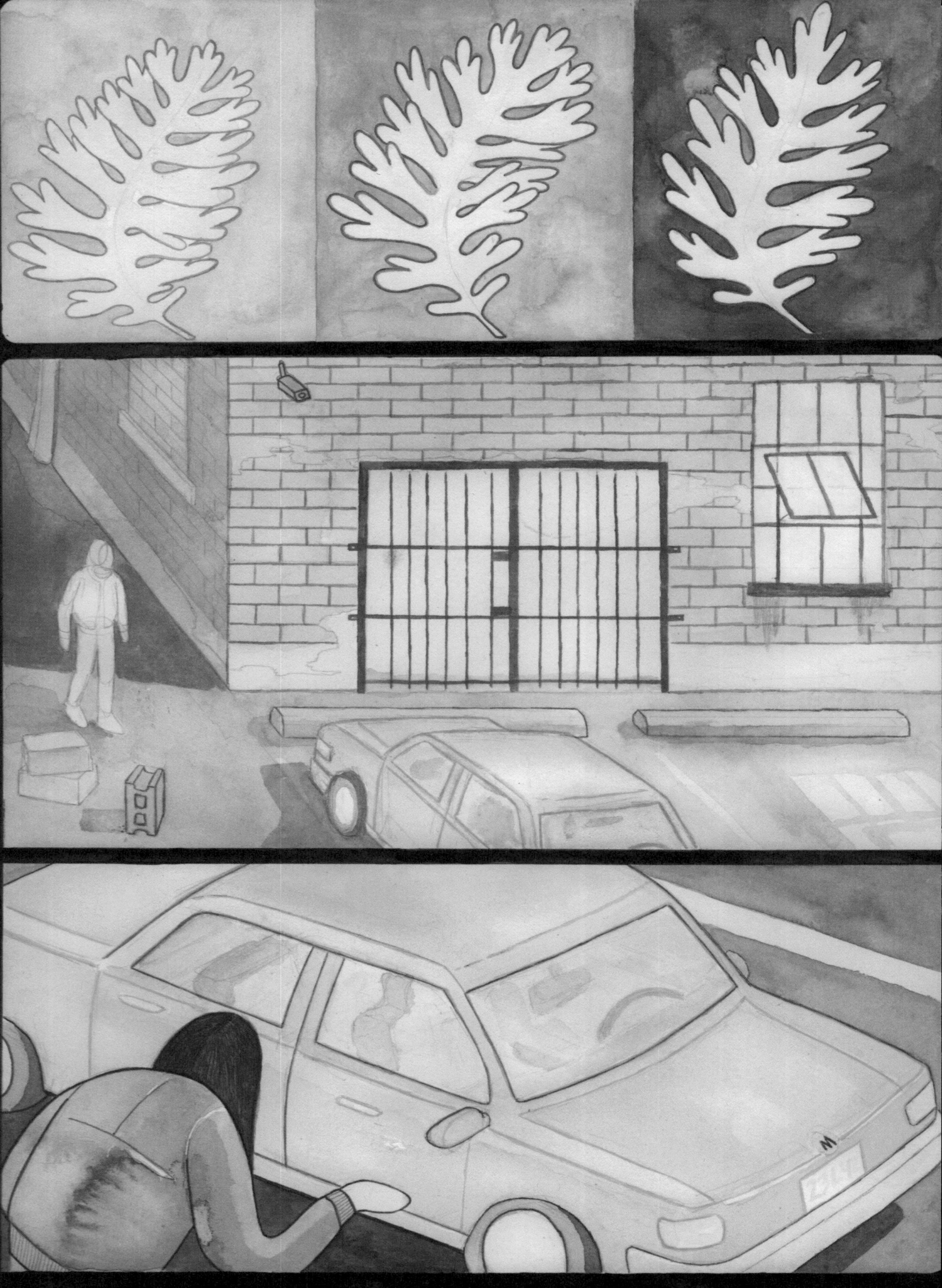

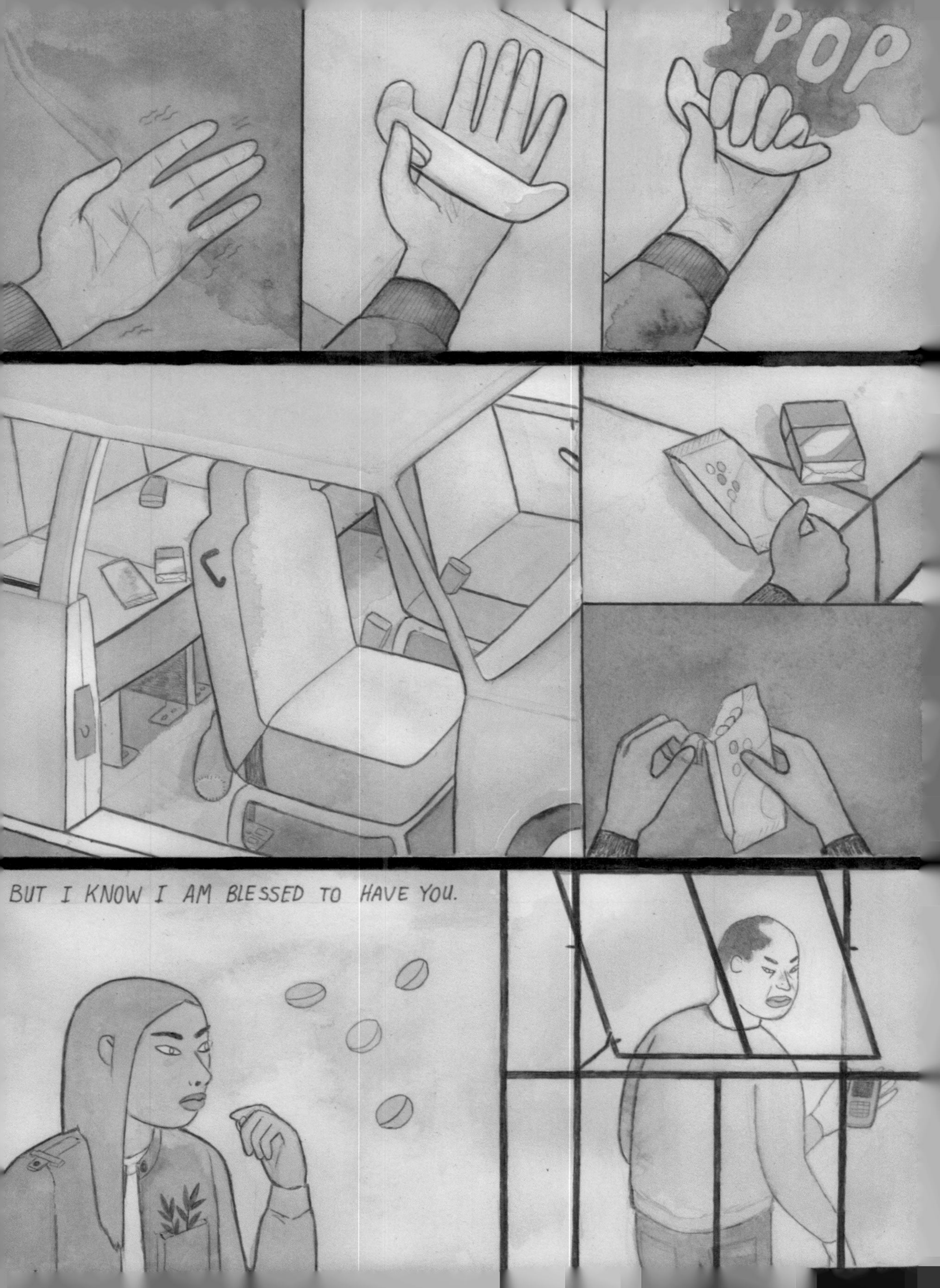
POP
BUT I KNOW I AM BLESSED TO HAVE YOU.

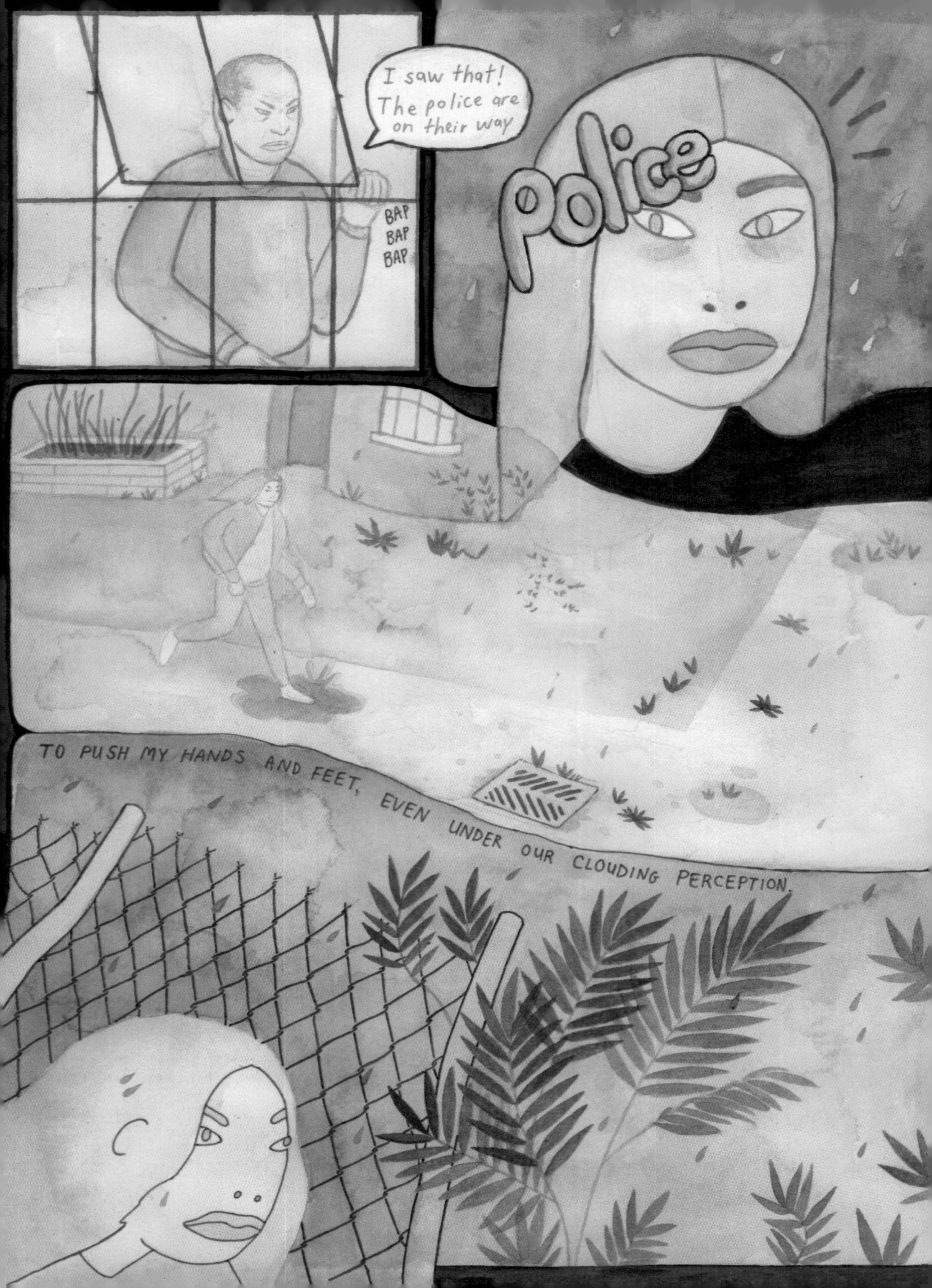
I saw that! The police are on their way
BAP BAP BAP
police
TO PUSH MY HANDS AND FEET, EVEN UNDER OUR CLOUDING PERCEPTION.

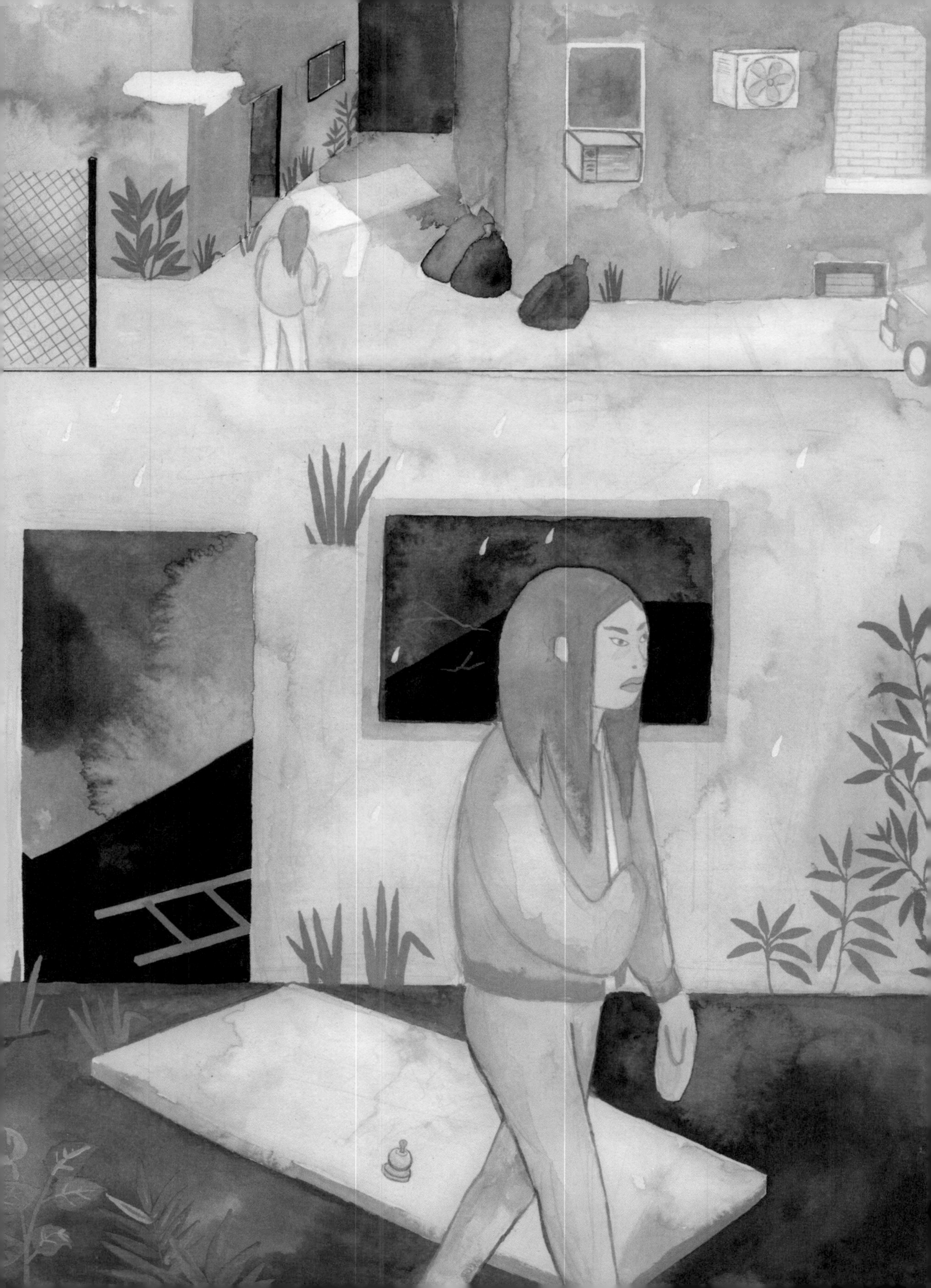

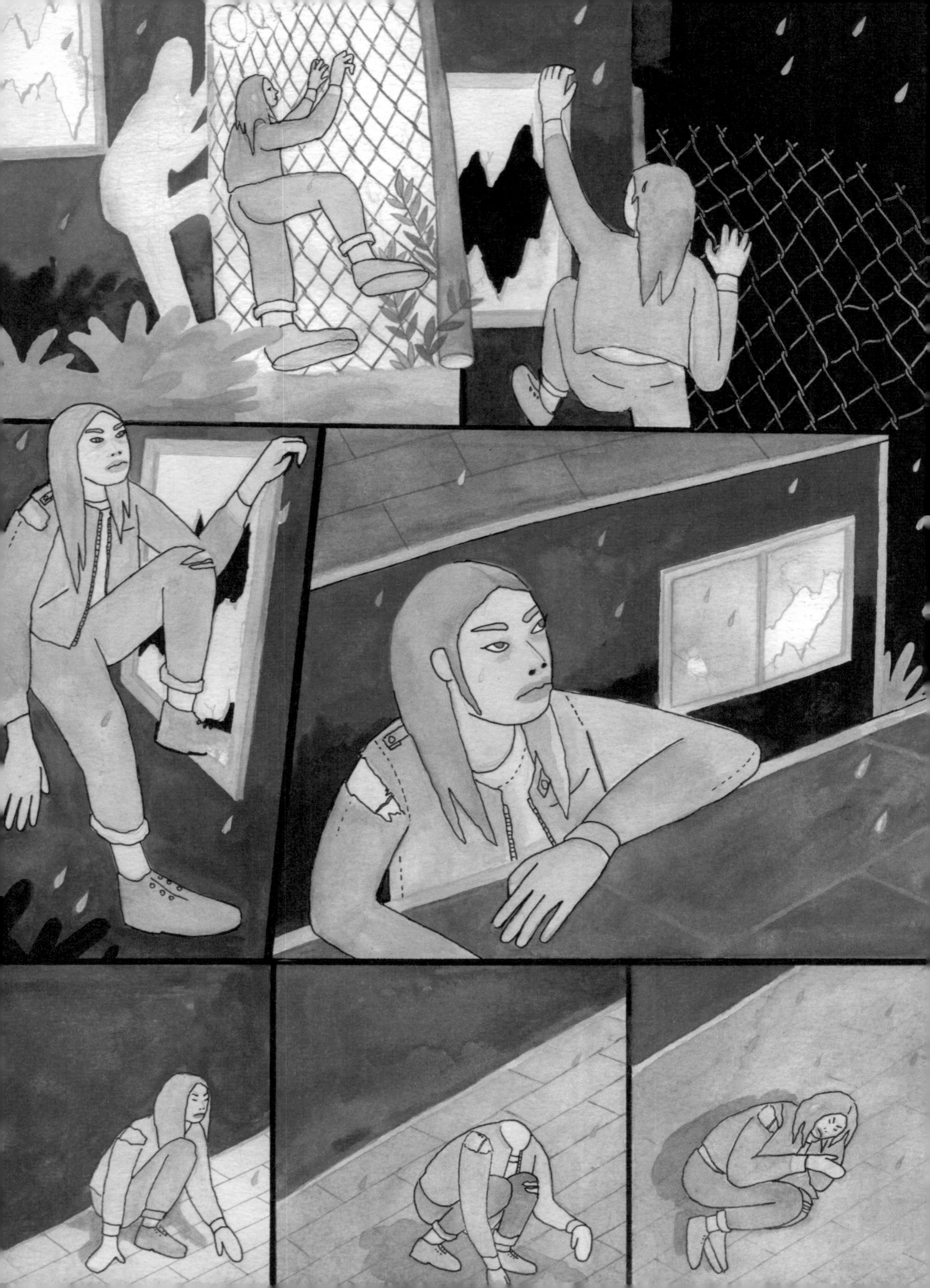

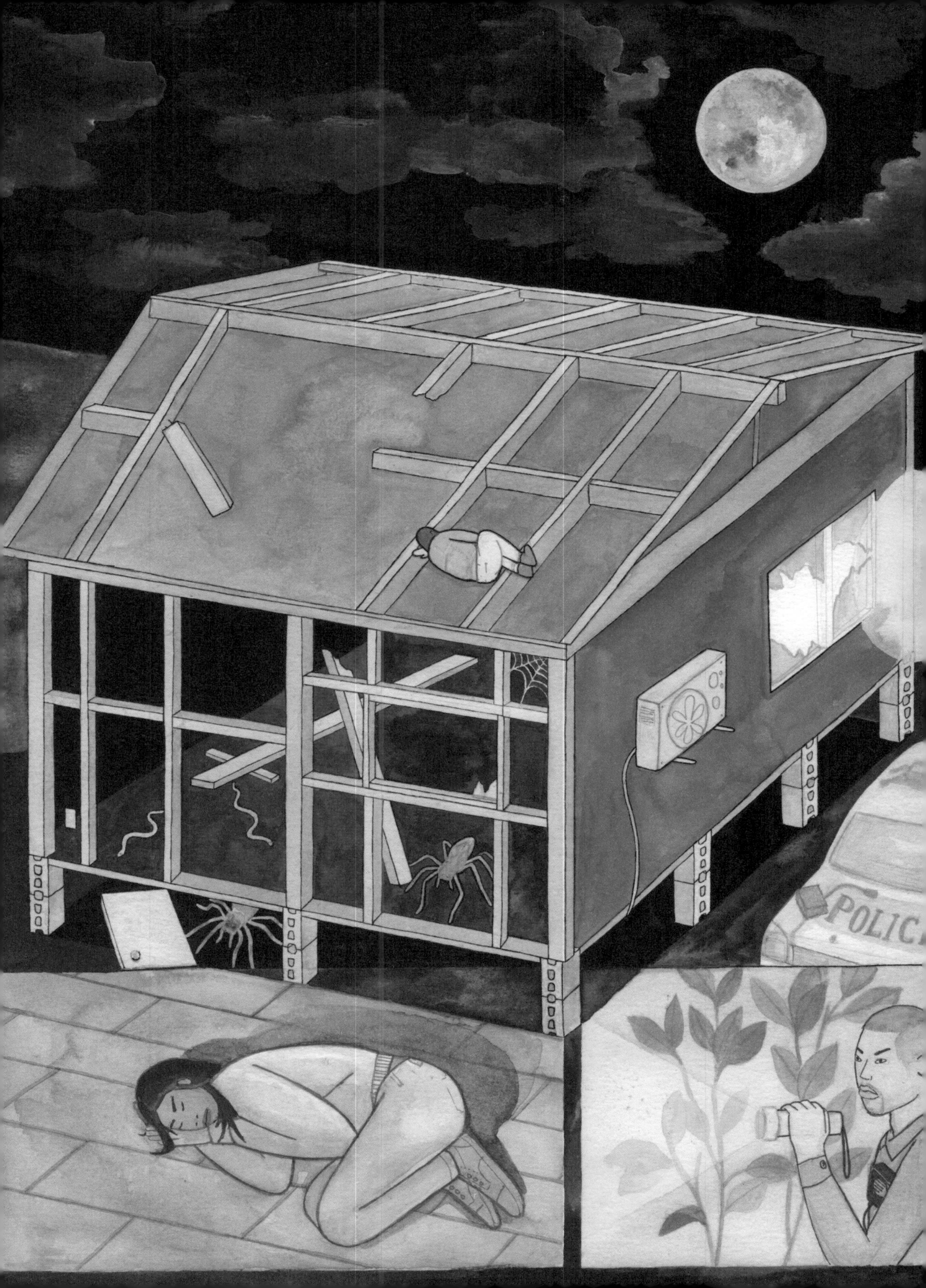
POLIC

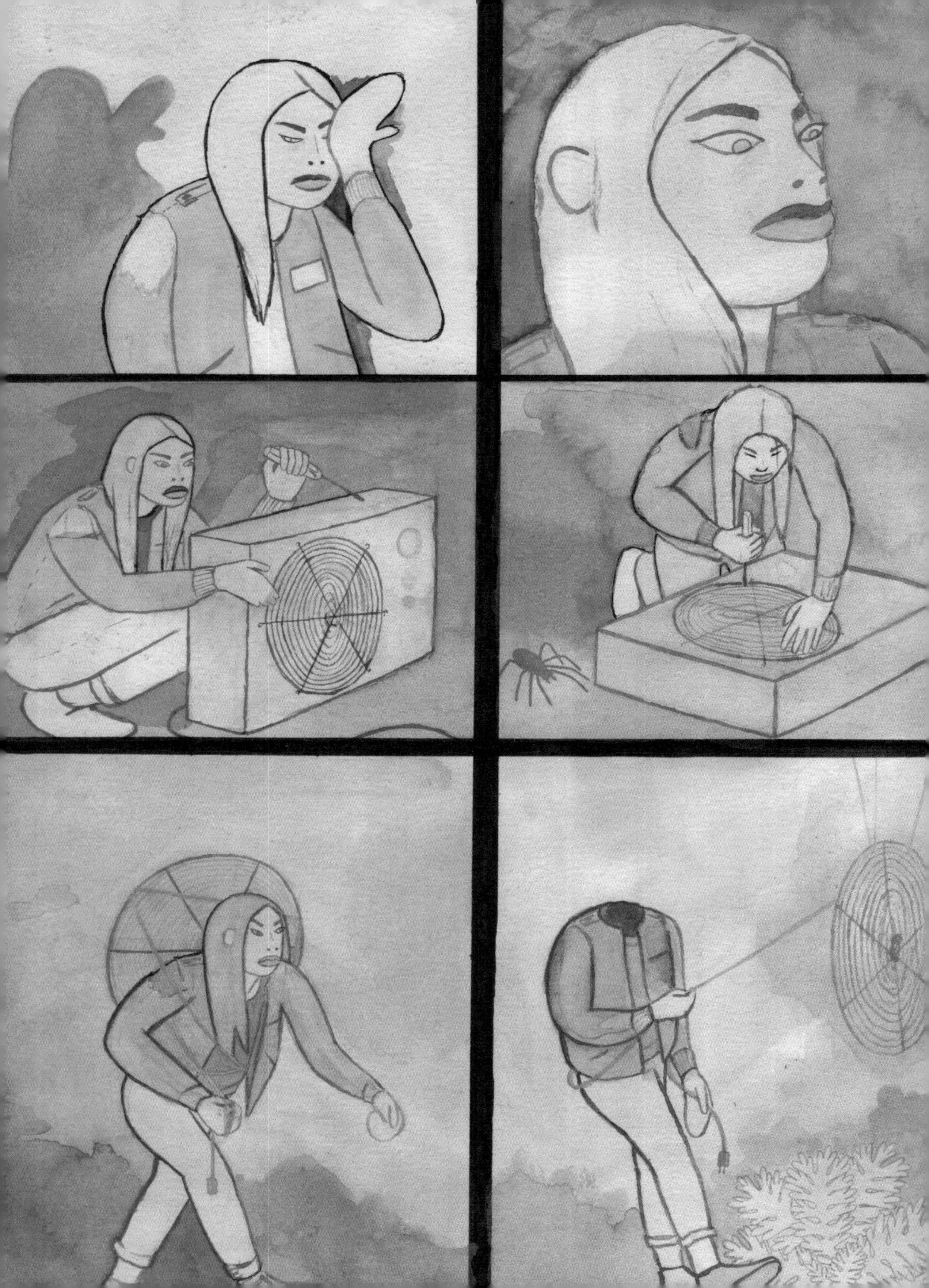

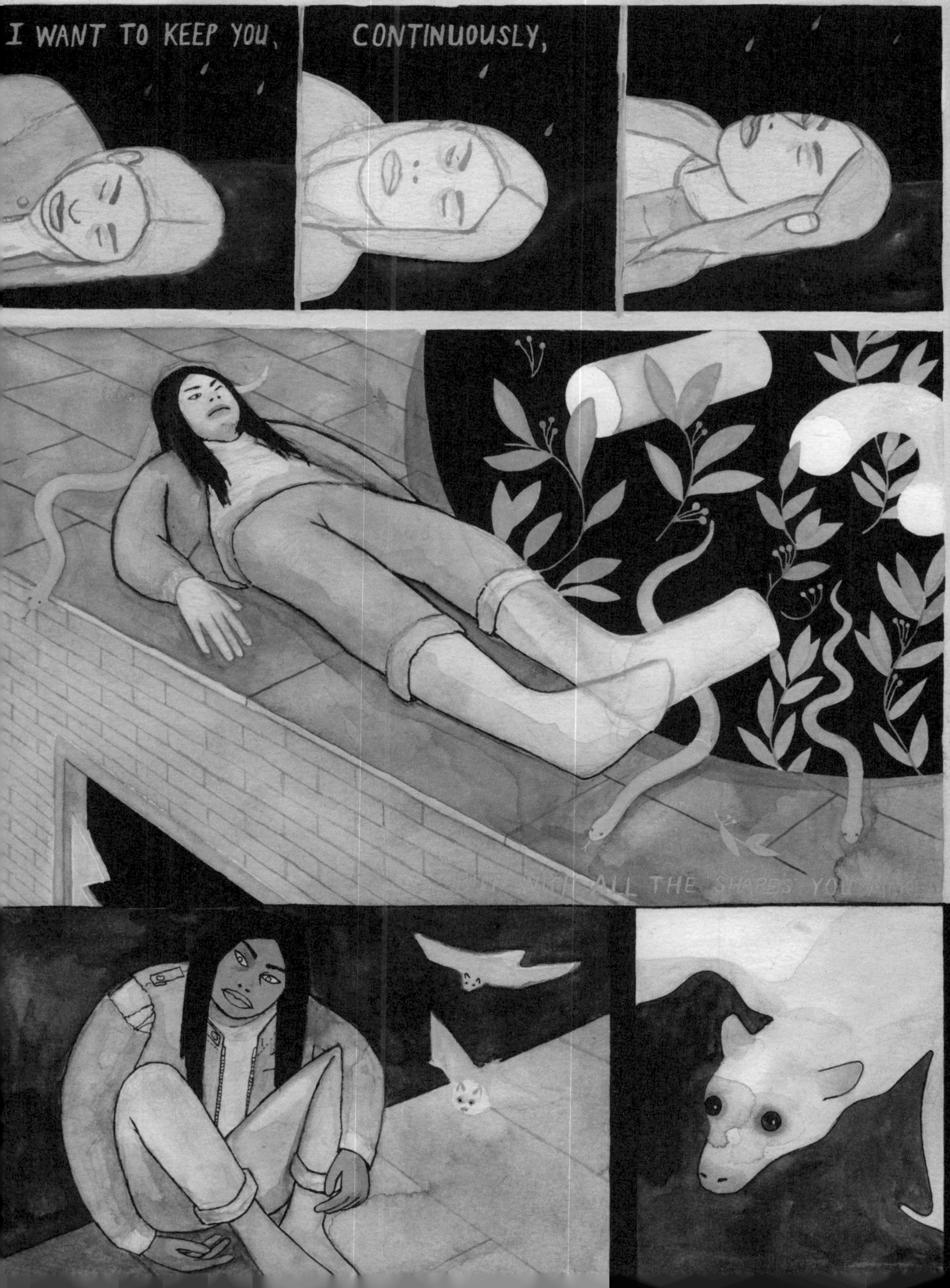

I WANT TO KEEP YOU,
CONTINUOUSLY,
ALL THE SHAPES YOU

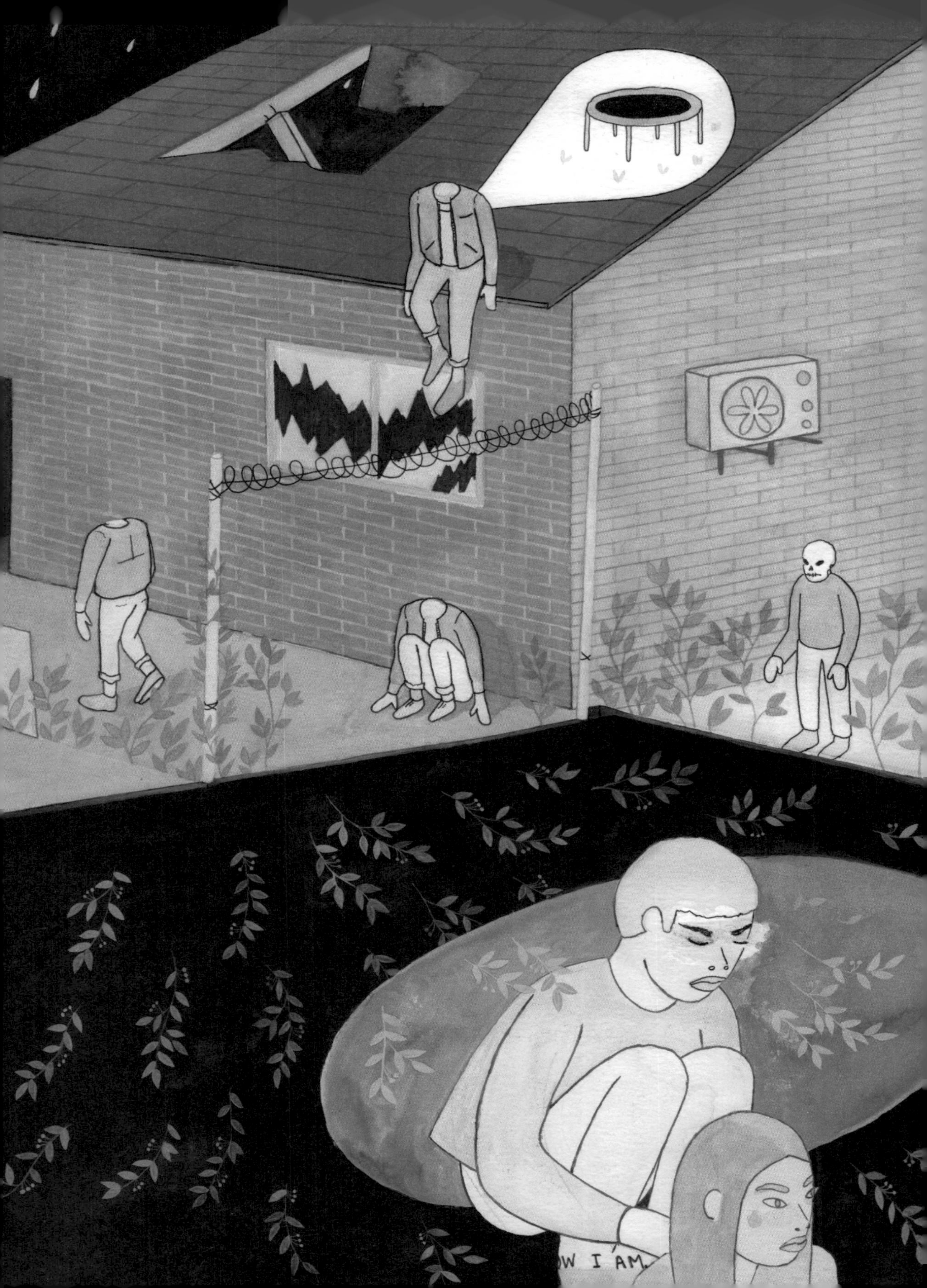
OW I AM.

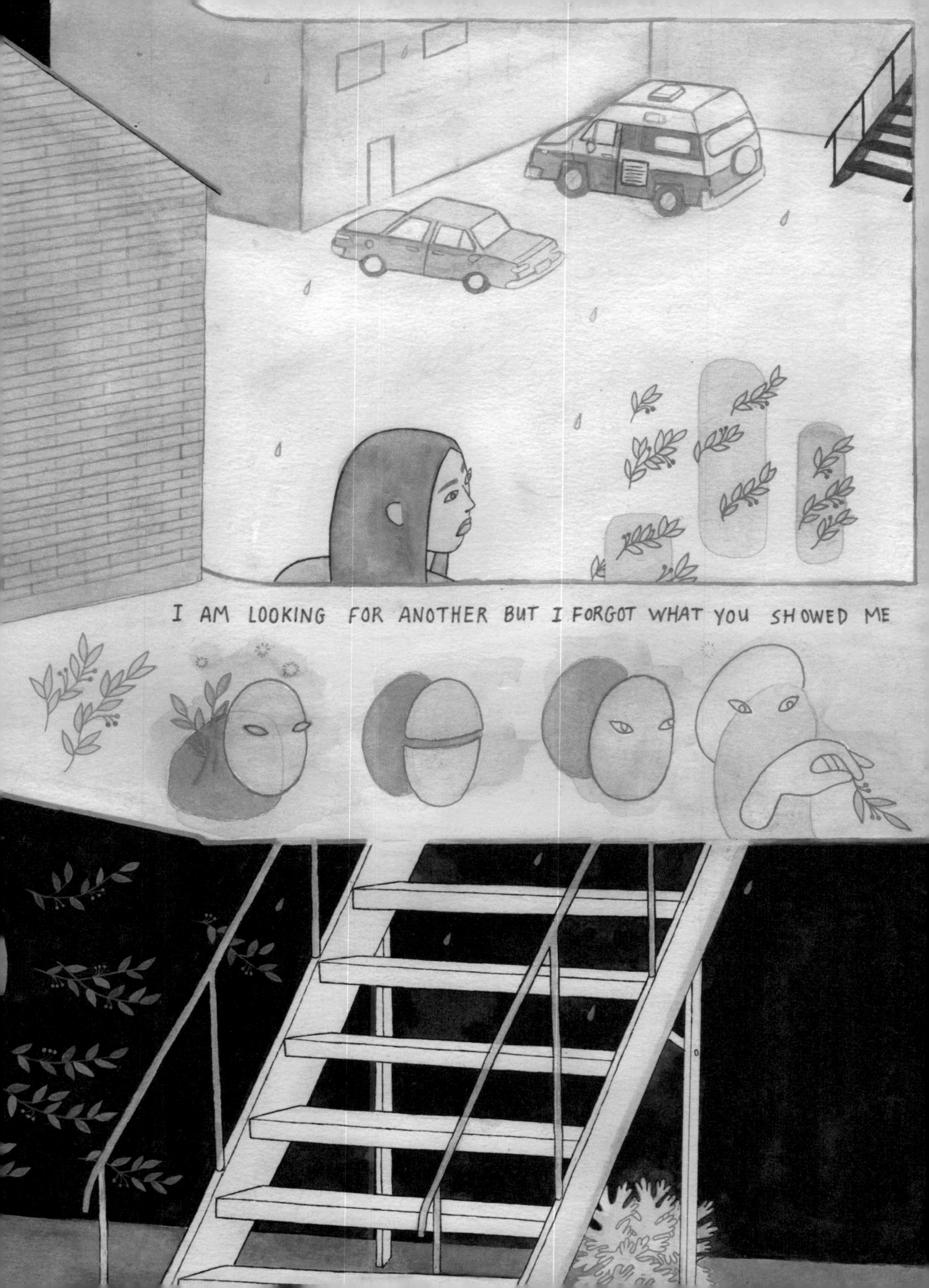
I AM LOOKING FOR ANOTHER BUT I FORGOT WHAT YOU SHOWED ME

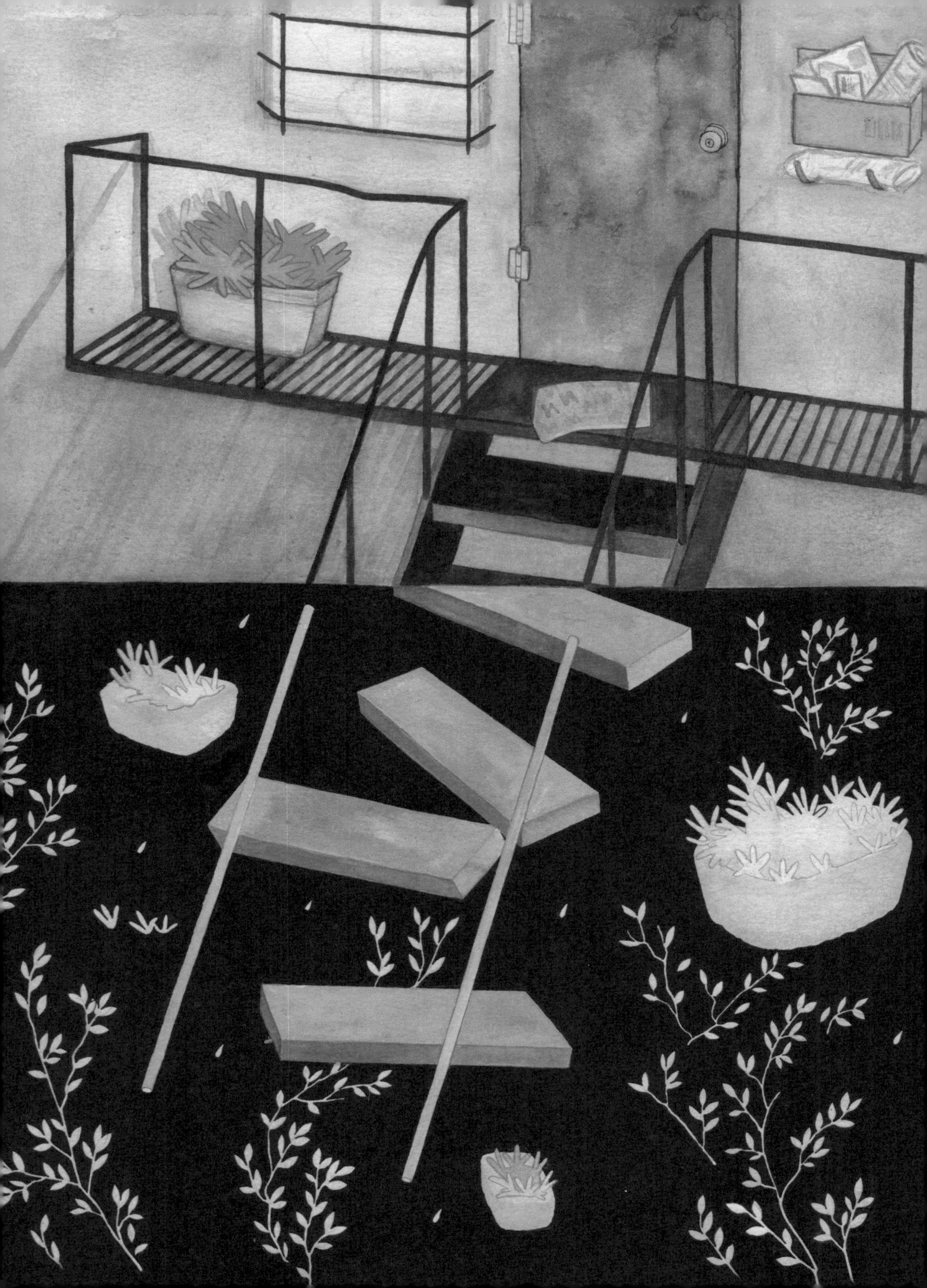

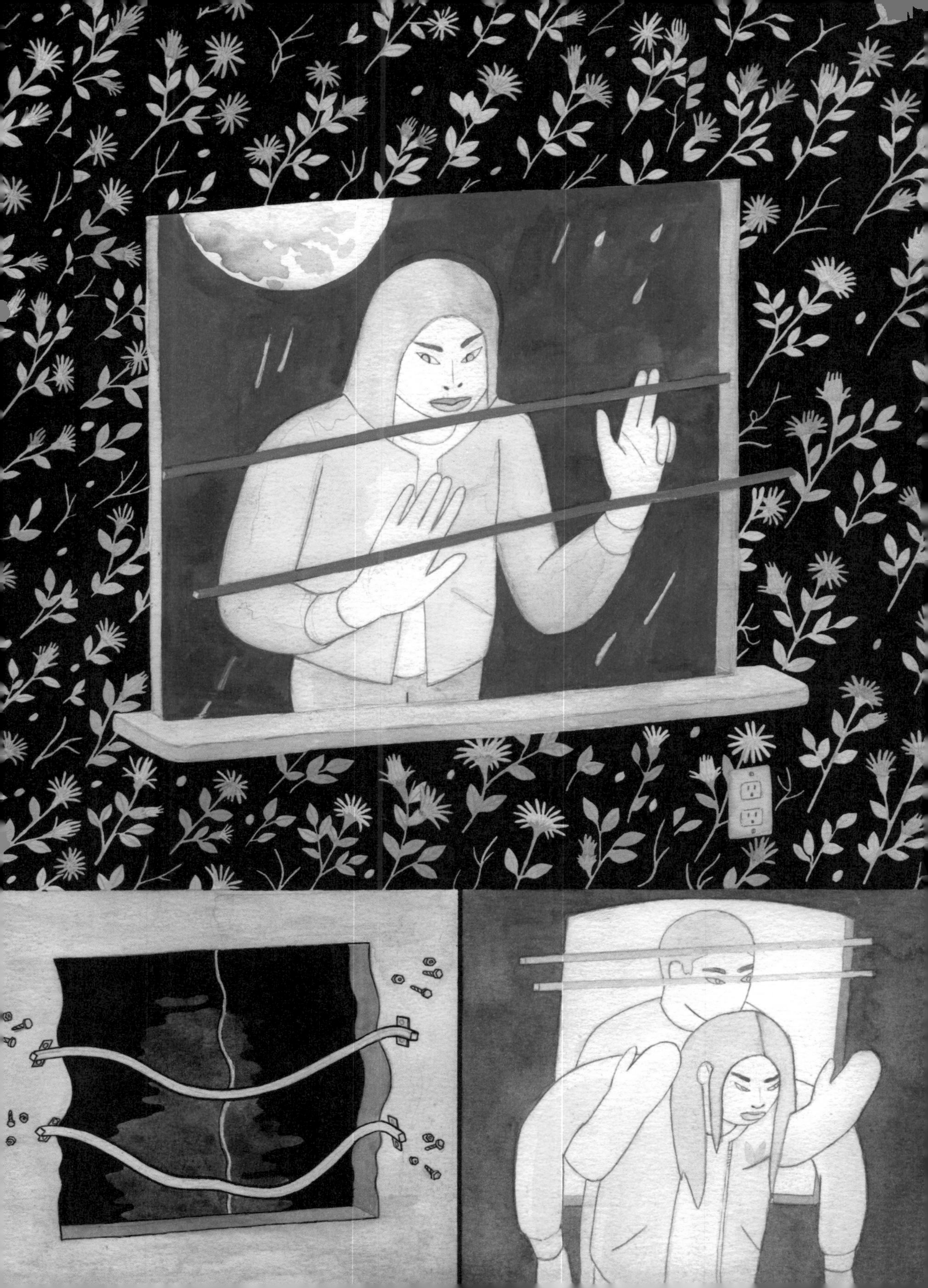

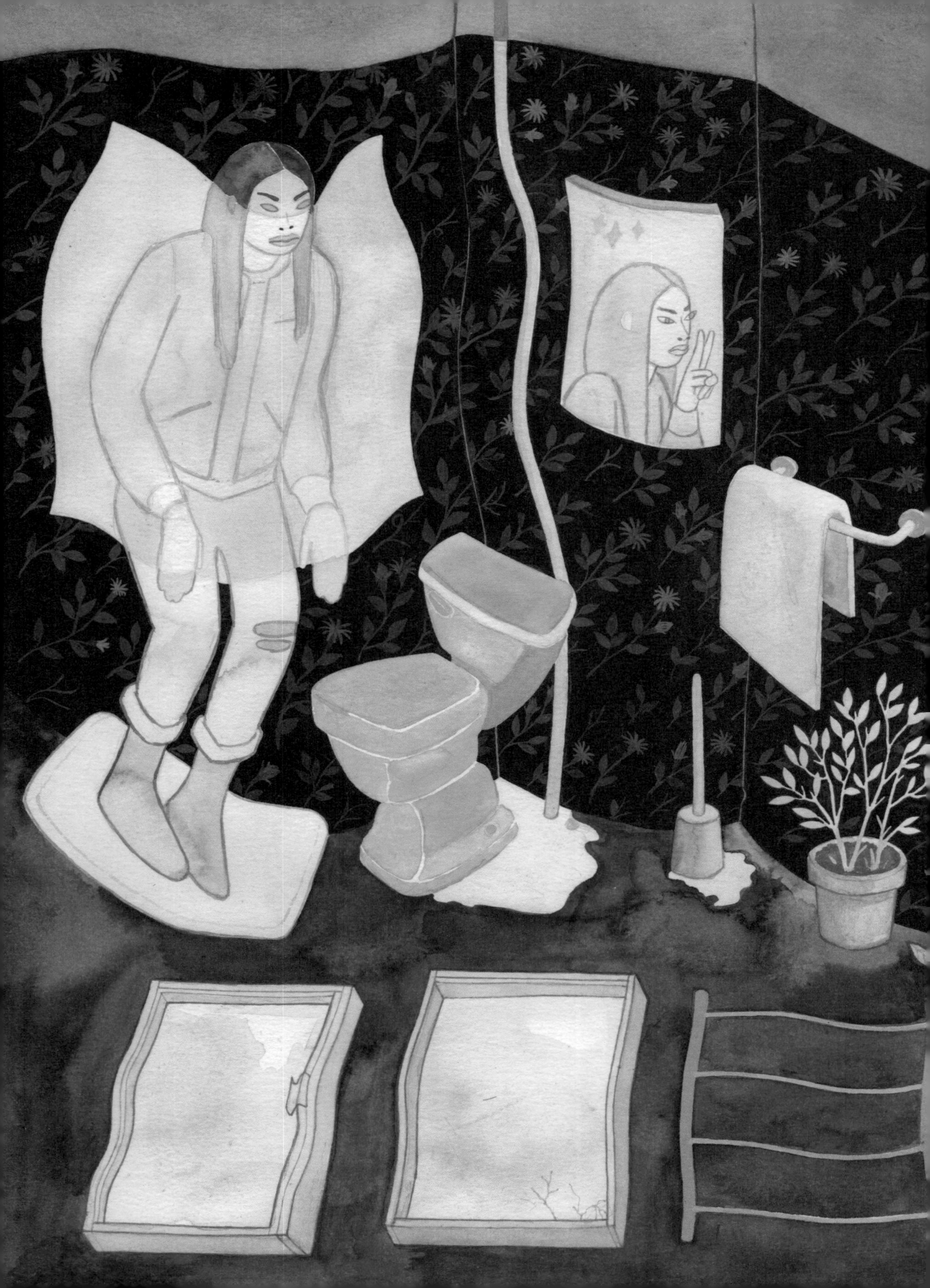

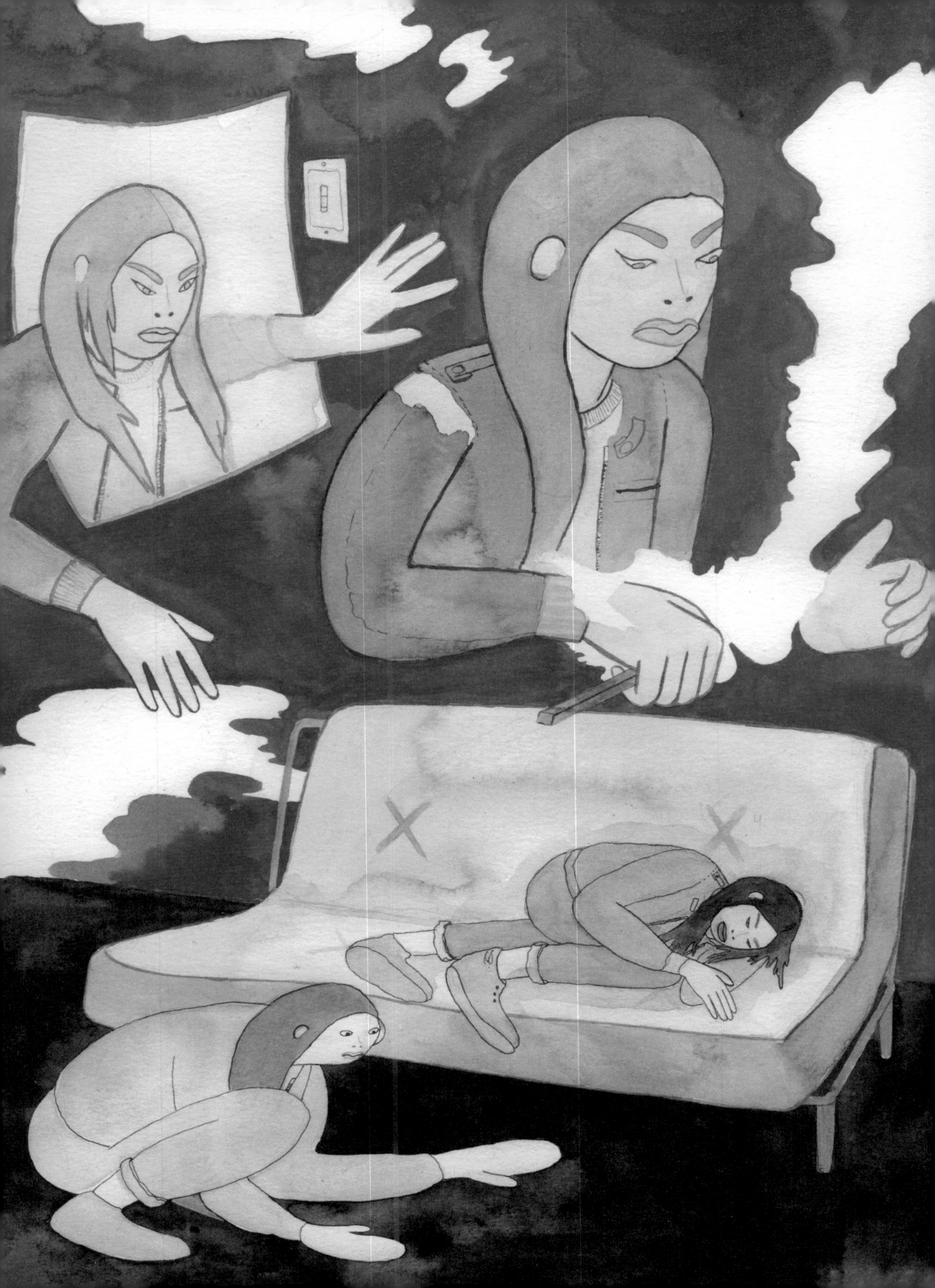

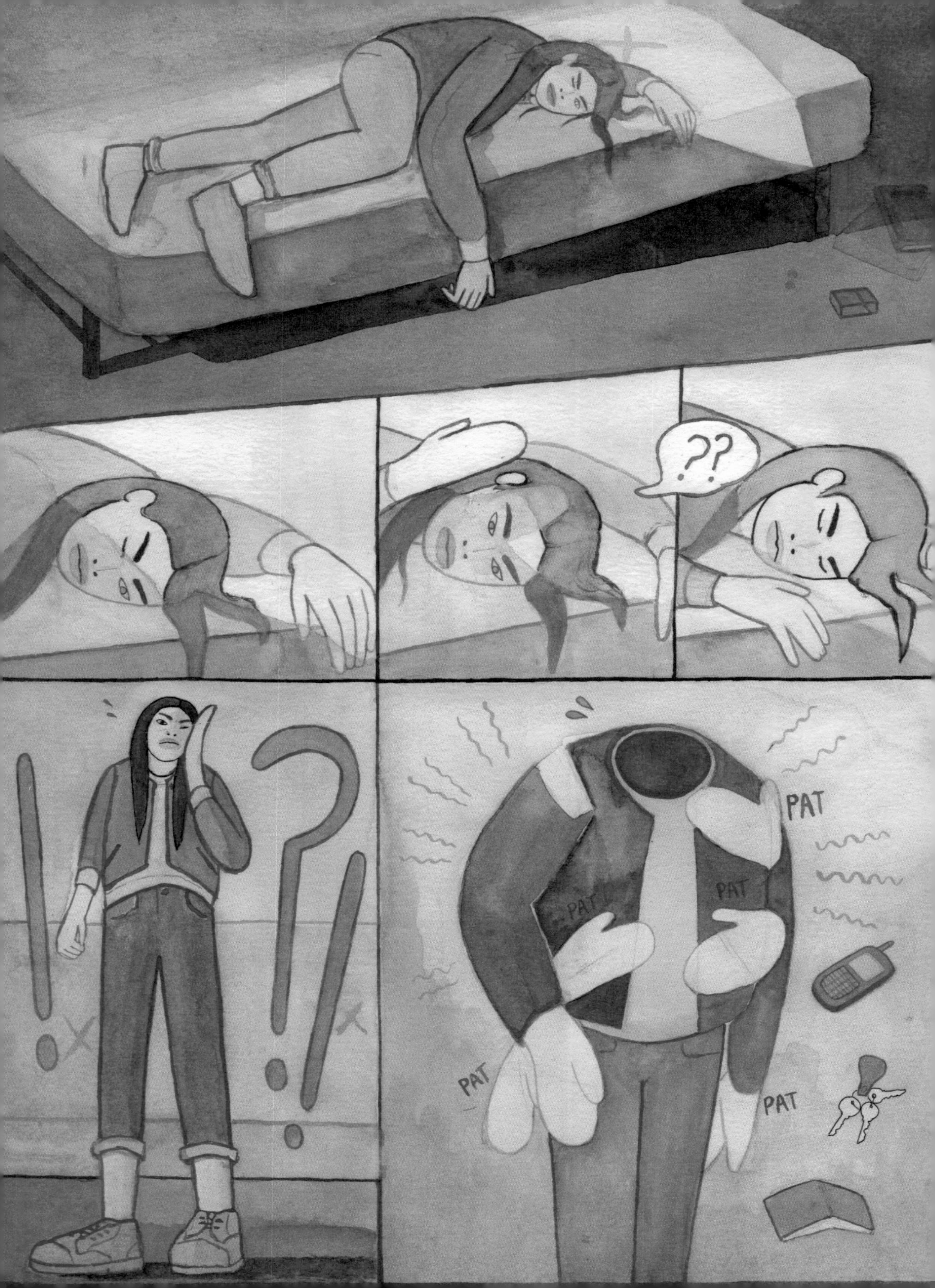
??
PAT
PAT
PAT
PAT
PAT

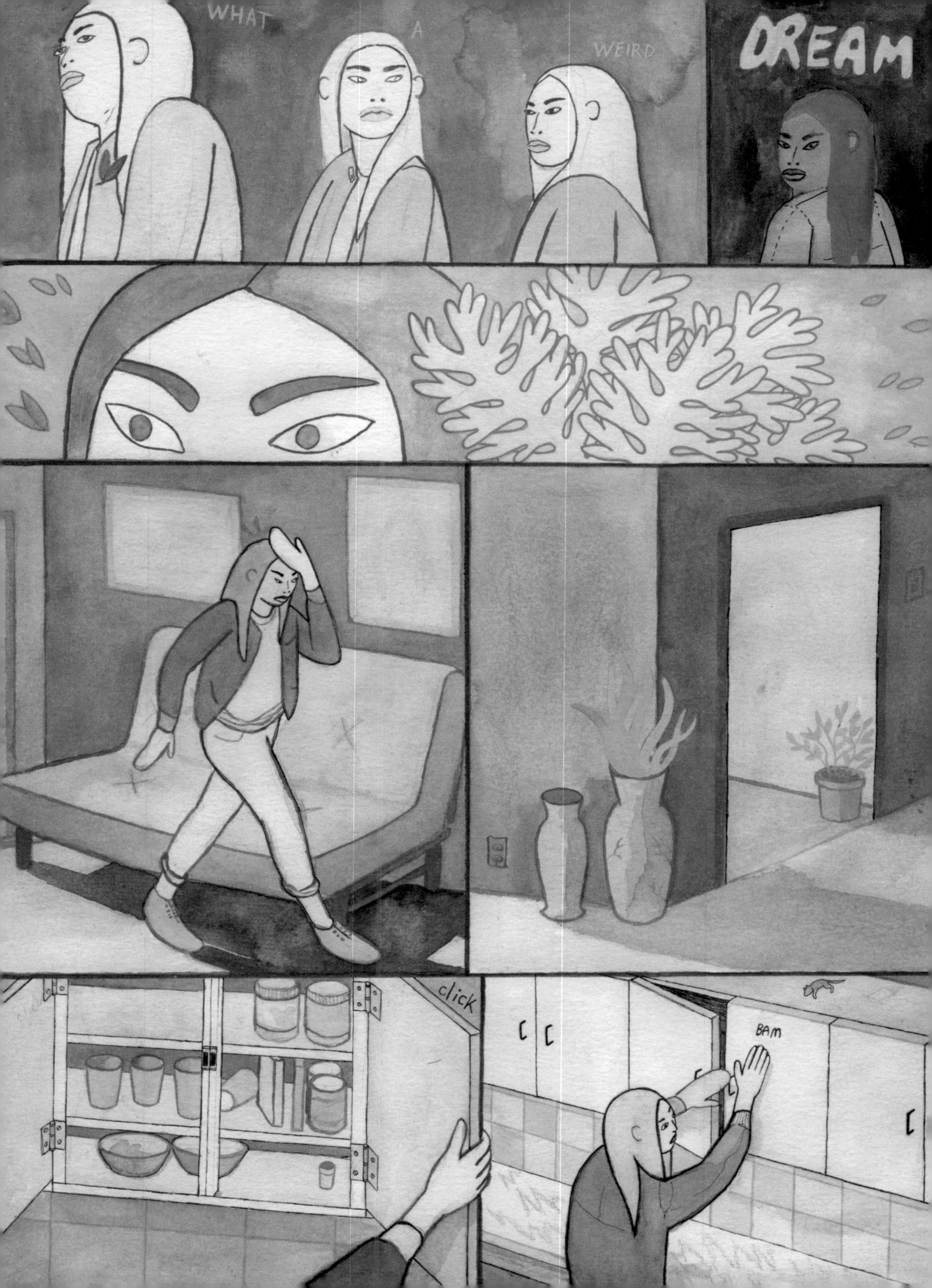
WHAT
A
WEIRD
DREAM
click
BAM

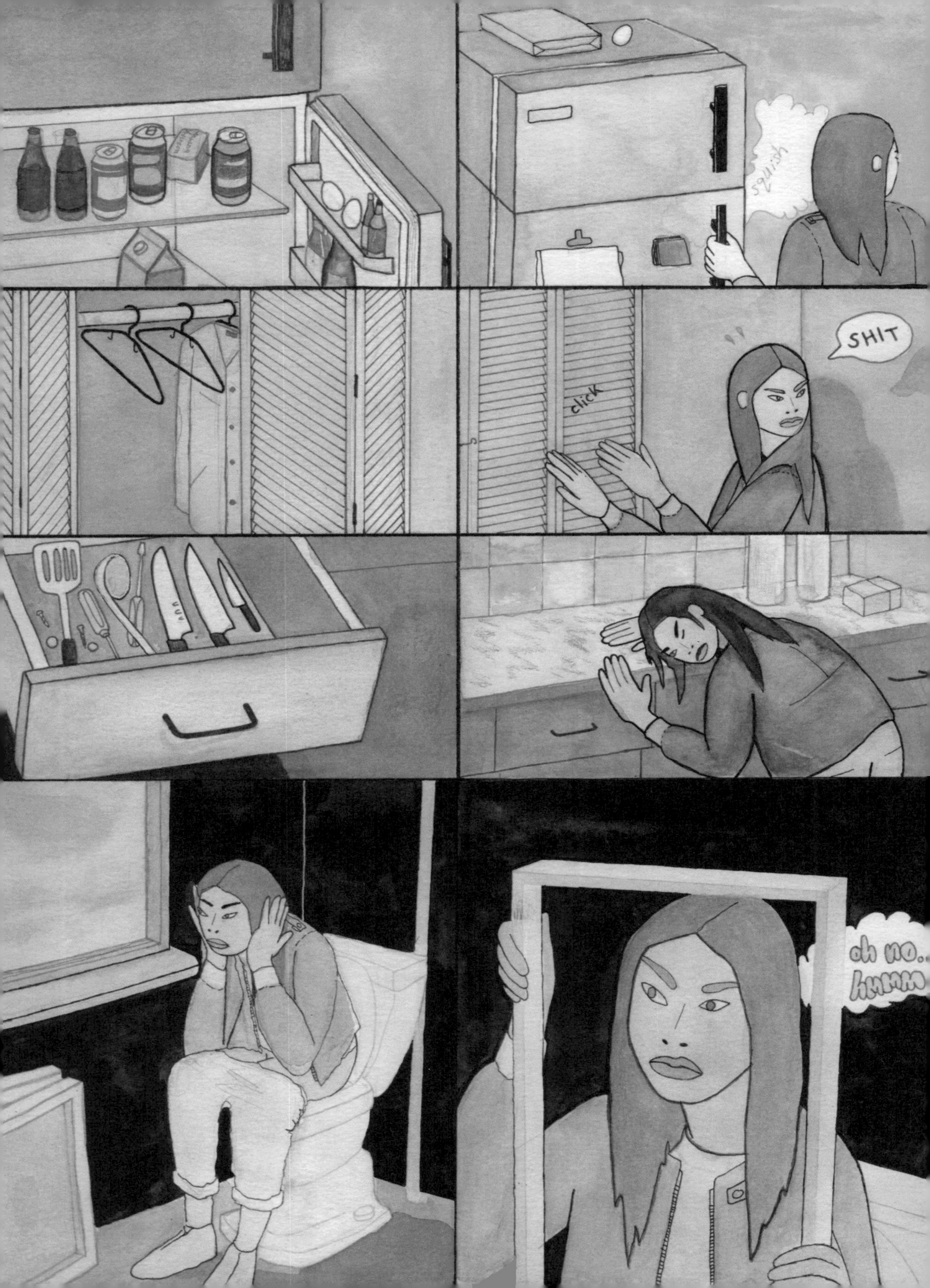
squish
click
SHIT
oh no..
hmmm

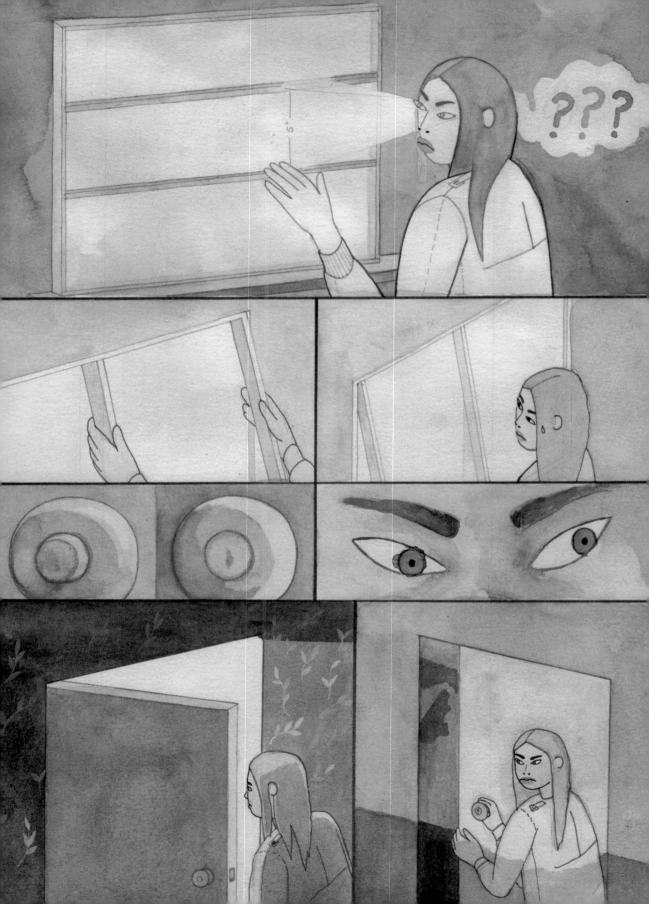

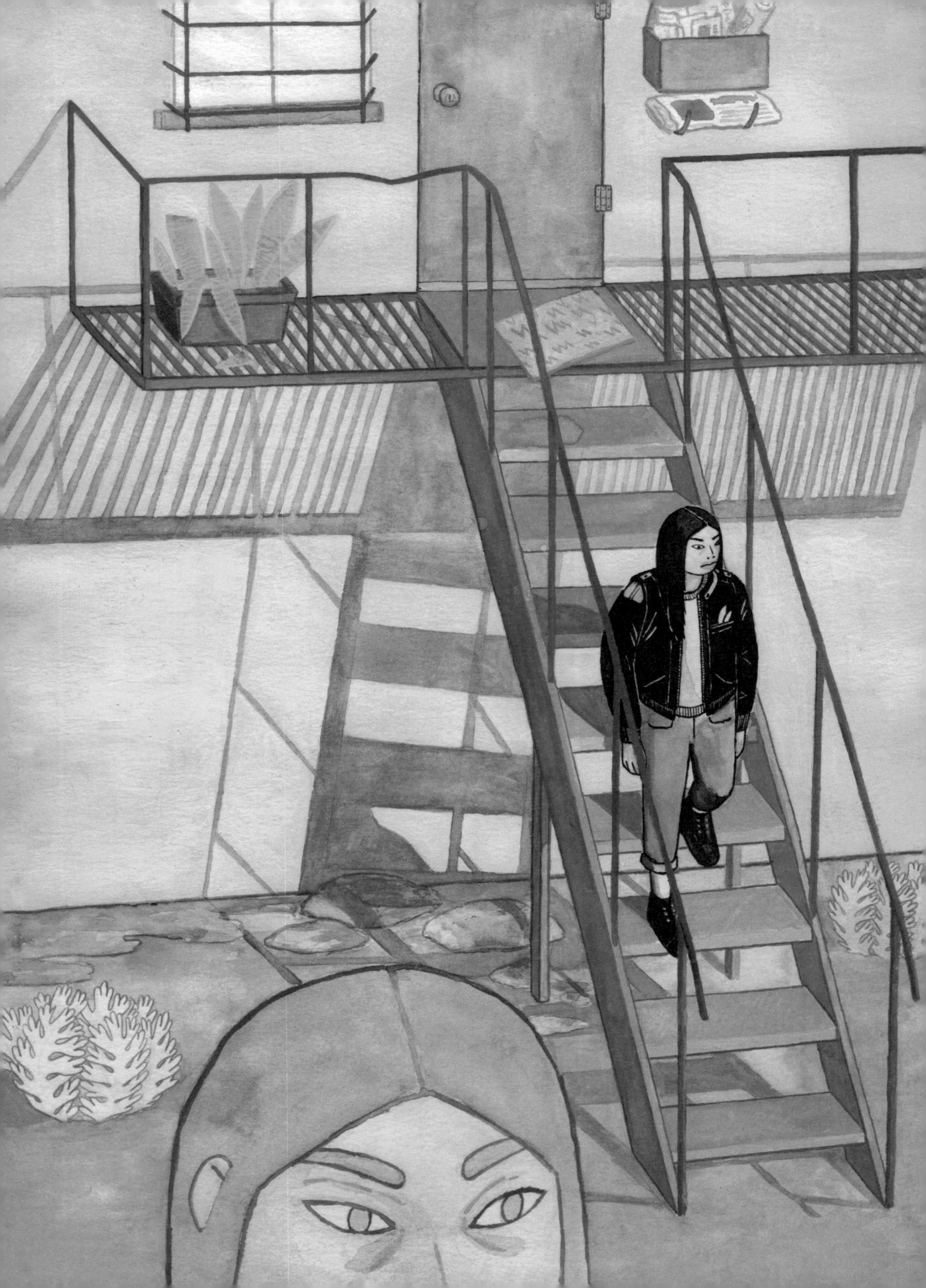

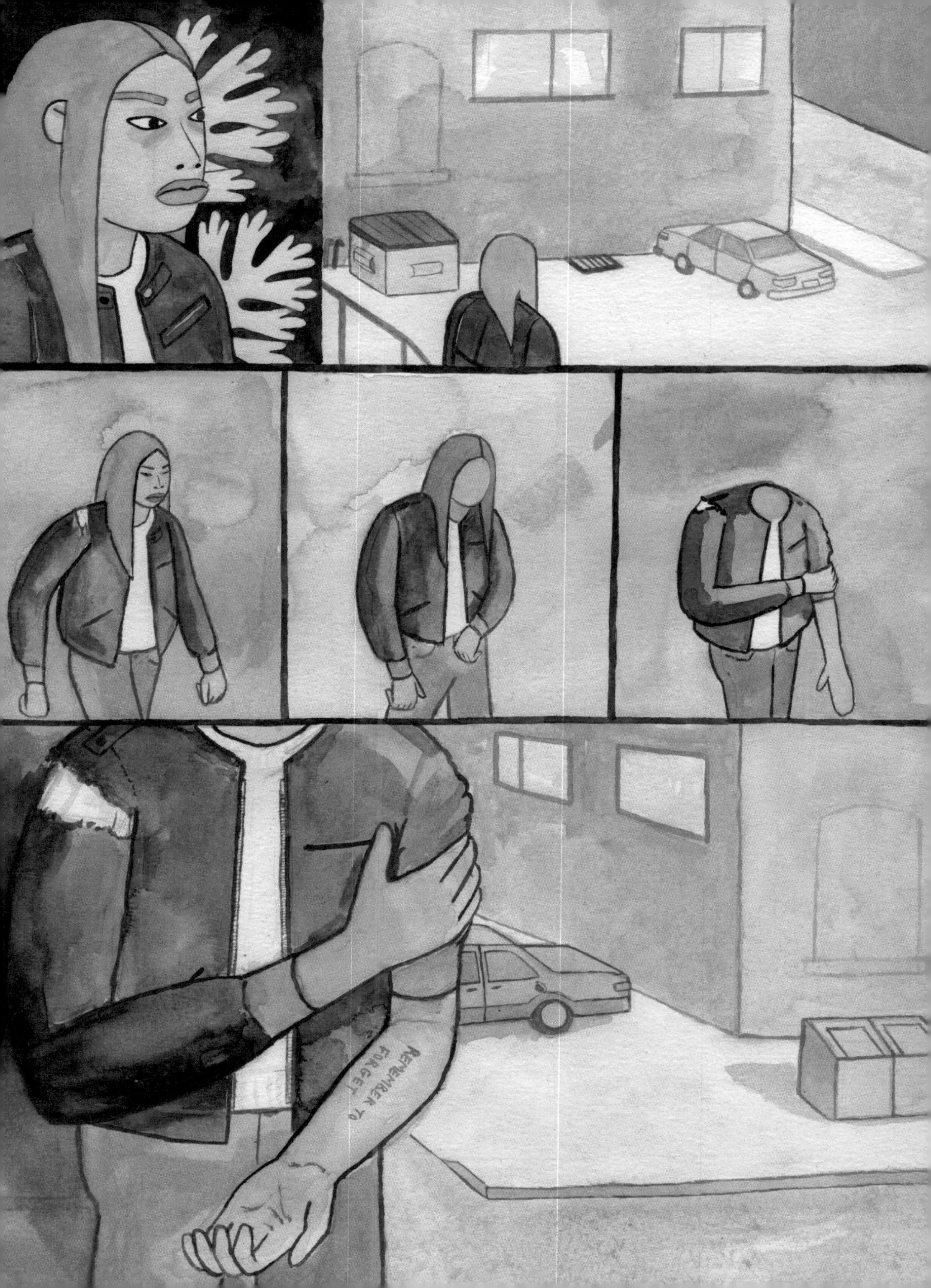
REMEMBER TO
FORGET

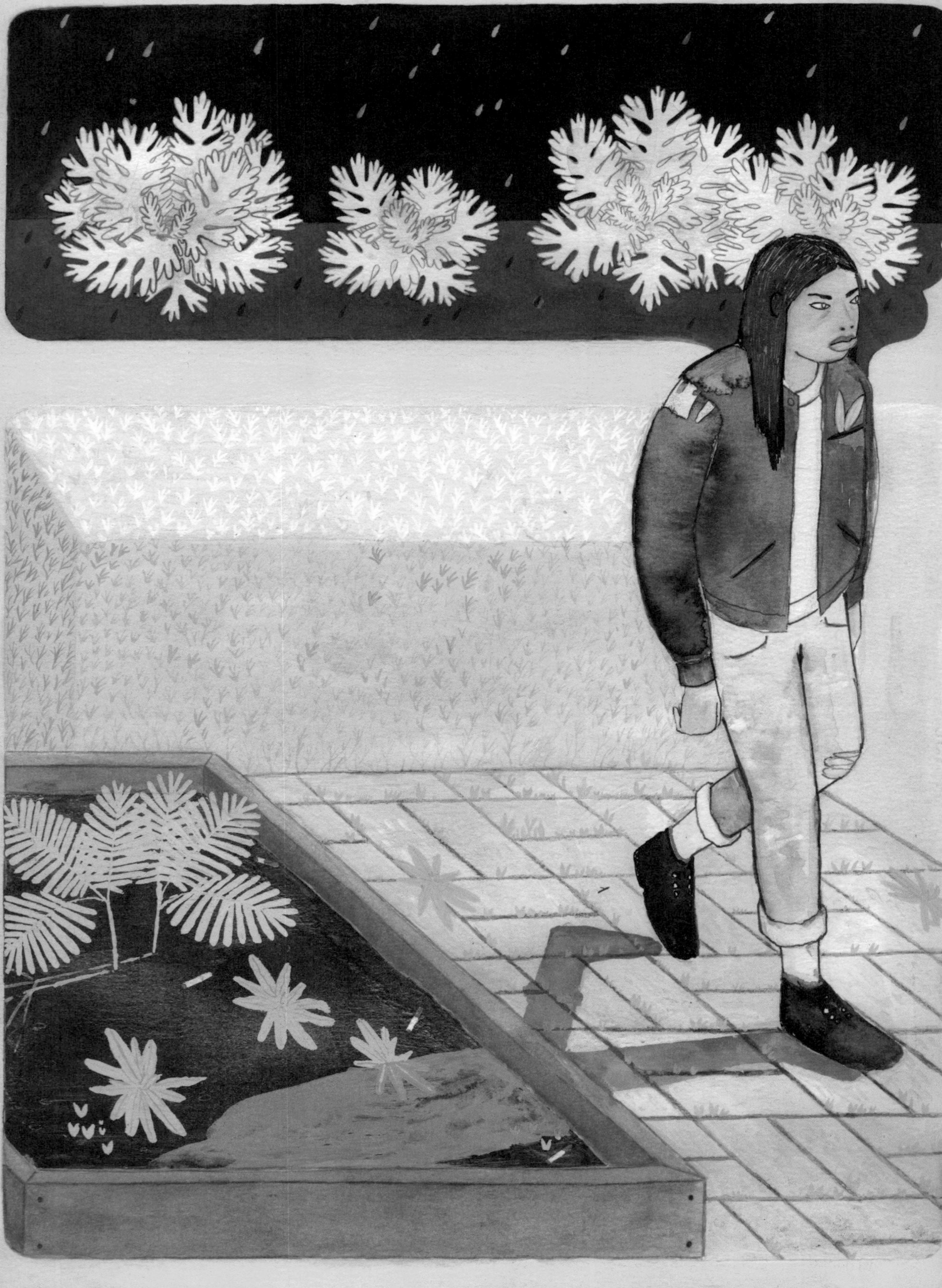